MOUNTAIN AND ASH

ENA OF ILBREA, BOOK TWO

MEGAN O'RUSSELL

Ink Worlds Press

To the ones who have been afraid.
You will destroy the darkness.

MOUNTAIN AND ASH

"Look at me." I took the child's face in my hands, blocking her view of everything but my eyes. "Look at me, love. Don't look at anything but me."

Her tear-filled gaze found my face.

"Good girl." I smiled.

A banging echoed from the street, but I couldn't tell the distance. The next house over, maybe the one beside that—my heart raced too fast for me to be sure.

"You are the bravest little girl in the world," I said. "Did you know that?"

She took a shuddering breath but didn't answer.

"You are so brave, you can do anything. I promise you can." I picked the child up. She weighed nothing in my arms. "Do you know what we do when we're brave?"

The girl looked over my shoulder toward the corner of the room.

"No, look at me." I balanced her on one hip, using my free hand to block the side of her vision. "When we are very brave, we look into the darkness, and we say, *I am not afraid.*"

A woman screamed in the distance.

The child gripped the front of my bodice in her little hands.

"We do not scream, we do not cry." I moved closer to the window. "We stare into the shadows and whisper, *I am not afraid.* Say it. Say, *I am not afraid.*"

Her lips wobbled as a fresh batch of tears glistened on her cheeks.

"Say, *I am not afraid.*" I slid the window open.

The crash of splintering wood carried from the street.

The child didn't look away from my eyes.

"Say, *I am not afraid.* Come on." I wiped the tears from her cheeks. "*I am not afraid.*"

"I am not afraid." Her voice cracked as she spoke with me. "I am not afraid."

"You are the bravest girl in the whole world," I whispered in her ear. "You will not scream when you're scared. Only whisper, *I am not afraid.*"

"I'm not afraid."

"Good girl." I held her out the window and let go.

She didn't scream as she fell, but a gasp came from the corner of the room.

"What have you done?" The woman cowering deep in the shadows shook with quiet sobs.

"What's best for your daughter," I said.

A bang came from close by, but the floor didn't rattle. The soldiers hadn't reached this house.

"Do you want to join her or not?" I said. "We're out of time. You have to choose."

"I…" The woman stepped toward the window. "I have five children. I have a home and a shop."

"May you find peace with the choice you've made." I lifted my skirt and climbed onto the windowsill.

"Please"—the woman grabbed my arm—"she's my baby."

"Not anymore. You have four children. Your baby does not exist."

"She needs me."

I took the mother's face in my hands as I had done with the child's. "She will never know fear again. She will not know pain or darkness. For the rest of your days, think of her in sunlit fields, running through bright spring flowers. You have given her endless peace, and she will always be thankful."

The woman fell to her knees, coughing through the sobs that wracked her chest.

"Remember her laugh and her smell." I turned toward the starless night. "Remember that it is still your duty to protect her." I stepped from the window ledge and plummeted into the darkness.

The warm wind lifted my hair from my neck as I fell. I exhaled all the breath in my body, bending my knees as I landed in the wide bed of hay.

"Ena?" Finn leapt up onto the front seat of the wagon. "Are you hurt?"

"Go." I scrambled through the hay, fighting my way to the front of the cart. "Is she under?"

"Didn't make a peep." Finn clicked the horse to walk. "I've seen grown men crumble at what that five-year-old faced silently."

"She's strong." I climbed into the seat beside Finn, brushing the hay from my skirt. "She'll make it."

"Of course she will. She's got us looking out for her." Finn steered the cart out of the alley behind the houses and onto the rut-covered thoroughfare of the tiny chivving town called Wilton.

"Halt." A soldier stepped in front of our cart.

"Whoa." Finn reined in the horse. "Happy to stop for you, sir. Is there something I can help you with?"

I clung to Finn, sliding my hand beneath his to coat to grip the hilt of his knife.

"We're searching for a sorcerer hidden in this village," the soldier said.

Four men in black uniforms stepped out of the shadows to surround our wagon.

"Sorcerer?" Finn said.

"Like magic?" I asked. "By the Guilds, you've got to find them. Are we safe? Is the sorcerer going to try to kill us?"

Two of the soldiers climbed into the back of our wagon.

"Do you really need to search our wagon?" Finn asked.

"Who cares about where they're searching?" I swatted Finn on the arm with my free hand. "We've got to get out of here. Unless the sorcerer is on the road. Oh, by the Guilds, do you know which way the sorcerer ran?"

The soldiers dug through the hay in our cart, tossing it out onto the dirt road.

"Hush, my love." Finn wrapped an arm around my waist.

"What if they're waiting in the dark?" Fat tears slid down my cheeks. "What if they're lurking by the road, waiting to attack? I told you I didn't want to leave home. My mother warned me of all the horrors that wait in the world."

"You're fine, my love." Finn wiped the tears from my cheeks. "I promise, I will not let any harm come to you." He brushed his lips against mine.

I pulled myself closer to him, letting my chest press against his as I parted his lips with my tongue.

"Hey." A soldier smacked his hand against our wagon.

"Sorry," Finn said.

"Sorry." I pulled away from him, tucking his blade under my skirt.

"The wagon's empty." A soldier hopped down from the back of the cart.

"Move on then."

The men stepped aside to let us pass.

"Thank you." Finn bowed his head. "Thank you for reminding

me there are some things in Ilbrea that are worth protecting." He laid his hand on my thigh.

"You are such a wonderful man." I leaned in to kiss Finn again.

"Get out of here before we have to take you in for indecency." The soldier had a smirk on his face as he waved us on.

"Sorry about that." Finn clicked for the horse to walk. "Have a lovely evening."

I clung tightly to his arm as the wagon rattled forward, smiling at the soldiers and listening for the sniffles of a small child coming from below.

It was well into the night by the time we'd gotten far enough away from Wilton to risk sleep.

Finn stopped by a stand of trees, cooing lovingly to our horse as he unhooked her from the cart.

"You are such a good girl." Finn patted the horse. "Such a pretty, kind girl."

"Should I be jealous of the horse, my love?" I hopped down from my seat, taking one last look around before heading to the back of the wagon.

"Never," Finn said. "There is nothing in this world that comes close to my adoration of you."

"Careful, you might make a girl blush." I ran my fingers along the back of the cart, searching for the latch to our hidey hole.

I slipped the metal aside and lifted the three long boards that made up the center of the cart. The compartment below was wide enough to fit two adults if they lay side by side, and just deep enough to leave a few inches of space above a person's nose.

I held my breath as I squinted into the shadows. I'd come up with a hundred different things to say to comfort the child and a dozen apologies for having locked her in the dark.

The child lay in the corner, clinging to a folded up blanket.

"You're all right now," I whispered as I climbed into the compartment. "Let's get you someplace more comfortable to sleep."

The child didn't move.

"You can come out now." I knelt beside her.

She didn't stir.

My heart skittered against my ribs as I laid my fingers on the child's throat. She gave a shuddering sigh and nestled her face into the blanket.

"Oh, thank the gods." I ran my hands over my face.

"She all right?" Finn peered in from the back of the wagon.

"Sleeping." I lifted her, cradling her to my chest. "I wonder how long it took her to drift off."

"Hopefully not too long." Finn reached for the child.

Part of me didn't want to hand her over. I'd taken the girl from her mother. I should be the one clutching her in my arms until we could leave her someplace where she wasn't in any danger. But her safe haven was still very far away.

She would be passed from hand to hand a dozen times before she'd truly be free of the Guilds. Finn and I were just one tiny cog in the massive clockwork that would ferry her south to a place where she would never need to be afraid again.

"Come on." Finn held his arms higher. "The sooner we get to sleep, the happier I'll be."

"Try not to wake her."

It didn't take long for us to get the tent up, a circle of stones placed around us, and the bedrolls down. I tucked the child in, and she still didn't fuss. Finn and I slept on either side of her, each with a weapon tucked beneath our heads. I stared at the canvas of the tent for a long while, waiting for sleep to come. I drifted into darkness, clutching the stone pendant around my neck.

"Mama."

A voice scratched against the edges of my mind.

"Mama!"

I sat up, tossing my blanket aside and grabbing the hilt of my knife. Finn was already at the flap of the tent before I could look around.

"Where is she?" the little girl asked.

"Who?" I crouched beside her, ready to leap to my feet. "Did you see someone?"

She shook her head. "No, but I want to see mama."

"Oh, darling"—I slid my knife back under my blanket and out of sight—"I know it's hard, but you can't see your mother."

"There's no one outside." Finn ducked back into the tent, curls of early morning mist lapping at his heels.

"Good," I said. "So we're safe. We've got our blankets and our tent, and we're perfectly safe."

"Is mama safe?" The child wiped her tears away with her fists.

"What name do you like to be called?" I held my arms out to her.

"Riesa." She buried her face on my shoulder.

"Well, Riesa, I think your mother is very safe." I lifted her and mouthed *pack up* to Finn.

He ran his fingers through his bright red hair but didn't argue.

"Do you know that you are special?" I asked Riesa as I slid out of the tent.

She shook her head, her face still on my shoulder.

"Well, you are," I said. "You are very special. You are a precious gift. Have you ever heard of someone stealing coins?"

"Yes." Riesa wrapped her arms around my neck.

"Well, you are a massive, shiny gold coin, and there are some who are very greedy and want to steal you from your mother. And in Wilton, she didn't have a way to keep you safe from people who might see how precious you are and try to take you. So she did the best thing she could. She asked us to come and take care of her beloved daughter."

"To take me away?" Riesa asked.

"Yes." I paced by the side of the wagon. "Finn and I are going to take you somewhere you can be very safe. Where there aren't any greedy people who might try to steal you. You will be protected and have every chance to be happy."

"Is mama going to meet me there?"

I took a breath, making sure my voice would sound strong. "No, Riesa, your mother isn't going to meet you. She has to stay in Wilton with the rest of your family. But there are going to be people who will take very good care of you. I promise you will have someone to look after you."

"Are you going to look after me?" Riesa stared up into my face.

"For now I will."

"But you won't stay with me?"

The wrinkles on the child's forehead stole the air from my lungs.

"I can't, darling." I made myself smile. "I have other precious children I need to protect. But you will never be alone. Finn and I will stay with you, and then you'll go on an adventure with someone else. You'll get to see so much of the world, and the place you are going is absolutely beautiful."

"Have you been there?"

"No, I'm not special enough. You are a gold coin." I bopped her nose. "Me, I'm nothing more than bronze."

Riesa gave a teary-eyed grin.

"We're ready." Finn climbed up into the front of the cart.

"I don't want to go in the dark." Riesa clung to me.

"You don't have to." I grabbed the side of the cart, hoisting us both into the front.

Finn gave a longing look to the patch of grass where our tent had been before urging the horse on. The animal seemed as pleased as Finn to be awake.

"Where are we going?" Riesa asked.

"The mountains," I said. "They are a beautiful place, and nothing at all compared to the wonders of where you're going."

"Oh." Riesa played with the end of my braid. "I don't think you're bronze."

"What do you suppose she is then?" Finn barely disguised his laugh.

Riesa shrugged.

"Hmm. If I'm not bronze, am I a fish?" I asked.

Riesa shook her head.

"Am I a tree?"

A giggle trembled in the child's chest.

"Am I a stone?"

I could hear her laugh that time.

"Am I a bird?"

The game lasted until Riesa fell asleep, nestled in my arms.

We let her rest for as long we could.

Wilton was farther west in Ilbrea than I'd ever been, though still far enough from the shores of the Arion Sea not to allow me a hint of salty air. A tiny bit of me, the part that could laugh through playing guessing games with Riesa, wished we had gone a bit farther west—far enough to have reached the beaches covered with powdery sand—and seen the tall sailing ships heading off on great adventures.

The more reasonable part of me, the portion that wished Riesa had chosen to fall asleep in a position that made it easier to reach the knife hidden in my boot, wanted to get back to the safety of the eastern mountains as quickly as we could. Riesa's life had been entrusted to Finn and me. The weight of keeping the child alive was much heavier than the girl herself.

"I don't like being this far west," Finn said as though reading my thoughts. "It feels like I'm naked."

"Naked?" I asked. "I thought you liked being naked."

"I do enjoy not wearing clothes, but without the mountains surrounding me, I feel like a fool who's walked into a bear's den with nothing but his skin on."

"Better than without your skin on."

"Fair enough."

We slipped back into silence as we passed a line of wagons heading west, seven of them in a row, all piled high with goods.

I held Riesa tighter and nodded at the drivers of each of the carts.

One held barrels of frie, another wide crates, but most held goods someone cared enough about they'd covered the loads with waxed canvas to keep the rain off.

Riesa stirred, fidgeting in my arms.

"Shh, darling, it's just some carts," I said.

My fingers itched to reach for my blade. I needed to know what hid beneath the canvas.

Was it weapons paun soldiers would be using against common folk? Was it books being sent to a scribe in some distant territory? Was it people being transported far from home against their will?

"Where are we?" Riesa whispered.

"Still on the road," Finn said. "And half-starved. Ena, can we have a bit of food? Riesa's a growing girl, after all."

I shifted Riesa to sit between Finn and me.

"Just be sure you don't eat all the food we have, Finn," I said. "Riesa, did you know that Finn would eat this whole cart if we let him?"

The road began to curve around a wide stand of trees. A pair of birds shot out of the branches and circled up into the sky.

"Would you mind me eating the whole cart, Riesa?" Finn asked. "Ena always says no, but I think she's being unfair."

Riesa laughed.

She's young. Her life before the Black Bloods will only be a strange dream.

The copse of trees ended, opening up into a wide field covered in tents and wagons. Men in black uniforms moved between the tents. A few wore red healers robes, and five wore map maker green.

I lifted Riesa back onto my lap. "Would you like to hear a story?"

Riesa nodded.

"A long time ago, there was a brave little fish." My heart thundered against my ribs as our wagon drew level with the Guilds' camp. "The fish had always lived in a tiny little pond, but it wanted to know if there was more to the world beyond the tall grasses and bugs."

"Afternoon." Finn nodded to a soldier who stood next to the road, watching us pass with narrowed eyes.

"But a fish can only travel by water, so there was no way for our little fish to hop out of his pond."

We passed the cluster of green-clad map makers.

"So the fish decided to ask a bear for help."

"Stop," a man commanded.

I tightened my grip on Riesa and looked up to find a soldier standing in the middle of the road.

"Hello there," Finn said in a cheerful voice. It was one of the beauties of him. He could stare a demon in the eye and greet him with a foolish charm. "Lovely day to be out, though I can't imagine it's ever nice being packed so close together."

The soldier stared at Finn for a long moment. "What is your reason for travel?"

"How do you mean?" Finn said.

"Why are you on the road?" The soldier stepped closer to our horse.

"Well…" Finn said, "we've got the cart, and I thought the road would be better than hoping for good luck in the woods."

"I don't have time for—"

"I'm sorry, sir," I cut across the soldier. "This one gets a tad slow when he's tired, and last night was a bit long for us."

"What business do you have traveling on the Guilds' road?" the soldier said.

"Had to move some things. We're coming from Gint's End," Finn said.

Riesa tightened her grip on my wrist.

"Hush," I whispered in her ear. "You're safe with Finn and me."

"Move some things?" The soldier nodded and walked around to peer into the back of our empty wagon. "What things are you moving?"

Finn's pulse beat quickly in his neck, knocking against his skin like a clock running out of time. "It's a bit of a complicated story."

"Take Riesa." I lifted the child, setting her in Finn's lap.

"Ena, no." Riesa clung to the top of my bodice, pulling it down low enough to catch the soldiers' eyes.

"You are brave, my love." I smoothed Riesa's blond hair, which wasn't close enough to Finn's red or my current black to hope for an easy claim to kinship. "Could I speak to you on the ground, sir?" I looked to the soldier.

"Why?" the soldier said at the same moment Finn said, "I can."

"There are some things best kept away from tender ears." I leaned over the side of the cart toward the soldier, giving him a fine view of the top of my breasts. "Please, sir. I'll only take a moment of your time."

"This had better be good," the soldier said.

"I can speak to him, my love," Finn said.

"Riesa is better waiting with you." I hopped down from the cart. Being on the ground somehow made the reality of being surrounded by a hundred paun soldiers more real. "Do you mind?" I nodded to the shadow cast by one of the map maker's tents.

The soldier's jaw tensed.

"Please, sir." I tried to speak sweetly, like a girl who relied on her pretty face for survival. The kind of girl a soldier would have dreams about—the sort of lurid dreams he'd hold on to until morning when he could brag about them to his fellows.

The soldier's neck eased. "Be quick."

"Of course, sir." I tucked my chin and headed straight toward the shadows. "Thank you for your kindness."

More men dressed in black had noticed me. They peered around the tents to watch me.

"Out with it." The soldier crossed his arms as he studied me. He didn't bother unsheathing his sword or asking one of his fellows to stand with him.

You are surrounded, Ena Ryeland. You will not be a chivving fool.

"We're coming from my sister's, sir," I said. "The child is my niece."

"And you can't say that in front of her?"

"Not really," I said. "She thinks we're just on an adventure. You know, taking her through the country for some summer air. But the crops in Gint's End were river flooded already this summer. There's no hope for a decent harvest."

"I've heard." A crease formed between the soldier's eyebrows.

For a moment, I wondered if he had been one of us. If once, a long time ago, before he donned his black uniform and became one the Guilds' demons, he had been a little boy on a farm where a flood could be as terrifying as an enemy's blade.

"They've no hope of paying their harvest taxes," I said. "My sister will lose everything. She doesn't want her child to be there to see it. She asked me to come get the girl and take her Frason's Glenn where I live. Raise the child on my own until things get better for my sister. *If* they get better for my sister. I just haven't had the heart to tell Riesa yet."

The soldier looked to the wagon.

Riesa had curled herself into a tight ball in Finn's arms.

"That's quite a thing to ask of someone," the soldier said, "even a sister."

"I wanted to say no, but I couldn't," I said. "And she's a good girl. Once she's settled, I think she'll be fine."

"What about the man?" The soldier nodded toward Finn.

Finn whispered something in Riesa's ear.

Riesa huddled closer to him.

"A suitor," I said, "and one with a wagon and the means to leave Frason's Glenn for a few days."

"A lucky man," the soldier said.

"At least until I get the child safely home. I hope you won't mind my being honest with you, but he flips between chattering like a bird and utter silence. Either end drives me mad."

"Poor fellow." The soldier's gaze slid from my face to my chest and back up again. "It would be an awful thing to lose a creature like you."

Heat rushed to my cheeks. "You're too kind, and I'm not sure you're right."

"I am." He leaned close to me. His scent of horse, sweat, and mud slammed into my nose. "My company travels through Frason's Glenn quite often. Perhaps you might allow me a moment to convince you?"

"I work in the market square." I held my hand out to him. "Look for the girl selling the best pastries in the city."

He took my fingers and pressed his lips to the back of my hand. "I look forward to seeing you in Frason's Glenn."

"And I look forward to expressing my appreciation of your generosity." I gave him the sort of smile I had learned in my brief time in Frason's Glenn. A hint of a joyful promise mixed with a joke no man could hope to understand.

"Safe travels." He stepped out of my way.

I kept my pace even as I strode back to the wagon. If I had been a sorcerer, I could have torched the camp with a snap of my fingers. If I had been a trueborn Black Blood, I could have shot a hailstorm of stones from my hands and cut the paun down where they stood.

But I was neither. So I smiled nicely as I let the men watch me walk, and gave a wave to the soldier who'd let us pass as Finn urged the horse to trot us away.

He kept Riesa in his lap, one arm wrapped around her as though he were shielding her from an oncoming storm.

I waited to speak until the road had twisted us out of sight. "We're safe, Riesa. You don't have to hide."

"I think she does." Finn loosened his grip just enough to allow me a glimpse of Riesa's hands.

Bright red sparks leapt between the girl's fingers. "I'm sorry."

"Don't be sorry, darling." I covered her hands with mine. Heat peppered my palms. "There is no shame in magic. Where you're going, you won't ever have to worry about how special you are."

Riesa hiccupped. Tears spilled down her cheeks.

"I need you to breathe for me." I scooted close to Finn and transferred Riesa onto my lap. Her sparks stung my arms, and Finn's shirt bore black flecks where he'd been scorched. "We're going to take nice, big breaths and calm down. I told you I would keep you safe, and didn't I keep my promise?"

"Yes." Riesa buried her soggy face on my shoulder.

"And I will keep protecting you." I held her tight. "All I need for you to do is take nice, deep breaths."

It took an hour for the red sparks to die entirely away. We didn't speak to anyone else the rest of that day and all through the next. I told stories until I couldn't remember the proper endings and sang silly songs until I thought I'd go mad. I kept Riesa jabbering and laughing, careful to stop her from noticing how Finn kept scanning the sides of the road for people waiting to attack, and how I kept shuddering, hoping it was a man who sold the best pastries in Frason's Glenn.

When I was a little girl in Harane, I believed in magic. In wishing on stars, fairies that danced in the moonlight, and beautiful spells made to save the world.

I learned very young that the sort of magic in stories does not exist.

I didn't know until much later that the sort of magic that does survive in Ilbrea is both more wondrous than fairies and more terrifying than Death's own axe.

Still, there was something about witnessing magic that always took me a little off guard. Like I was a character who had fallen into the wrong story. My tale was that of an orphan from a small village. A girl who was destined to watch everyone around her die until it was her turn for the grave.

Somehow, I had ended up in a saga of bravery, murder, and magic.

I had spent the last four months ferrying sorci children away from the hands of the Guilds. Taking them from Ilbrea to the woods of the eastern mountains, where they would meet the sort of Black Bloods that did not venture into open territory.

Finn and I would hand over the children we'd gathered and

never see them again. They would become a part of a different tale, venturing to a faraway, hidden realm where magic reigned above all.

My part in Riesa's story ended before her tale truly began.

I would do as I had with all the other children. Give her a hug, tell her to be brave, and pray to the stars she would find a happier place than Ilbrea.

Repeating my role in the prologue of someone else's story did not make playing the part any easier.

"I don't want to be blindfolded." Riesa squirmed away from me.

"Believe me, you do." Finn leaned against a tree.

"I'll make you a deal." I knelt in front Riesa. "We'll tie your blindfold on, and I will hold you tight the whole time you have to wear it. I won't let go of you, so you'll know how safe you are."

Riesa pursed her lips at me and wrinkled her forehead. She'd been in a sour mood since we'd left the horse and cart with a friend of Finn's.

"Riesa," I said, "I know it's been a difficult few days, but I promise it will be worth the hardship when your journey is done. You can be brave, I'm sure of it."

"I can be brave." Riesa nodded.

"Of course you can." Finn pulled a cloth from his pocket.

I lifted Riesa onto my hip.

She gave a giant sigh and scrunched her eyes closed.

Finn tied the cloth around her eyes and leaned back against the tree to take off his boots.

"What happens after this?" Riesa asked.

"You're going to go with some of our friends who will take

you farther along on your adventure." I twisted to turn Riesa's closed eyes away from Finn.

"But what happens to you?" Riesa asked.

"We go home and take a hot bath and eat awful food." Finn pulled off his shirt, tossing it onto his boots and socks.

"Where is home?"

"Far away where the Guilds can't find us." I looked up to the canopy of leaves as Finn dropped his pants.

"And I'm not allowed to come with you?" Riesa asked.

"I'm afraid not, darling," I said. "See, where we live, there aren't any other children. If you lived with us, you would get very bored and lonely."

Finn's footsteps crackled across last season's debris on the forest floor. I looked down from the leaves in time to see his bright white, naked bottom disappear through the trees.

"I wouldn't be lonely." Riesa nestled her head onto my shoulder. "I'd be with you."

A tiny pang shook what little was left of my heart. "But I wouldn't be there all the time. There are other people I have to help." I slid the cloth from around Riesa's eyes. "It'll be better for you to stay where the same person will be there to feed you breakfast every morning."

Riesa made no move to scramble down from my arms. "When I'm older, can I come and be with you?"

"Maybe." I held her tight even as I kept my gaze fixed on the woods where Finn had disappeared. "You'll have to see what you want to do with your life by the time you're all grown up. You might have fallen in love with a merman by then and decided to live your whole life at sea."

Riesa giggled. "I am not a fish."

"Too right you're not."

She played with the end of my black braid.

I strained my ears for any sign of Finn.

A small creature rustled through the rotting leaves trapped under a bush. A bird chirped high above.

"Will we have a new horse for traveling?" Riesa asked.

"I don't know. But I'm sure you're going to have a grand time either way."

A branch cracked in front us.

"Hop down, darling." I pried Riesa's arms from around my neck and set her down behind me. I pulled the knife from my boot, savoring the weight of the blade in my hand.

"Ena"—Riesa clung to the back of my skirt—"are soldiers coming?"

"Of course not. We're perfectly safe," I said, though the racing of my heart screamed I was lying. "I have a horrible fear of rabbits, so I like to be ready to defend myself."

"Rabbits?" Riesa stepped in front of me, staring up with a furrowed brow. "What's frightening about rabbits?"

A crackling came from closer by and farther east than the first sound.

"It's the way their noses twitch," I said. "I've never managed to figure out what they're smelling that I can't."

Riesa scrunched up her whole face. "Probably rabbit food."

"I think you're right. You may have just cured my fear of rabbits."

A bright smile lit Riesa face. "That's good! I'm—"

"Another tiny one." A woman stepped out of the trees. She was small, barely breaking five feet, though she might have managed to look larger if the man behind her weren't a good head taller than Finn.

"They keep showing magic younger," the giant man said.

"Honestly, it makes it easier on us." Finn stepped out from behind them, a thin blanket wrapped around his waist. "Easier to ferry someone small."

"Finn, why did you take off your pants?" Riesa asked.

"The seams were too itchy." Finn shrugged. "Needed to give my legs a break."

Riesa giggled for a moment before looking to the tall man. She backed up to lean against my legs.

"Come on." I scooted her far enough away to be able to tuck my knife back into my boot. "Let's meet your new friends."

The tall man knelt down. "What's your name?"

"Riesa." She kept her cheek pressed to my leg as we walked toward him.

"Well, Riesa, I'm like you." The man circled his finger along the ground.

Riesa knelt, peering at the dirt.

A sprout of green appeared, poking up through the brown. Before Riesa had managed to crawl all the way to the man's side, a tiny blue flower had blossomed.

"We're going to take you south," the woman said. "We're going to stay in the woods and move very quietly. Do you think you can manage that?"

Riesa nodded.

"Good girl." The woman stroked Riesa's hair. "We should get going, then."

"But…" Riesa turned to me, tears sparkling in her eyes.

"Don't cry, little one." I bent down and kissed the top of Riesa's head. "You are the bravest little girl, and you are heading off on an amazing adventure."

"I am not afraid." Riesa tipped her chin up.

"Don't forget that," Finn said.

"Goodbye, Riesa." I pressed my face into a careful smile. "May you always enjoy your freedom."

She clung to me for a moment before reaching for the woman's hand.

"Up we go." The woman lifted Riesa onto her hip, and the three of them disappeared through the trees.

Finn and I stood quietly for a long while.

"Put your chivving pants back on."

"Really?" Finn nudged me with his elbow. "I thought you liked me better naked."

"Don't be a fool." I couldn't tear my gaze from where Riesa had disappeared. It seemed too awful for a sane person to consider sending a child off with strangers.

Her mother sent her away with you.

"She's going to be all right, isn't she?" I asked.

"Sure." Finn tossed his cloth at my feet. "Henry and Jess are old guard in the Brien Clan. They've been running children south since I was young. They're two of the best."

"Then why haven't I seen them before?"

"Don't know. Lots of work to be done during the warm months. My pants are back on."

"Good." I turned to face him as he raised his arms to pull on his shirt.

The dark outline of a mountain range marked the right side of his ribcage. I wanted to touch the image, not for the sake of being near Finn's skin, just to promise myself the mountains were where I belonged.

"It does get easier." Finn tugged on his boots. "The sorci saving runs aren't my favorite activity, either. I'd rather be sticking a blade between a soldier's ribs than smiling and being nice to one. But we're helping, Ena. We're getting these children beyond the reach of the Sorcerers Guild. We're saving them from a lifetime trapped in the Lady Sorcerer's stone tower."

"It still feels awful to take a child from their home and then abandon them to people I don't know." I untied the end of my braid. Bits of my hair had already fallen loose from Riesa's fidgeting with it. "I know we're just one part of the beast that saves the sorcis, but doesn't Riesa deserve more than to be tossed from hand to hand?"

Finn wrapped his arm around my waist. "We're doing good work. Let that be enough."

I leaned my forehead against Finn's shoulder. "Right. You're right. We are doing important work, and we are quite excellent at getting the chivving thing done."

"Chivving true." Finn tipped my chin up and kissed my forehead. "Just do me a favor. Next time we have to separate, let me be the one to walk away with the soldier."

"Why?" I picked up my pack. The weight seemed heavier than it had on our walk into the woods.

"If he had suspected anything and decided to murder you—"

"Then I'd have begged for mercy until I got a chance to stab him in the throat." I shooed Finn east.

The mountain sloped up in front us. She would make us climb to find the riches she hid.

"I can see where a proper throat stabbing would come in handy. But what about when word got around camp that you'd shoved a blade into a soldier's windpipe?"

"I suppose I would have to deal with being the toast of the camp." I took a few quick steps to walk by Finn's side. "Just imagine how proud Cati would be of her favorite student."

"And what would I do when Liam and Emmet came to murder me for letting you put yourself in danger?"

An ember of anger flared to life in my stomach. "The two of them aren't allowed to have a chivving opinion about anything I chivving well do."

"Liam is the trueborn in charge of our camp, and Emmet is your brother."

An involuntary growl rumbled in my throat.

Finn held up both hands. "You want nothing to do with them, fine. That wouldn't stop them from coming for my hide if anything happened to you. And quite frankly, either one of them angry is bad enough without having to worry about their anger being rightfully directed at me."

"I'm running sorcis with you." I lifted my skirt to leap over a thin stream that cut through the slope. The sunlight caught the water as it danced downhill, leaving specks of gold shimmering on the surface. "They've got to accept there are risks involved. And if the slitches don't like it, they can very well go marching on a bed of hot coals."

"I appreciate your imaginative punishments."

"I've had time to ponder."

Finn stopped beside a tree bearing little white berries. He sniffed carefully before pulling a berry free.

"Don't even think of eating those."

Finn frowned.

"Trust me," I said. "It's not worth the fever and chills you'll get."

"To distract you from your vengeance on members of my clan? I might chance it."

"I'm not dragging your trembling body through the mountains." I knocked the berry from his hand. "Now get a move on before I decide to tell Neil you couldn't stop talking about how much you missed his root stew while we were traveling."

"You'd condemn the whole camp to eating sludge just to punish me?" Finn clutched his chest.

"Definitely. So don't test me."

"Fine." Finn let his hand fall, all hint of pretense gone. "Just be careful, Ena. Believing in a cause doesn't mean you have to take unnecessary risks for it. You're amazing with the sorcis—their families, too—but I'm better with a blade. If someone is going to have to try and stab a soldier, it should be me."

"No." I started climbing again, grateful for the distraction of the burning in my legs. "If you had died, Riesa and I would have been stuck. I couldn't hand her to the Briens without you. I couldn't take the way home without you. Like it or not, you are more valuable than I am."

"That's a chivving lie, and you know it." Finn took my elbow, steering me north. "This way if you want to get back to camp."

"See." I winked at him. "You, Finn, are irreplaceable."

7

We chatted off and on as we climbed through the mountains, Finn mostly asking if every new plant he spotted could be eaten. He nabbed some sour grass as we passed through a wide clearing, a few mushrooms not too far above a waterfall that tossed enough mist into the air to dampen my clothes, and a handful of leaves, I'd only have chosen if starving, from a twisted tree growing out of a cliff face.

The mountains had bloomed with their full summer bounty. Birds chattered, animals scurried, and it seemed hard to believe there could be anything wrong in the world.

When darkness came, we both pulled our lae stones from our pockets, trusting their blue light to lead us until we found a nice place to rest. I didn't miss the tent we'd left behind with the horse and wagon. Now that we were in the mountains, the rocky over-hang we chose suited me perfectly.

Finn carefully surrounded us with dark rocks as I laid down our bedrolls.

"We'll be back to camp by tomorrow afternoon." Finn stretched out under his blanket.

"A bath will be nice." I untied my boots and laid my knife at the top of my bed.

"Are we taking bets on how long we get to stay before they send us back out again?"

"Do you think they'll send us together?" I crawled under my own blanket. "They might give you another partner."

"I don't think so," Finn yawned. "There are so few people willing to put up with me."

"I do tolerate you rather well." I wrapped my fingers around my pendant and closed my eyes.

"You're a gift from the gods, Ena Ryeland."

I don't think I finished laughing at Finn's words before drifting into darkness.

Crack.

The sound yanked me from sleep.

Crack.

It came from right in front of our camp.

I sprang to my feet, my knife gripped in my hand.

"Finn," I whispered his name, hoping it was him I was hearing moving through the dark.

"I hear it." Finn's voice came from right beside me.

I glanced down.

He crouched on top of his blanket, a blade in each hand.

I swallowed my instinct to call out or reach for my lae stone.

A scuffling and a rustling carried from the right.

A growl came a moment later.

My heart slowed a little.

Not a soldier. A soldier wouldn't make a sound like that.

Another crack came, and then another.

"Do you see it?" Finn whispered.

I squinted into the darkness. "No."

A sighing growl sounded like it was coming from just beyond the trees.

I stepped forward, to the very edge of the stone-marked barrier.

A thing moved in the shadows, taller than any person and broader than two men put together.

The beast opened its mouth and gave a snarl that sent my heart racing.

Still gripping his knives, Finn slid an arm in front of me, pushing me away from the stones.

Thump, thump. Thump, thump.

The ground shook as the beast charged forward.

I caught a glimpse of massive claws as the monster swiped for us. It struck our boundary, sending a shimmering blue light blasting out into the night.

The beast roared and swatted again.

I tried to get a clearer view of the monster, but again the light flashed, dazzling my eyes and leaving bright spots in my vision, blocking out the details of the massive beast.

Over and over, the monster battered our protection. I caught a glimpse of it between every flash.

Sharp teeth in a mouth big enough to bite my head clean off. Dark fur matted with something that smelled like old blood. But not on the head. The monster's scalp had barely any fur. Thick scars on black flesh left ridges down its muzzle.

"What is it?" I whispered.

"A monster."

The thing roared, the strength of its rage shaking the leaves above us. It slammed its head into the barrier over and over again, sending flashes of bright blue into the night.

"What do we do?" I asked.

Finn stepped forward so his toes nearly touched the rocks.

The beast growled and gnashed its teeth.

"Hope it's gone by morning," Finn said. "Pray to the gods there aren't any paun in the woods for the light to attract."

"Wonderful."

The beast gave a bellow that sounded almost human.

"Are you sure it's real?" I asked.

"I mean…" Finn tipped his head to the side as the beast attacked our protection. "How do you mean?"

"Not a ghost or figment of our imagination?"

I stood on top of my blankets, feeling like a child woken by a nightmare as Finn slowly stepped side to side, squinting at the monster.

The beast roared.

"Don't know what it is." Finn sat down on his bedroll. "Don't honestly know if it matters."

"You're a Black Blood. You have the mountain running through your veins. Shouldn't you know every creature that roams this range?"

"Yes. I should also know every plant I'm allowed to eat, and we've seen how well I do on that end."

"Shouldn't you have heard of a great beast roaming the woods?" I sat with my back pressed to the rock wall.

"That's the problem with being a Black Blood. There are so many myths and legends, it's hard to keep them all straight."

The beast bellowed and moved to the cliff face on the side of our shell of safety. Stones clattered to the ground as the monster tore at the rock.

"You've got the myths that really are myths"—Finn raised his voice to speak over the scratching and clacking—"and the myths that are real. And the legends that are no better than fairy stories, and the legends that are about my great uncle, which my family swears are true."

I laughed and dared to set my knife down by my side.

"And that's just in the Duwead Clan," Finn said. "There are five Black Blood clans, and I promise you not all of our stories line up. This is probably Narek the Bumbling or some such nonsense."

"What?" I laughed louder this time.

Narek snorted his displeasure.

"Sure"—Finn scooted back to sit beside me—"flitted around on his lover and got turned into a great smelly beast so no one would let him into their bed. Poor Narek here is probably only trying to get in because he finds you so unbelievably attractive."

"Finn!" I swatted his arm.

"You're right," Finn sighed, "it's me the cursed bloke is after. Should I let him down with kind words, or just tell him right off I know better than to mess around with chivving curses?"

We kept laughing and chatting until the beast lost interest and left.

Finn and I drifted in and out of sleep, both leaning against the stone wall, knives by our sides.

I was glad Riesa wasn't with us. I didn't have enough left inside me to bear protecting an innocent against the horrors of the world.

Better to laugh at the monster in the dark than to face how truly terrifying the beast is.

8

I held my hand up to one of the scratch marks in the stone. The gouge cut three inches deep and was longer than my forearm. "Do you think he'll know what it was?"

I couldn't bring myself to say Liam's name, even if he was the person I wished were standing beside me as I ran my fingers through the gouges.

"We can hope." Finn passed me my pack. "I don't want to sound as though I'm a Black Blood who fears the mountains, but I'd rather not have that beast come sneaking up on me in the forest."

"Narek might steal you away," I said in a hushed voice. "Keep you in his cave forever."

"Don't test the gods." Finn started climbing the rock face.

I checked the knife tucked in my boot before following him.

In the daylight, all fears began to seem foolish.

Birds soared overhead, taunting us with how easy it was for them to fly from place to place.

I didn't envy their wings, not really. Not as I once had.

My arms were strong enough to help me scale the side of the cliff, and my balance good enough that I beat Finn to the top. My legs had ample strength to carry me wherever I wanted to go, even if they did burn in protest as the soft forest floor gave way to scree and the ground began shifting beneath our feet with every step.

Wings are delicate things. They can be broken. Then the bliss the birds sing of in their love ballads is gone. Having something as wonderful as wings only gives a person something precious to lose. In a world where the Guilds reign, everything you treasure can be ripped away from you. Everything you love is a weakness the paun will use to shatter you.

Better to have normal, sturdy limbs than beautiful wings. Better not to have anything it would break your heart to lose.

We'd already passed midday by the time we reached the high wall of stone even I wouldn't have had a chance of climbing. Sheer and more than a hundred feet tall, any normal traveler would have seen the cliff and tried to find a way around.

While I waited for Finn to woo the mountain, I amused myself by trying to think through a path up the cliff face. I couldn't do it.

I leaned against a tree fifty feet away as Finn paced back and forth in front of the rock, trailing his fingers along the cracks.

I loosened the cord on the pendant around my neck and retied it so the stone hung below my bodice and out of sight. The wind bit my skin, freezing the place where the pendant had lain. I felt naked without the stone resting above my heart. But I would rather have strolled through camp actually naked than let people see me wearing it.

Finn cursed at the rocks.

"Did you lose your way, Black Blood?" I shaded my eyes to stare at the rock face. "Did we end up at the wrong cliff?"

"No." Finn smacked his hands against the stone. "Though sometimes getting through this entrance is as bad as convincing my grandmother to give me a fourth helping of pie. I know she'll give in eventually, she just likes to make me beg for it."

"I think I'd like your grandmother."

"Stay with us until winter and you'll meet her." Finn stepped back and stared up at the top of the rock wall. "Though I will warn you, I get vicious when asked to share her pie."

"Warning taken."

Finn froze, like he had heard a noise that didn't exist to my ears. He looked to his right and beckoned me forward.

I crept slowly toward him as he slunk to his right. Before I'd made it thirty feet, most of Finn had disappeared. The only part of him I could see was his left arm reaching out through a crack in the stone I would swear to the gods and stars had not existed a moment before.

I took Finn's hand and slipped sideways into the slit in the rock. The world went black.

The birds' singing, the warmth of the sunlight, the smell of the forest, all vanished in an instant.

I took a deep breath, letting the scent of the stone soothe the instinct that shouted I would be crushed by the darkness.

The scent held more than just stone, though. The air was damp. I could smell the moisture on the rock, but it wasn't a stale thing like a puddle in a cave. The air was alive, as the mountain was alive.

I took a second breath. My body stopped panicking at the sudden loss of the outside world, and a strange feeling began. A pull right in the center of my chest. An ache that penetrated the bone above my heart as though the mountain itself had tied a string to me and would drag me through the darkness, whether I liked it or not.

And I wanted to follow the pull.

There was a longing deep inside me that wanted nothing more than to follow wherever that magic led, even if it meant walking into my own destruction.

After a third breath, I managed to shove the longing down.

Push it aside with all the other things I was smart enough to know I couldn't bear to feel.

I squeezed Finn's hand.

He pulled his lae stone from his pocket. The walls were close together this time, like the mountain had barely bothered to give us safe passage.

I waited for a nod from Finn before daring to pull out my own light.

Neither Finn nor I spoke as we wound our way through the tunnel. The ground beneath our feet was clear with not a pebble in sight to trip us. The dark stone of the walls was packed close together, leaving scarcely enough room for Finn's shoulders to pass.

I trailed my fingers along the walls as we traveled. Most of the stone was cool, as you'd expect from a rock kept out of the sunlight, but every now and then, there would be a warm patch, like a vein running to the heart of the mountain.

Magic.

I wanted to ask if I was right, but there was only one person I knew who was a trueborn Black Blood and really understood the way the magic of the mountain worked. Strong as my curiosity was, it couldn't make me go to him.

The tunnel opened into a wider space. The chamber's walls looked like they'd been cracked by time, and debris lay along the sides of our pristine path.

A gentle, blue light glowed off to one side, barely peeking out from behind a boulder.

I squinted at the shadows, trying to see where the light might be coming from. Something white lay on the dark ground. I took a step toward the glow.

Finn grabbed my arm, keeping me on the path. His red scruff glinted in the light of his lae stone as he shook his head. He kept his hand on my arm as we passed the boulder.

There was white on the far side, too.

Human bones lay on the ground, as though whoever had died while trapped in the mountain's embrace had been intentionally stripped of everything else.

I bit my lips together and stared at the back of Finn's head until we entered a tunnel three times as wide as the first. I walked by Finn's side as the tunnel twisted around itself, as though avoiding some unseen barrier.

A rumble of rushing water joined the sounds of our footsteps.

My heart leapt into my throat. I slid my arm from Finn's grip and held his hand as the sound became louder.

I have come too far to drown in a tunnel.

I gritted my teeth, sending the thought up to the gods and stars or down to the root of the mountain itself. I didn't really care where my plea went, so long as I didn't die buried deep beneath the ground.

Finn held my hand tighter as flecks of moisture filled the air. He stopped short and took a shuddering breath before holding his light close to the ground.

A foot-wide stretch of stone continued uninterrupted in front of us, but on either side, the rock disappeared. A torrent of water rushed beneath our feet with enough strength to wash away an entire village.

Shaking out his shoulders, Finn gave himself a nod before stepping onto the stone bridge.

The ground was slick beneath my feet. I clung to Finn's hand just as much for his safety as for mine. He was born a Black Blood—the strength of the mountains ran through his veins. The mountain itself recognized him as kin and gave him passage through the darkness. But I didn't know if the mercy of the mountain would go so far as to save Finn's neck should he slide into the racing water.

The torrent raged under us for a long time, reaching wider than any river I'd ever seen. Then suddenly, it was over, and the ground was solid rock once more.

Finn looked back at me, giving me a strained smile and a kiss on the cheek before striding quickly through the darkness.

As it always was when traveling beneath the mountains, just when I thought we would never see the outside world again, the tunnel narrowed and twisted, and then we were back out in the forest as though nothing strange had happened.

The sun sinking in the west gave away how long we'd been underground. The terrain was different as well. Tall trees surrounded us. Some even grew from the rock face we'd stepped out of, though I'm not really sure how they survived the vertical stone.

Finn let go of my hand and took a long moment studying the trees before heading north.

"You know," Finn said once the rock face was out of sight, "I'd find being swallowed by the mountain to be a much more pleasant experience if I knew there was decent food waiting on the other side."

"Don't be too harsh with Neil," I said. "You and I are lucky. We get to run off on adventures and save children from terrible fates. Poor Neil waits for us all to come home. Hungry, tired, sore, cranky, and he's got to feed the lot of us. I don't envy Neil."

"I never said I *envied* Neil, or that I thought I could do a better job. I just wish that whatever brave soul had Neil's job would also have some talent when it came to food."

I laughed louder and harder than I had since we'd left the camp more than a week before. A feeling of being home settled into my stomach, easing my fears and lifting a terrible burden from my shoulders.

We both walked more quickly in the last hour before we arrived at the camp.

I tucked my hands behind my back as we passed between two of the giant boulders that made up our boundary, steeling myself against the warmth that filled my chest as we stepped through the magic that protected us.

"Finn?" a man shouted from high up in a tree.

"Indeed it is." Finn bowed to the unseen person. "We have returned from yet another triumphant journey."

I balled my hands into tight fits, pushing away the heat that felt like a terrible hunger had taken over my soul.

"Good to hear." A man dropped from the branches of a tree, keeping an arrow nocked in his bow even as he fell. "Not all who've come back have fared so well."

"What do you mean?" I asked.

"We lost one." The man, Patrick I think was his name, put away his arrow and scratched his beard. "And another party is late in coming back."

"Were they all sorci runs?" Finn asked.

"Don't know." Patrick shook his head. "I try to keep my nose out of who's running what into the open. I have enough to worry about just with the people who are coming back."

"Right," Finn said. "Thanks for keeping watch."

I wanted to ask who had been lost and whose party was late coming home, but there was something in the way Finn strode toward the center of camp that kept me silent.

I'd only been with the Black Bloods since the spring. They'd accepted me as one of their own to a point, but there were rules and funny little ways of doing things I still didn't understand.

If it had been Emmet who'd been hurt, Patrick would have told me. I was new, but the Black Bloods nigh on worshiped my brother, and they all knew we were related.

Cati and Marta hadn't left camp all summer, so it couldn't be either of them.

Liam.

Panic pinched my lungs, making my head swim.

It's not him.

Liam was the trueborn Black Blood who commanded our camp. Patrick would have said if it was Liam. I resisted the urge to pull out the pendant I'd tucked into my bodice.

He's fine, Ena. They are all fine.

I stayed close enough to tread on Finn's heels as we took the path to camp. The scent of food and clatter of pans were the first signs of life.

A wide tent with all the flaps tied open came into view. A few hearty souls had already lined up to be fed. Neil glared at them as he stirred the stewpot, which was large enough for me to sit in.

Finn sidestepped so I could walk next to him. "It doesn't smell too bad. But I suppose I still shouldn't get my hopes up."

There was an unnatural tension beneath his words.

I opened my mouth to say something funny back but couldn't manage it. Not even to see Finn smile.

We entered a wide clearing surrounded by benches and chairs carved out of wood. A few of the seats were filled. A woman stitching in a patch of sunlight, an older man flipping through papers, a younger man staring into the shadows.

The largest chair, with a great bird carved into the back, sat empty.

There were more signs of life on the far side of the clearing, down the path that led to the tents where all of us lived. Voices carried from within the canvases. A man worked his way down the row, placing lae stones in each of the lanterns that hung along the trail.

The largest sleeping tent waited at the end of the path. My small tent sat right beside it. I wished I could go and hide inside my tiny fabric home, but someone had died. Delaying finding out who it was wouldn't keep the people I cared about any safer.

9

"Liam," Finn called out when we reached his tent.

I raised my fist and banged on the tent pole.

"Liam, are you in there?" Finn asked.

"Finn." Liam's voice came from behind us.

The pinching let go of my lungs.

"They told me you were back," Liam said. "How did it go?"

I turned to look at him. His skin shone from sweat. The edges of his hair had curled from it. He'd rolled up the sleeves of his shirt, and the beginnings of a giant bruise marked his arm.

"Well," Finn said. "The tracker was dead right with the location of the girl. Mother gave her to us, but the rest of the family stayed behind."

Liam dragged one hand along his jaw. The other rested on the hilt of the sword attached to his belt.

"It's probably for the best," Liam said. "The fewer we move, the fewer chances of being caught."

"Who was caught?" I asked.

Liam barely glanced at me before shifting his gaze to the palm of his hand. "Roland."

"Roland?" Finn asked. "What was he doing?"

"We needed supplies," Liam said. "His source turned him in. Mary barely made it back."

Roland and Mary, I could put faces to both of their names, but I'd never had a proper conversation with either.

I was grateful for it. My gratitude brought bile to my throat.

"Are we going back out to make sure the slitch never betrays our people again?" Finn asked.

"Emmet's already gone." Liam glanced at me again before looking to Finn. "He left two days ago."

"Good," Finn said. "Some need to be taught the consequences of betrayal."

"What party is late returning?" I asked.

"Sorci run," Liam said. "Kian and Erin—they left before you did. They should have been back two days ago."

Kian and Erin I knew. They liked to sit together at night in the clearing. Kian was fond of ale, and Erin loved to laugh loud enough for the whole camp to hear.

"Maybe they just got held up," I said. "We nearly had to lie low for a bit. They could be hiding in a barn somewhere, waiting the paun out."

"Why would you have to lie low?" Liam turned to me, actually keeping his gaze on me for more than a second.

"The soldiers were searching for the girl," I said. "We got away from them and met a pack of paun on the road."

"Shocking thing is," Finn said, "we didn't have to use our knives once."

"Come in, Finn." Liam stepped around me to his tent. "I want to talk through what you saw."

Finn moved to follow him.

"Have fun, boys," I said. "I'm going to try and figure out how eyes are meant to work. Since I clearly didn't see anything."

"Ena," Finn began.

Liam cut across him. "I just need Finn for now. I'll have things to speak to you about later, Ena."

I gave Liam a low curtsy. "I am honored, trueborn Liam."

Finn's eyes widened at me as Liam went into his tent.

I winked at Finn and ducked into my own tent.

The blankets were still carefully folded just as I had left them days before. A bag with the few extra bits of clothing I owned sat on the foot of the bed, safe from the ground's moisture. My comb lay on the little table made of a cut log, and the shorter log I refused to ever sit on waited beside it.

That was the funny thing about the Black Bloods' encampment—it was all permanently impermanent.

The tent was the closest thing to a home I'd had since Harane. It was my space, but only for now. When the cold came, it would be packed up, and all the people from camp would retreat to Lygan Hall, a place I still had trouble believing existed.

We would be gone, but life in Ilbrea would go on. Sorci children would be caught, and we wouldn't be there to stop it. The army would move, and we wouldn't know.

I didn't blame the Black Bloods, or even Liam, for fleeing from the snow. If we tried to stay in tents in the mountains, we'd all freeze to death well before the spring thaw. But the thought of Riesa being taken by soldiers with swords and shipped off to live in a stone tower because I was keeping warm in some mythical hall, made me so angry I thought I'd be sick on the dirt floor of my tent.

"Don't be a chivving fool, Ena." I dug through my sack of clothes, grabbed my comb, and left my tent.

The low rumble of Finn and Liam talking carried through the canvas as I strode past Liam's tent. Part of me wanted to smack the canvas and tell Liam he could chivving well cut his toes off if he thought I would be running around helping him if he didn't want to speak to me after.

But Liam was right to only want to speak to Finn.

Finn had been making sorci runs for three summers. Finn was a Black Blood. Finn was familiar with the maps. Finn understood things lowly little me wasn't supposed to know about. Finn hadn't kissed Liam and had his bleeding heart handed straight back to him.

I tried to slow my steps as I walked down the narrow path that led to the cave.

Humid air filled my nose before I reached the mountainside. The scent of dried flowers drifted out of the dark.

"Hello," I called into the shadows. I waited a moment before calling out again. "Anyone in there?"

I peered into the cave. Dim blue light left shadows drifting through the space, but there was no one inside.

"Thank the gods."

I dug into the back of one of the stone niches and fished out my soap, setting it beside the bath before sitting to unlace my boots. Dirt from the forest clung to my hands and dusted my bare legs above the ankles of my boots. I set my knife beside my shoes and stood to finish undressing.

The hot water of the bath wasn't enough to melt my anger away, but it did help to smooth out the edges. Scrubbing the filth from under my nails made me want to scratch Liam's eyes out just a little less.

I washed my hair and was just beginning to make a list in my mind of what I'd need to gather to give it another coat of black dye when a voice called from the entrance.

"Hello? Ena, are you in there?"

I ducked my head under the water.

You can't hold your breath forever.

I let my head drift back up above the surface.

"Ena?" A stone clacked under Marta's foot as she peered around the corner. "Ena?"

"Marta." I pushed my hair away from my face. "Come to have a bath?"

"Come to find you, more like." Marta's gaze swept through the corners before she stepped all the way into the cave. The light played across her pale blond hair as she walked to the side of the bath, carefully checking the floor before sitting beside me. "How are you?"

"Fine." I scrubbed my already clean arms. "Had a nice, healthy trek through the mountains and it's almost supper time. What more could a girl ask for?"

"Hmm." Marta pursed her lips, making her dimples disappear. "I could make you a list if you like. It would start with big, soft bed. There would be fine chamb and a proper dinner table included as well."

"And here I thought you liked ruling over our camp." I flicked water at her.

"I rule over nothing." Marta brushed the droplets off her skirt. "I just like to be useful wherever I can. Helping in Liam's work, even if my part is only making sure the lot of you don't fall into chaos and starve, makes me feel needed. I like it."

"You are most definitely needed. I don't know what we'd do without you."

"Good." Marta smiled. "How did it go out there?"

"Didn't you already get a full report from Liam?" I almost kept the edge out of my voice.

"A report from Liam doesn't tell me how you're actually doing. You went out into Ilbrea and had more than one run in with soldiers."

"It's not as though I never had to deal with them before I joined the Black Bloods. Honestly, the lot we met were downright gentlemanly."

"Ena, I'm being serious. When I found out about Roland and Mary, I was worried about you."

"Marta, it's kind of you." I took her hand. "But I promise, I was fine."

"It wasn't just me who was worried."

I climbed out of the tub, not caring as water sloshed toward Marta's skirt, and headed for the pile of folded cloths in the corner. It was probably Marta who made sure there were always some there waiting for us. I don't know who else in camp would have thought through such comforts.

"Emmet was worried sick, Ena." Marta snatched a cloth from the pile and handed it to me.

"Should I thank him for his concern?" I dried my arms so hard, my skin turned pink. "Perhaps a nice, heartfelt letter?"

"When he and Liam found out what had happened, it looked like both of them had seen a ghost." Marta beat me to my comb and handed that to me as well. "Losing Roland was a huge blow, Emmet was angry about that, but the fear was for you."

"And I'm sure he's taking that fear out on whatever cact of a demon spawn—"

"Ena."

"—betrayed Roland and Mary."

"Yes." Marta handed me my clean shift. "If I'm being totally honest, someone is going to die at Emmet's hands before he returns to camp. And whoever the poor fool is won't be leaving this world in an easy manner."

"Do you pity the one who caused Roland's death?" I grabbed my skirt before Marta reached for it.

"No, but I do wish your brother hadn't torn out of this camp as though he were off to slay the world."

"Then Liam should have stopped him."

"Liam sent him."

My hands shook as I threaded the laces on the front of my bodice.

Marta batted my fingers away to do the work herself.

"No one can bring Roland back," Marta said. "No one but the gods can save the fool who betrayed us from Emmet's wrath."

"No one can stop the Guilds from tormenting the tilk or the winter from coming. Don't you think I know that?"

Marta tied off my laces and started combing the tips of my hair. "There is precious little we can control in this world. I can't give the Black Bloods a homeland that will always be safe from the Guilds, but I can make sure our fighters don't have to worry about a warm bed or supplies. You can't bring Roland back, but you could stop resenting the fact that people worry about you. That your brother worries about you."

"Don't." I snatched the comb from her hand. "It's bigger than that. It's so much more than Emmet thinking I'm incapable of keeping myself alive. I'm grateful to have you as a friend, but my problems with him are too large for even you to fix."

"He's your brother, Ena. Doesn't that count for something?"

"It used to."

Marta didn't say anything else while I gathered my things and left the cave.

I wasn't fool enough to think she was done with me.

10

The fire crackled merrily in the corner of the clearing.

Neil stood beside the barrel, doling out ale to anyone brave enough to withstand his withering glare. He hadn't brought a pot of stew or a basket of bread from the cook tent. I suspected that was how you could tell what sort of a mood Neil was in. If he brought food, he was vaguely unhappy. If he didn't bring food, he was miserable and wanted all of us to be miserable with him.

Of course, I had no way of proving I was right, since Neil glowered no matter the occasion.

Two fiddle players had brought their instruments to the clearing. They took turns playing and drinking, so a cheerful tune always filled the air.

Did they play the night they found out Roland had died?

Probably.

I watched the shadows shift as people drifted in and out of conversation. The night was still young, and no one had settled into true frivolity.

"Going to lurk like a lump?" Cati sat beside me. The knife tucked in her boot glinted in the light of the lae stones.

"I just climbed a mountain for two days." I raised my mug to her. "I think I've earned a bit of sitting."

"I don't buy it." Cati took my mug from me, stealing a long drink of the ale I'd braved Neil to claim. "You love scrambling up and down the mountains. Holding you in one place for too long might wear you down, but not climbing."

"Does it matter?" I took my mug back and had a sip. I was grateful they managed to get any ale at all to camp, but I still couldn't help but wrinkle my nose at the perfumed taste of the brew.

"Sure it does," Cati said. "I'm to take you to the training field tomorrow. If you're ill or injured, I might have to go easy on you."

"Never." I laughed. It was a small laugh, but at least it was sincerely felt.

The fiddlers seemed to have decided they were sufficiently lubricated to begin playing in earnest. They set their cups down and began a dancing song. Within the first chorus, four couples had moved to the center of the clearing.

"I'm not Marta, Ena," Cati said. "I don't have the fortitude to sit here all night trying to slowly wheedle out what's wrong with you. If you're not ill and you're not injured, why under the stars are you sitting all alone?"

Finn appeared from the shadows, yanking Case off a bench and weaving him into the dance.

"I shouldn't be here." I ran my hands over my face. "I should be down in Ilbrea, helping. I should be ferrying the sorci children south. I should be doing something."

"Ahh." Cati drank from my mug again. "The first time Liam forbade me to leave camp, I almost murdered him. I had a sword in my hand and everything. I was going to run my blade straight through his gut then stomp down the mountain to kill as many paun soldiers as I could manage."

"Then why is he still alive?"

"Because"—Cati downed the rest of my ale—"I'm not the hero of our fight. No one is going to sing songs about me. I am one tiny piece in the little clockwork that is trying to keep the Guilds from gaining enough power to destroy my people's home while the bastards decimate everything in their wake. And my little cog is most useful teaching the other little cogs how not to die in a fight. Each of us has to do our part if we want any good to come out of all our work, and sadly enough, not all our parts involve getting to kill the chivving bastards."

"But what's my cog meant to do? Because sitting in this clearing doesn't seem to be helping anyone."

"Your part of the clockwork isn't in use at the moment." Cati knocked her shoulder into mine. "So have a bit of fun, forget about the world, get some rest. Then, when it's time to do your bit, you'll be ready. You'll have a recent memory of something in this chivving world that's actually worth fighting for. Now get some more ale and dance hard enough that you'll hate me on the training field tomorrow."

I didn't move.

"Go." Cati pressed my empty mug into my hand. "Be merry, whether you like it or not."

I swallowed my sigh as I stood and headed for the line of brave Black Bloods waiting for ale.

A shout rose from center of the clearing. Finn and Case bounded through the growing number of dancers, lifting and twirling each other with an enthusiasm to make Cati proud.

Join them, Ena. Abandon everything and jump into the dance. Just keep going until you're too tired to remember the outside world exists.

"Back again?" Neil grumbled at me when I reached the front of the line.

"Yes." I held my mug out. "My drink was pilfered, and I wanted to talk to you anyway. I'm going to go foraging tomorrow. If you like, I can keep an eye out for anything special you might be looking for."

In the light of the lae stones and fire, I could almost make out a gleam in Neil's eyes.

"Of course, if there isn't anything you need—"

"I'll think on it." Neil filled my mug to the brim. "Can't say I really do, but I'd be a fool not to spend a moment thinking on it."

"I'll stop by in the morning and see if you've come up with anything." I hid my smile as I turned back toward the clearing.

"What do you want more for, you lout?" Neil railed behind me. "Is your aim to be a no good drunk? Because I won't have any part in it."

I laughed through my sip of ale.

"Maybe I don't need any more," Pierce said as I crossed behind the end of the line. "Is he actually in that bad a mood?"

"That depends," I said.

"All I want is a drink, Neil!" The shout came from the front of the line.

"On what?" Pierce looked at me, his forehead creased in something between concern and amusement.

I considered Pierce for a moment. He was on runs into Ilbrea as often as I was, so I'd only spoken to him a few times. I didn't know him well enough to be sure what he considered a funny joke.

"On whether he likes you or not." I sipped my fragrant ale. "I didn't have a problem."

"You're cut off," Neil shouted. "For the rest of the season. If you want a drink, march to Lygan Hall."

"I don't think I need another ale tonight." Pierce stepped out of line.

"You're drunk on power!"

I peeked around to watch one of the older guards shouting at Neil.

"Probably for the best," I said. "You can have mine if you like. I don't really enjoy it."

"No." Pierce shook his head, his pale blond hair shimmering

in the faint blue light. "Doesn't seem worth it now. Would you like to dance instead? Then I don't have to worry about anybody's wrath."

"I..." My mouth had gone suddenly dry. I winced as I took another sip of the ale.

"Can I have that, Ena?" Cati appeared by my side. "I'm thirsty, and I don't think I could speak to Neil without punching him."

"Sure," I said after she snatched my mug away.

The fiddlers struck up a new tune.

Finn whooped his joy.

"You two should dance," Cati said. "It'll keep you out of the way if a brawl comes."

"Shall we?" Pierce offered his hand.

Cati winked at me and sipped my hard won ale.

"Sure."

Pierce took my hand, leading me toward the other dancers. His skin felt foreign against mine. His calluses lined up in places I didn't recognize.

He twirled me under his arm and led me into the circle with the other couples.

Finn and Case had given up on moving with the rest of the pack and danced in the center all by themselves.

I forgot to worry about following Pierce's steps as I watched their pure joy.

Finn tipped his head back, laughing to the sky. Case joined in as they tripped over the dance steps in their mirth.

By the time I realized I should be paying attention to where I was going, my body had already adjusted to Pierce's hold on my waist. He spun me faster, and I leaned back against his hand, letting him take all my weight.

His smile creased the corners of his bright blue eyes. Their color, along with his light hair, made my heart forget to beat for a moment. It was like a ghost from the life I'd left behind had somehow found his way to the mountains.

Pierce spun me under his arm, and the world disappeared in a blur of shadows and glowing blue lights.

I hadn't tied my hair back, so the black sheet of it floated out around me.

Pierce laughed as he spun me back in and lifted me in a circle.

I liked the sound of his laugh. It was easy and low, as though joy somehow came naturally to him.

The song ended, and Pierce held me tight, one arm still around my waist, as I caught my breath.

In the quiet between songs, Marta's voice rose above the rest of the chatter. "Now, Neil, no one is trying to steal ale from anyone. It's for everybody. If you don't want to work the tap, you can just go to bed."

The musicians started back up, playing louder than before as Neil began shouting.

"Again?" Pierce's blond eyebrows rose up his forehead.

"Best not to risk being caught in that mess," I said.

Pierce laughed as he swept me into the new dance.

I glanced toward the center of the clearing, wanting to see if Finn had noticed the sound of Pierce's laugh.

Finn and Case had disappeared.

The new dance had a series of jumps scattered through the pattern. Pierce's hands shifted from my back to my waist as he lifted me so easily I might as well have been flying.

"Just a bunch of ungrateful—"

Neil's shout startled me. I missed a step. Before I could even begin falling, Pierce had clutched me to him, shifting us out of the path of the dancers.

"Are you all right?" Pierce asked.

"I work my fingers to the bone to feed you lot," Neil shouted. "Does that not earn me a bit of respect?"

"I'm fine," I said.

"It's not about respect," the older guard said. "I do my job. Why can't you mange yours?"

"Everyone here is grateful for everyone else's work." Marta held her hands up between the two men, like a dimpled doll trying to hold back two angry hounds.

"Should I do something?" Pierce asked.

"I don't know." I took his hand, drawing him farther away from the dancers, whose weaving pattern had broken down as more of them stopped to watch Marta and the men.

The music broke on a foul note.

I looked to the bench where the fiddlers perched, but they were both staring at the path to the sleeping tents.

Liam stood at the edge of the light, behind his chair with the carved bird.

"Oh no," Pierce breathed as Liam strode across the clearing toward the fight.

I kept Pierce's hand in mine as I backed away from Liam's path.

Liam didn't even glance at me. He kept his dark gaze fixed on Marta.

"We should go." I turned to hop up and over a bench. A bit of me expected Pierce to let go of my hand. He didn't.

He kept our palms pressed together, even as he placed his free hand on the back of my waist, like he was ushering someone important into the woods.

"The last thing I need is one more man trying to fix a problem started by male egos!" Marta shouted.

Peirce and I laughed together as we ran farther into the woods.

11

We didn't stop running until the lights of the clearing had faded and the only sounds were the leaves rustling in the trees. The wind picked up, lifting my hair off my neck.

I sighed and slowed my steps.

"That happy to be away from the clearing?" Pierce matched his pace to mine.

"Yes," I said. "Maybe. It would be nice to watch sweet Marta give every man in this camp what for."

"Do all of us deserve it?" Pierce stopped to look at me.

"Probably." I ran my fingers through my hair, getting the stray strands away from my face.

"Do I?" Pierce lifted my hand away from my hair.

"I don't know. I'm not sure I know you well enough to have a clear view of what you might have done to anger Marta."

"I don't argue over ale." Pierce kissed the back of my hand. "And I was raised to be kind to ladies."

"Ladies?" I tipped my head back to stare up at the sky. Stars shone around the glimmer of the moon. "What about the women who don't really qualify for that title?"

"But you do qualify." Pierce stepped closer, halving the space between us. "You're brave enough to go into Ilbrea to save sorci children. You're beautiful enough to turn every head in camp. You're hard enough to have survived what life has given you, and you're a fine dancer besides."

"You seem to know a lot more about me than I know about you."

"You're fascinating. I'm not." Pierce smiled. The corners of his eyes lifted, and creases appeared. Not lines of anger or worry, just little hints of joy.

My fingers buzzed as I reached up to touch their texture.

He turned my other hand, kissing my palm. "We can head back if you like, cut around the great ale brawl."

I didn't want to head back. I didn't want to see Liam and wonder if he was ever going to truly look at me again.

"No." I closed the gap between us, tipping my chin up.

He let go of my hand and wrapped his arms around my waist.

Slowly, he lowered his mouth, brushing his lips against mine.

A tiny flare of something like hunger bubbled up from my spine as I leaned closer to him, letting my chest graze his.

He kissed me in earnest.

He'd shaved not long ago. There was no stubble on his chin to rake across my skin.

I wrapped my arms around his neck, teasing his lips with my tongue. I couldn't taste him beyond the fragrance the ale had left on both of us.

He held me closer, pinning his hips against mine, as his left hand roamed up my side, his thumb caressing the side of my breast.

I wound my fingers through his hair, kissing him more deeply, letting what my body craved drown out the aching of my heart.

He lifted me, carrying me to a wide tree. The bark cracked as my back pressed against it.

His lips roamed, kissing down my neck and back up to my

ear. I took his face in my hands, guiding his mouth back to mine as he undid the tie at the top of my bodice.

He trailed his lips back down my neck, kissing the soft spot beside my collar bone.

The thrumming in my body extinguished all thought beyond wanting to be touched.

He pulled the laces of my bodice loose, lowering the neck of my shift as he kissed the top of my breasts.

I shuddered a gasp as he ran his hand up the side of my thigh, lifting the hem of my skirt.

"Ena," he whispered my name.

"Ena." A voice boomed through the trees.

Pierce straightened up, clutching me to his side as though protecting me from the noise.

A shape appeared between the trees, the shadow of the first and last person I wanted to see.

"Who's there?" Pierce pulled his knife from his belt.

My heart froze and shattered as Liam stepped into a beam of moonlight.

"Liam?" Pierce squinted at him. "You nearly gave me a heart attack."

"You shouldn't be out here, Ena." Liam's gaze drifted over me, from my falling off top to my mussed up hair, before locking onto Pierce. "She doesn't know the mountains well enough to be wandering in the dark."

"I won't leave her alone," Pierce said. "I can see her safely back to camp."

"I'll take care of her," Liam said. "We still haven't talked about her last sorci run."

"Right." Pierce eased his hold on my waist. "Can't afford to wait. Lives could be in danger." He kissed my temple. "I'll see you tomorrow, Ena."

The chill of the night air sent a shiver up my spine as Pierce turned and walked back toward camp.

"What do you want to know?" I tucked my hands behind my back, resisting the urge to retie my bodice.

Liam glowered up at the trees.

"Oh," I said, "you didn't want to know anything? You just wanted to follow me to be sure poor, incompetent little Ena didn't get lost in the scary woods?"

"The girl," Liam said, "you should have left her in the compartment below the wagon."

"Left her terrified and alone in that tiny space? No." I stepped closer to him. "I didn't know enough about her magic to risk her panicking out of my sight a moment longer than necessary. Was I supposed to leave her back there and wait for the cart to catch fire or for lightning to strike? Better to keep her where I could see what I was facing.

"That and I'm not a heartless slitch who wants to snatch a little girl from her mother only to leave her locked up and terrified. That's what the Guilds would do, and I am not like them."

"And what if Finn hadn't been able to hide her magic when the soldiers stopped you?" Liam looked down at his hands.

"Then I guess we would have had to fight."

"Against a hundred soldiers?"

"I didn't say we would've survived."

"You can't do that, Ena." He finally looked at me. His dark eyes held none of the warmth I longed for. "You have to be careful."

"Careful?" I crossed my arms over my chest. It made my unfastened bodice look worse.

"Yes." Liam stepped away from me. "I am trying to protect you."

"Like you protect Emmet?" I walked straight up to him, stopping with barely a foot of air between us. "Do you think he's being safe right now? Do you think he's carefully doing everything he can to avoid a fight?"

"That's different."

"Because I'm a sad little girl who might get lost in the woods at night? Do you think I'm incapable of accomplishing the tasks you've given me? Do you think I'm dumb or weak—"

"I'm trying to keep you alive!"

"Why should my chivving life matter more than Emmet's or Roland's?"

Liam scrubbed his hands over his face.

"I am not a child. I am not innocent. I don't need you coming into the woods to make sure I can find my own chivving tent."

"Ena—"

"If I die, it's my life that's ended. Let my death be my own concern. It wouldn't matter to you any more than losing anyone else in this camp. Go find someone else to protect."

I turned and strode off through the trees.

"Ena," Liam called after me, "we're not done here."

"Find me tomorrow."

I didn't look back. I couldn't manage to mask my hurt any longer.

The fire in the clearing had been put out for the night, leaving only the blue glow of the lae stones.

I searched the shadows, hoping Pierce might be waiting for me.

There was no one.

I wanted a mug of ale, but the barrel had been rolled away.

"Just sleep, Ena." I forced myself down the path to my tent. I dragged my fingers through my hair, picking out the bits of bark caught in the strands.

A few people lingered outside their tents, whispering in gleefully hushed voices.

I should have retied my bodice, or at least cared as gossipy Nessa spotted me out of the corner of her eye and her face lit up like the King himself had died.

I ducked into my tent and tied the flaps shut behind me, like a thin bit of fabric could somehow serve as a barricade between the night and me.

My comb waited on the stump table. I sat on my bed and brushed my hair until there wasn't a hint of forest left behind. I placed my knife under my pillow and my boots under my bed, then folded my bodice and skirt so cleanly, no one could have guessed they'd been mussed in the woods.

When I had nothing left to occupy myself, I lay down, clutching the stone pendant, wondering what would have happened if Pierce had kissed low enough to find it.

I lay there for hours, waiting for exhaustion to claim me.

I never heard Liam return to his tent.

There are some people you love so deeply they remake your entire soul.

It is not a beautiful process. It is painful and permanent.

I remember the girl I was before. I think like her. My face is the same as hers.

But my soul is different.

Where the wind through the trees once called to me, now I long only for him.

His scent is what fills me, and I would follow it to the end of the world.

"Better." Cati planted the tip of her staff on the ground and reached down to help me up. "But you've got to learn to attack, not just defend."

"Right." I took Cati's hand and jumped to my feet, doing my best to pretend I couldn't feel the stinging pain behind my knees where her staff had pummeled me. "I'll try and attack you and see how much faster I end up in the dirt."

"Survival isn't meant to be easy." Cati handed me my staff. "If learning to fight wasn't hard, the Guilds would have overrun the mountains last century."

"Then I will take the pain, knowing the paun feel it as well."

Before Cati could respond, I twirled my staff over my head, bringing one end down toward her shoulder.

Cati swiped her own staff through the air, knocking my blow toward the ground.

I slackened my grip on my staff and let the momentum of her strike kick the bottom of my weapon toward me. I grabbed the staff with my free hand, spinning it toward Cati's neck.

She ducked just in time.

Before I could tighten my grip on my weapon, a blow caught

me right above my shoulder blades, and I was on the ground again.

I pushed myself to my knees and spat the dirt from my mouth.

Clapping carried from across the field. Finn strode toward me, his sword sheathed at his side. "Nicely done!"

"She'd still be dead." Cati held my staff out to me.

"But she'd have gone down in a blaze of glory I could recount around the fire in my old age," Finn said.

"All of my wishes granted." I brushed the filth from my face.

"You've improved so much." Finn clapped me on the shoulder, barely avoiding my growing bruise. "I think it must run in your bloodline. The Ryelands are a deadly crew."

"Am I a deadly Ryeland? Or am I just a child who gets tattled on for doing her job?" I glared at Finn. His mirth melted away. "Is there even a reason for me to learn how to fight if my place is just to sit prettily in the wagon? In fact, I think the Black Bloods and all Ilbrea would be better served if I sat by the fire sewing. I can make dolls that look like women. You can take one on your next sorci run. Prop it up in the front of the wagon to sit beside you. No one will know the difference. Don't worry, if you don't like how the pretty doll handles herself, you can just tell Liam."

Cati let out a low whistle and lifted the staff from my grip.

"Cati"—Finn looked to her—"I think you've hit Ena on the head a bit too hard. She seems to be confusing me with a chivving slitch instead of the partner she's run through Ilbrea with more than once."

"If you didn't tell Liam about my keeping Riesa out of that chivving trap and speaking to the soldiers, who did?" The heat of anger rushed through my chest. I enjoyed the way it filled me.

"Of course I told him what happened." Finn stepped close to me, speaking in a low voice. "He's the commander of the camp. I also told him what a brilliant job you did, and that I would be pleased to keep making sorci runs with you, because I stand a better chance of getting those poor children out with you by my side."

A tiny hole punctured my chest, deflating my anger.

"If Liam's giving you a hard time, it's got nothing to do with me," Finn said. "But sort yourself out quick. We're two pairs of runners down, so it won't be long before they send us out again."

He strode away, back toward the ring where the Black Bloods practiced their sword fighting.

"Damn," I breathed.

"Go," Cati said. "I've bruised you enough for today anyway."

"Thanks." I ran after Finn.

He stopped before I reached him.

"I…" I bit my lips together, wishing Lily had spent more time teaching me the proper way to apologize. "Did you tell Liam about the beast we saw?"

"I did." Finn turned to face me. "He said he'd send a message to Lygan Hall, see if any of the elders or story keepers had heard of such an animal."

"Right." I took Finn's hand and pressed his palm to my cheek. "I'm sorry. I shouldn't have snapped at you. I just—"

"Came home last night with your top untied?" The glimmer of mirth returned to Finn's eyes. "Had your fun interrupted and got to see Liam's better side all at once?"

"More or less."

Finn kissed my forehead. "Like it or not, you Ryelands have the same chivving temper. At least when you're angry, I only have to worry about my feelings getting hurt instead of needing to protect a small village from destruction."

"Give it time." I poked Finn in the ribs. "I'm getting better at fighting. Next warm season, maybe I'll go take out my wrath on Ilara."

"I believe it of you. The destruction of Ilbrea's mighty capital at the hands of a beautiful raven. Just remember who's fighting on your side, little bird."

He wiped a streak of dirt off my chin and headed to the boundary of the sword ring where Case waited with his blade drawn.

Case's face lit up as Finn approached. I wished I could hear the words they exchanged before facing off to fight.

The sun beat down on my shoulders, warming my skin as I listened to the clanging of their blades. They fought with such fury, it seemed as though they were deadly foes.

Do your work, Ena.

The words echoed through my head. The voice sounded like Lily, or at least, the way I remembered Lily speaking.

I didn't remember the sound of my parents' voices. They had been gone too long. Soon enough, time would steal Lily's voice from me, too.

The need to move and climb burned through my legs. I had to get out, away from the clanging weapons and people of the camp.

I ran all the way back to my tent, but the effort didn't lessen my need to flee.

The bag I'd carried with me from Harane waited under my bed. I snatched it up and darted back out of the tent as though the canvas had caught fire.

Nessa stood on the path between the tents, leaning toward Marta, whispering in her ear. Glee filled Nessa's face when she spotted me.

I bolted through the trees, heading south.

"Ena," Marta's call followed me, but I didn't look back.

I ran and ran, not bothering to loop around to see if Neil wanted me to search for anything in the woods. I didn't care about having an excuse to escape the camp. I just needed to get out.

My breath tore at my throat and stung my lungs.

I ran harder, leaping over fallen logs, not pausing as tree branches ripped the skin on my arms.

I didn't stop until I reached the boulders that marked the edge of camp.

Even gasping for breath couldn't mask the longing that filled my chest as I neared the great rocks. No moss or filth marred their surface, as though the stones were meant to be solitary and perfect, untouchable by the realities of mortal life.

I rested my palms on a boulder, letting the ache that pulled at the place just above my heart tear through every other horrible thing I didn't want to feel.

The cool surface of the stone welcomed me. I pressed my forehead to the rock, savoring the knowledge that my touch couldn't warm it.

The mountain had made the boulder. The mountain didn't care about my fate. I was nothing to the magic that lived deep below the ground.

A knot pressed on my throat as the pull in my chest threatened to shatter me.

I let out a long breath and stepped away from the stone and beyond the spell that protected us all.

I had fled from camp often enough to know the mountainside well. My feet carried me to the mushrooms Neil always asked me to gather and to the tiny clearing where the roots I wanted to grind into tea grew.

My path had become so familiar to me, I began untying my bodice before I even heard the faint rumble of the waterfall.

The trees changed as I drew near the river's narrow banks. The moisture allowed the trunks to grow thicker and the leaves broader. The scent of damp earth hung heavy in the air, and the ground gave gently under my feet.

The waterfall itself wasn't massive, only twenty feet high. But time had created a deep basin at the bottom. I'd found my secret swimming place a month before when I'd dodged out of camp after Emmet had a fit about my coming back from a sorci run with a bandage on my arm.

I sat on a wide rock to untie my boots. The sun caught the mist off the falls, sending little rainbows dancing in the air. I slipped out of my clothes, using the heft of my knife and bag to protect them from being stolen by the wind.

A breeze played across my naked body, not caring which bits

of me were bruised or scarred. The stone pendant hung low around my neck, its warmth a constant comfort against my skin.

A bird swooped through the sky, chirping his joy at the freedom he'd found.

"Fly on, little bird," I whispered to the wind.

I didn't let myself run to the side of the waterfall. I picked my way through the rocks and moss, careful not to let any thorns pierce my bare feet.

A stone cliff reached to the top of the falls. Time had created enough cracks that scaling the twenty feet didn't hold enough difficulty to make my arms ache. I wished the cliff were higher—fifty or a hundred feet, enough to make my head swim and my body burn from the effort.

I pushed myself up onto the ledge and rolled onto my back, shutting my eyes against the bright sunlight.

The rocks beneath me were warm.

"Does the mountain want the boulders it presses magic through to be cold?" I ran my fingers along the rock. "Is it only some stones in the mountains that hold magic, or is it all of them?"

The bird swooped overhead again but didn't offer an answer.

Liam would know. Liam could tell me all about the magic that surrounded me.

I leapt to my feet and ran along the rumbling riverbank.

Not far from the ledge, the path of the water twisted, arcing north. I stopped at the curve, turned, and sprinted back toward the falls.

The thin mist coming up from the cascading water blocked my view of the pool below. The drop could have been a thousand feet, or an infinite plunge into a vast darkness. There was no way for me to be sure the earth hadn't opened up to swallow me whole.

I took a breath as I reached the edge of the cliff and leapt into the open air.

The rush of falling, the way my stomach surged up into my lungs, pummeled every other feeling from my body before I hit the cold water below.

The river surrounded me. The rumbling of the falling water was the only sound left in the world. My limbs were weightless, nothing more than bits of debris to be pushed around at the current's will.

First, the cold stole the soreness of my limbs, numbing the aches and bruises. My feet grazed the rocks at the bottom of the river as the current carried me away from the world.

I didn't fight it.

Then, the calm of the nothing began lifting away other, deeper hurts. Pains I was too terrified to even begin to name. A bit of anger drifted downstream. The jagged edges of a longing that could never be fulfilled were smoothed.

A vice wrapped around my ribs, squeezing all the air from my lungs.

I kicked back, fighting to free myself, but the horrible pressure only increased. I grabbed at my ribs, finding an arm wrapped around me as my head broke through to the open air.

I coughed, gasping for breath.

"You're all right." A gravelly voice spoke in my ear. "I've got you."

I elbowed back, knocking my captor in the stomach.

He grunted from the impact but tightened his grip.

I twisted to the side, ready to bite, but it was Liam who held me.

"Stop fighting me," Liam panted as he shoved me toward the shore.

"What are you doing?"

He tossed me onto the bank, sinking out of sight for a moment before dragging himself up after me.

"Are you hurt?" He swiped his soaking hair away from his eyes.

"Why would I be?"

"What under the stars were you thinking?"

"That this was nice spot to have a swim." I sat up, wringing the water from my hair.

"You could have died." Liam got to his feet. His whole body shook right down to his sopping wet boots.

"I was doing quite well until you tried to drown—"

"Do you have any idea how long you were down there?" Liam shouted. "I thought you were dying."

"Well, I wasn't." I stood and headed back toward the rock wall. "I was having a grand old time, so you can feel free to leave."

"What are you doing?" Liam chased after me, the water in his boots squishing as he ran.

"Climbing." I dug my fingers into the rock and began pulling myself up.

Liam grabbed me around the waist, lifting me off the stone. "No, you're not."

"Why?" I rounded on him. "Is it against some Black Blood rule? Is this a sacred waterfall from some myth that happens to be true?"

"Don't be ridiculous."

"What's ridiculous is you trying to save me." I brushed away the moss that clung to my ribs. "What are you doing out here anyway?"

"Put your clothes on, we're going back to camp." Liam turned away from me.

"Why? Do you need me for a run into Ilbrea? Am I supposed to be leaving now?"

He stalked over to my clothes.

"Are you afraid I won't be able to find the camp by myself?" I leaned back against the stone cliff. "I promise I can. I don't need you to hold my hand and lead me through the scary woods."

He pulled my clothes from under my knife and bag and held them out to his side. "Get dressed."

"Why?" I strolled toward him. "The weather is lovely, and I'm enjoying being naked."

"Just put your chivving clothes on."

"Why do you care if I'm naked or not? It's not like you look at me anyway."

I watched the sides of his neck tense. I stopped right behind him.

His shirt clung to the muscles of his back. My fingers burned with the urge to touch him, just for a moment. Just long enough to memorize the contours of him.

"You don't care anything about me," I said.

"That's not true."

"Of course." I dodged around his outstretched arm to stand in front of him.

He tipped his gaze up to the sky.

"You are the trueborn Black Blood in charge of our camp," I said. "You care for all your people. Even the ones you won't look at."

The line of his jaw hardened as he looked at me. Not a glance or a glare.

For the first time since we'd come home from Marten, he actually saw me.

"It's better if I don't." He spoke just above a whisper.

I froze as his gaze searched my face.

"I have to keep you safe, Ena." He reached out, his fingers barely grazing my cheek.

"Why?" I wanted to lean into his touch but was too afraid I might shatter whatever magic kept him near me as his thumb slid down the side of my neck.

"I have to protect you. Sending you out into Ilbrea is bad enough, but the most dangerous thing I could do is let you anywhere near me." He stepped away, pressing my bundle of clothes toward me.

"That doesn't make sense." I shoved the clothes aside.

"You don't understand."

"Understand what? What have I done to make you believe I am so foolish or weak that I can't understand, that I need to be protected?"

"I'm a trueborn." Liam tossed my clothes back onto the rock. "In camp, that makes me important, in Ilbrea, it's a death sentence, and in Lygan Hall, it puts a target on my back."

"What's that got to do with—"

"The safest place for you is far away from me. I put you in danger by bringing to the Black Bloods—"

"You saved my life."

"Your place is with us now, but letting you stand by my side is one thing I will not do. I have to protect you, and that means keeping you away from me." He dug his fingers into his hair, pulling at the roots.

I held my breath as I stepped toward him. I took his hands in mine and lowered them between us.

"You don't want me," I whispered. "You kissed me, and you walked away."

He stared down at our hands.

"Tell me you don't want me, Liam." I moved his hands to my waist, then lifted his chin so his eyes met mine. "Just say it."

"I…"

My heart shuddered and stopped.

"I want you safe. I want you protected." Pain filled his dark eyes.

"What about what I want?" I stepped closer to him, my bare chest touching his. My skin burned as his hands tightened around my waist.

"I'm not worth it. You are better off far away from me."

I rose up on my toes so my lips skimmed his. "No, I'm not."

The world froze as I kissed him. His scent flooded through me, and everything else vanished.

He trailed his hand up my side, and fire filled my stomach.

I laced my fingers through his hair and deepened our kiss.

My body hummed as he held me tighter. Wanting pulsed through me as I began to unbutton his shirt.

If the gods had destroyed the world in that moment, my story would have had a happy ending.

Fate is not that kind.

Liam broke free from our kiss and took my hands in his. He met my gaze before pressing his lips to both my palms.

"It isn't about wanting you, Ena." He touched the pendant hanging around my neck. "It can't be."

He let go of my hands and picked up my clothes.

"I followed you because I need to talk to you. I received a message from a trueborn Brien."

"Is Emmet all right?" I took my clothes from him.

"It wasn't about Emmet." Liam looked into my eyes. "The Briens have heard about your poison, the way you took care of Drason."

"How?"

"The death of a monster like Drason was never going to go unnoticed."

"An entire village was slaughtered." I pulled my shift over my head. "Do they want vengeance for the innocent blood on my hands?"

"They want your poison."

"What?" The world froze again. There was no bliss this time.

"There's a problem on the route they use to ferry the sorci children. The Brien need to get rid of the problem."

"And they've never heard of a sword?" I fastened the back of my skirt.

"It needs to happen quietly."

"A knife, then."

"They want the poison."

"No."

Liam took my hand. "They need it, Ena. Just a dose, maybe

two."

"Absolutely not." I pulled away from him. "I'm not going to package up a nice vial of death to murder a stranger."

"You never met Drason."

I wiggled into my bodice, yanking at the laces to keep my hands from shaking. "Drason was different."

"How? One paun monster is the same as the next."

"I don't know the Brien. I don't know their definition of a monster. I don't know how careful they'd be to get the poison to the right person."

"Ena—"

"Drason was different because I trust you." The words tore at the back of my throat. "Blame the stars if you want, but I do. I won't have a stranger die by my hand based on the word of a person I've never met."

I sat on the rock to yank my boots on. My nerves finally gave out, and my fingers started shaking as I tied the laces.

"I'm sorry to have to ask you." Liam knelt beside me.

"I can't have another massacre on my head. I can't survive it." I shoved my knife into the ankle of my boot. "You want to protect me from you but think I should help the Brien? By the gods, you're a chivving fool, Liam." I snatched up my bag and headed for the trees.

"Ena, wait."

"If the Brien really want to poison someone, it's not that hard to figure out." I rounded on him. "Line up a batch of volunteers and start feeding them every plant from the forest it looks like they shouldn't eat. When one of the slitches dies, they'll know what to use for murder."

Liam stared at me, his expression a mix of pain and confusion.

I wanted to comfort him, to soothe away every worry.

Before I could move, he nodded and turned toward the waterfall. I swallowed my hurt and walked back to camp.

16

My hair had nearly dried by the time I reached the cook tent.

Neil had a bruise blossoming around his left eye and was busy chopping roots with such fury I didn't even speak to him as I laid the mushrooms on the table and dodged back out into the open air.

I thought of trying to find Marta so she could tell me what had happened the night before, then I remembered Nessa whispering in her ear.

No sooner had the dread at what Nessa might have said dripped into my stomach than Marta appeared on the path in front of me.

"Ena." She gave me a bright smile, setting her dimples on full display. "I've been looking for you."

The dread in my stomach doubled.

"I was out gathering some things." I patted my bag. "I left goodies with Neil, and I'll be able to make some nice tea for the next batch who have too much to drink."

Marta circled around to loop her arm through mine before leading me on toward the sleeping tents.

"Winnie will be so grateful. She's a fine healer, but having you to gather things for her is such a help. Especially when people bother her with silly problems of their own making," Marta said. "It is funny the things that can happen when people get too deep into their cups. Honestly, if I didn't think I'd be killed in my sleep, I'd stop allowing the stuff in camp at all."

"That would be a dangerous decision." My laugh came out close enough to genuine that Marta continued.

"Take last night, for example."

"What happened to Neil's eye?" I stopped to look at Marta.

"Nothing." She waved a hand through the air. "Old men with bad tempers. Those two would like to punch each other stone sober and well fed. There are some people who love being miserable, and there's not a thing you can do about it."

"That's still a nasty black eye."

"There are worse things than black eyes." Marta tugged on my elbow, guiding me off the path to a stand of trees just out of the way of anyone passing by. "And some choices made in the dark can have awful consequences."

"Sure." I nodded before adding, "What are you talking about?"

Marta reached into her pocket and pulled out a little glass bottle. "I don't want to interfere, but I can't let this sit on my conscience."

"I still don't know what you're talking about."

"Pierce isn't a monster or anything, but deciding to run off into the woods with him because Neil's having a tantrum? That's a dangerous thing to do, Ena."

"Yes, Pierce might have left my corpse for the wolves."

"It's not funny." She pressed the bottle into my hand and closed my fingers around the glass. "I'm not overly fond of gossip, but I'm glad I heard about this before it was too late. Consider whose child you'd be willing to carry before running into the dark next time. Or at least be prepared for morning."

I opened my hand to stare down at the glass bottle. "I don't know what you think happened—"

"What I think doesn't matter. Just know there are people who genuinely care for you and want to keep you safe." She kissed my cheek. "Best to drink it when you've got a bit of water on hand. It's nasty stuff."

Marta patted my shoulder and strode away.

I stood for a long moment, staring down at the little bottle. The sun peeked through the leaves above me, glinting off the glass.

A deep anger bubbled in my stomach, seething up into my throat. I let out a yell as I threw the bottle against the tree, smashing the shining glass into shards.

I went into my tent and lay down on my cot, counting the minutes until Finn would come bursting in to tell me it was time to go back out into Ilbrea and far away from the den of chivving Black Bloods.

17

The first day, I stayed in my tent, hiding from whatever rumors Nessa had started.

The second day, I went out to the training field and let Cati beat my rage out of my body.

The third day, I realized I wasn't insane. Pierce had started avoiding me. He wasn't as subtle about it as Liam.

Liam had at least managed to start looking at me again. He even gave me a nod when I nearly ran into him as I stumbled to the breakfast line, my eyes barely open.

Pierce, on the other hand, caught sight of me, turned sheet white, and left without getting any food.

That afternoon, I convinced Finn to start training me in sword combat.

The fourth day, I finished training, bloody and bruised, and walked far enough into the forest that I could scream my rage without anyone hearing.

The fifth day, a little stone bird flew into camp and landed on Liam's shoulder. Word had finally come—Kian and Erin would never be returning to camp. They had been killed by paun soldiers while fighting to protect a sorci child.

Finn didn't dance with Case that night. He sat on a bench with me, holding my hand.

It took six days for Liam to finally speak to me again.

"It's not that hard a job." Neil banged his spoon against the side of his massive metal pot with a clang that pounded into my ears.

None of the three of us working in the cook tent were foolish enough to speak.

"Go out into the woods, find an animal, and kill it," Neil railed. "Bring the chivving thing back, and I'll do the real work of preparing the chivving beast to feed the hundred-odd ungrateful chivving mouths I've been charged with."

I tucked my chin and kept my gaze fixed on the dried root I was shredding.

"But when the meat doesn't come"—Neil picked up his knife and began hacking his way through a tuber—"it's not the useless hunters that get blamed. It's me."

A brew for an ill temperament, that's what he needs.

Lily had grown herbs for such things in her garden in Harane. She usually doled them out to soothe women who found dealing with their chivving husbands nigh on impossible. I hadn't seen any such plants in the mountains, but I was sorely tempted to find myself a few seeds the next time Finn and I ventured out into Ilbrea. Start brewing Neil a morning cup of tea.

"Ena." Liam's voice broke through my thoughts.

I looked up to find him standing outside the tent, his face unreadable.

"Liam"—Neil stepped forward, still clutching his knife—"I will not be blamed for the lack of meat. You've got to do something about these hunters."

"I'll send Marta by," Liam said.

"But you're the trueborn," Neil said. "It's you who's in charge of this camp. It's you who can make sure the slitches get what's coming to them."

"Marta will handle it," Liam said. "Ena, I need to speak to you."

I swallowed the fear that balled up in my throat. There was something in his tone, in his stillness, that didn't seem natural.

"People are going to be hungry, but by all means." Neil bowed me toward Liam.

I stood, leaving my half-shredded root on the table, and stepped out of the tent. Being closer to Liam didn't make his manner any less disconcerting.

"This way." He nodded toward the path that led to the sleeping tents.

Neil's angry mutters followed us as I walked beside Liam.

He didn't speak until we were out of hearing distance of the others. "It's not Emmet."

The knot of fear in my throat dissolved a little.

"Then what am I supposed to have done?" I placed my hand over my heart. "I've been keeping my clothes on, I swear it."

Liam winced and shook his head.

"Have rumors of my running wild in the woods become enough of a bother that I'm in trouble?" I asked. "Am I being thrown out and sent back to Ilbrea to take my chances with the Guilds?"

Liam stopped and turned toward me, his shoulders and jaw tense. "That wouldn't happen. I would never let that happen."

"Then what is it?" I reached out to touch him.

He flinched again.

I tucked my hands behind my back. "Whatever you need to tell me, you're just going to make it worse by brooding like this."

"We have to meet with the others first." Liam cut off the path and into the woods.

I swallowed my questions as I followed him, studying the trees we passed instead of letting my mind race through the hundreds of horrible things that could have possibly riled Liam so badly.

We reached a small clearing in the trees with a giant stone sitting right in the center.

If we had been in Ilbrea, I would have said that someone had taken a great deal of time to grind the top of the rock into a perfectly flat surface. But we were in the mountains, and though it sent a shiver through my shoulders, I was quite sure the stone had been smoothed by magic.

"Liam." Cati stepped out of the trees. Her gaze locked on me, but she offered me no greeting.

Finn stepped out of the shadows beside her with the horse minder, Tirra, close behind.

Tirra glanced between Liam and me. "Why's Emmet's sister here?"

Liam laid his palm on the flat top of the stone. He stayed that way for a moment, his eyes shut tight.

I held my breath, waiting for some great magic to happen.

"I received a message from a trueborn Brien." Liam opened his eyes and pulled a tiny stone bird from his pocket. He ran his finger down the bird's spine, and the creature came to life, wiggling its wings and tipping its chin up so a tiny scroll could poke out from the front of its neck.

Liam handed the scroll to Tirra.

"The trueborn wants to meet Ena," Liam said.

"What?" Finn stepped around the stone to stand beside me. He wrapped his arm around my waist, keeping me close to his side. "That's ridiculous. If the slitches think it's going to happen, they're out of their chivving minds."

"Why?" Cati asked.

"The poison," Tirra said. "They want to meet her in person to ask for her help."

Cati gripped the hilt of her sword and looked to Liam. "You told them no, of course."

"With the first request," Liam said. "I don't know if I can deny this message."

"Why should you?" I asked. "If someone wants to meet me, that's fine. Have the trueborn come with the next pair to ferry a sorci Finn and I rescue. I'll meet them, tell them to find their own chivving poison—"

"That wouldn't work," Finn said. "The Brien trueborn don't leave their camps."

"So they want me to go to them?" I asked. "Is it far?"

"It's not about far," Cati said. "The Brien are worse than most when it comes to who they allow to enter their camp, and how, and what they consider to be proper hospitality."

"Which is why she's not going," Finn said.

"We don't have a choice." Tirra read aloud from the scroll. *"The risk of ferrying the children grows with each passing day. We are committed to protecting all Black Bloods from the threat of a magically-dominant Ilbrea. But, if we cannot trust the Duwead Clan to stand fully with us, to commit every available asset, we can no longer allow our own clan members to take on the dangers of moving the children south. We will have to find other ways to deal with the sorcerer threat."*

The wind picked up, rustling through the trees.

"What does that mean?" I asked. "Is there another path to take the sorci children on?"

"No," Finn said.

"It means they'll kill them." Cati kneaded her knuckles into her forehead.

"The children?" A horrible, freezing fear settled into my lungs.

"That's not true. Cati, it can't be. I've met some of the Brien. They're kind to those children. They promised they would take care of Riesa."

"They will," Finn said. "Riesa will already be far enough south by now."

"But not the others." I leaned on the flat stone. It didn't feel like the boulders that surrounded our camp. There was no pull drawing me to the stone table. The cold, flat surface offered no distraction from the fate of the sorci children.

"How many are left to be taken?" Tirra said.

"There's one I've been sent word of, but there's nothing to be done without Brien runners to take the child south," Liam said. "I don't know how many more might be found before winter sets in."

"So we find a way to take them south ourselves," Finn said.

"We can't cut through the Brien lands," Cati said. "That sort of fight would end badly for all of us."

"We could write to Lygan Hall," Tirra said. "See if the elders would be willing to let us take the children straight there."

"Orla would never allow it," Liam said.

"So then let's go." I pushed away from the table and ran my fingers through my hair, gathering the mass of it over my shoulder.

"Go where?" Finn said.

"To the Brien trueborn." I began weaving my hair into a braid. "If we're going to have to travel to them, it's best to get started. How far away are they?"

"It's not that easy," Cati said.

"Yes, it is," I said. "They want to see me, or they'll slaughter the children we're all living in tents to try and save. It's incredibly simple, actually. I have to go, so let's just do it."

"You can't," Finn said.

"Are you going to put on a wig and pretend to be me?" I asked.

"You're not a Black Blood," Liam said. "Not by Brien standards."

Finn reached into my pocket and pulled out the string I always kept tucked away. "You know how when we give the children to the Brien, I always go prancing into the woods naked?"

"I have noticed," I said.

"The Brien are picky about who they'll appear to." Finn tied the string around the end of my braid. "I go bare to prove I have no weapons."

"I know that."

"I'm marked as a Black Blood so they'll know I'm not just a naked paun," Finn said.

"The mountains on your ribs?" I said. "I thought you just liked them."

"No. Though I mean no offense to the artist." Finn nodded to Liam. "I was given the mark when I swore my allegiance to the Duwead Clan—"

"But you were born into the Duwead Clan," I said.

"And gave my oath to the trueborn Black Blood." Finn bit his lips together. "It's not an easy choice to make. Most people in this camp haven't even taken the oath. It's not something you can ever back away from."

I covered my face with my hands, wishing I could jump back into the river and make the world go quiet, if only for a minute. I took a long breath. As my chest rose and fell, I could feel the weight of the pendant hidden under my shift.

I allowed myself one more breath. "All right. How do I take this oath?"

"Ena—" Liam began.

"Do you need a blood sacrifice or something?" I asked. "Is there a test I have to pass?"

"There is no test, only an oath," Liam said.

"And a bit of pain," Finn said.

"Sounds fascinating." I stepped away from Finn. "When can we start?"

"This isn't something to just dive into," Cati said.

"There are children who need us in Ilbrea," I said. "There are children who will be taken by the Sorcerers Guild if we don't get to them. You're telling me the Brien would rather kill those children than take them south if I don't go meet their trueborn. Is there anything I've misunderstood?"

"No," Tirra said.

"Then how is there any question?" I asked.

"You don't want to help the Brien," Liam said.

"I don't want innocent blood on my hands," I said. "If those children die, it would be on me."

"It wouldn't." Finn took my hand. "You can't blame yourself for the way the Brien do things. It's best not to even try to understand it."

"I don't—"

"Ena," Cati spoke over all of us, "are you prepared to swear allegiance to Liam? Do you offer your life as payment for disobeying our trueborn? Are you willing to die at the command of our trueborn? Will you fight to your last breath for the cause our trueborn has chosen?"

I met Liam's gaze. My heart thundered in my chest. "Yes."

"Then we had better do this before Emmet gets back," Cati said. "We'll be lucky to survive his wrath when he finds out."

"Tonight then?" Tirra said.

Liam nodded. The solemnity of the motion stilled my heart, replacing fear with deadly acceptance.

"I'll have horses ready for you in the morning," Tirra said.

"Two," Liam said.

"Three." Finn took my hand. "She's not going without me."

Liam nodded again.

I wished I could hear whatever thoughts brought such darkness to his eyes.

"You should get some rest," Cati said. "It'll be a long night."

"Sure," I said.

Finn kept a tight hold on my hand as he led me away from the stone table and into the trees.

I glanced behind to watch the others go their separate ways.

"What sort of ceremony is it?" I asked.

"Nothing fancy," Finn said, "but don't let that fool you. You'll be making a vow that can't be broken."

"How does that even work?" I whispered.

"Liam will explain everything." Finn took me by the shoulders and turned me to face him. "You don't have to do this."

"Yes, I do."

"In theory, sure. You would be a chivving awful person not to."

"Then why are you arguing with me?"

"Because you can't save everyone." Finn tucked a stray hair behind my ear. "I know it's a horrible thing to say and an even worse thing to understand, but not everyone gets to live, regardless of how innocent they might be."

"Do you think I don't know that? I understand that good people die. I probably know it better than most Black Bloods."

"Knowing the facts and accepting there are some sacrifices not worth making are two different things."

19

As the shadows of dusk darkened my tent, I began to pace the tiny space. Finn had told me not to leave my tent until Liam came for me. His words had turned my little home into a cage.

Cati brought me dinner and a good-sized mug of frie. I tried asking her about the ceremony, but she wouldn't answer. All she did was urge me to eat before she slipped back out of my tent.

Her words didn't make eating the sour, chopped tubers she'd brought any easier. I wanted to go to the clearing and see if everyone else had been given the same food. See if Neil was still raging about the hunters not bringing in any meat.

But Finn had said to stay, so I'd set my lae stone on my table and perched on my cot, drinking the frie and shifting the tubers around my plate.

The pacing had begun when I'd run out of frie and couldn't stand staring at the tubers any longer. I don't know how many passes I did, pacing the six feet of ground in my cage, before a sharp knocking shook the front pole of my tent.

"Come in." My voice sounded strong. Cati had been smart to bring me the frie.

Liam stepped into my tent. The same darkness I'd seen in the woods still filled his eyes.

"Is it time, then?" I slipped my hands into my pockets to hide their sweating.

"It doesn't have to be," Liam said. "You can still change your mind."

"From what I've been told, this is going to be a long night. As we're meant to ride to meet the Brien in the morning, I'd just assume skip you trying to convince me not to swear an oath to you and get started. There's no point in wasting time."

Liam stared at me for a moment before nodding.

"So where do we go?" I asked. "Is it back to the fancy flat stone? That seemed like a nice place for a ceremony."

"We can stay here if you like," Liam said. "Or go to my tent if you'd be more comfortable."

I studied him standing in my tent, a little rounding in his back as he hunched to fit his height under the canvas. There was only a few feet of space between us.

Suddenly, it seemed like there wasn't enough air in the tent for me to breathe properly. Like the heat of him, the magic hidden so deep inside him I'd rarely even noticed it, had somehow absorbed everything around him.

I didn't mind the sensation.

"What sort of a ceremony is it?" I asked. "If it's going to involve flinging my blood all over the tent, we can use yours instead."

The tiniest hint of a smile played at the corner of his lips. "Very little blood will be spilt."

"Then here's fine." I looked toward the stump that was meant to be my chair. "Do you need a seat?"

"Not yet." He didn't move.

We stood, staring at each other for a long moment.

The music began in the clearing. Faint notes of the tune drifted all the way down the path to find me.

"By swearing your loyalty to me…" Liam's voice faded away.

I stepped forward, taking Liam's hands. His skin was warm against mine. My fingers longed to twine through his. "There are far worse people I could be swearing my loyalty to."

"By swearing your loyalty to a trueborn Black Blood, you accept their cause as your own. You accept their word as your law. You give your life and death to them." He tightened his hold on my hands. "By giving you my mark, I accept you as one of my own. You are a member of the band of brothers that will fight by my side even as the sky falls. Your victories and shame shall be mine in equal measure.

"The mountain herself gave the magic in my blood that makes such a bond possible, and the stones that shield my people shall be your death if you break your oath."

A chill trickled down the back of my neck.

"Is this a burden you are willing to bear?" Liam asked.

"Yes."

A crease formed on Liam's brow. "I've spent the whole day trying to think of a way out of this."

"Are you afraid I'll shame you?" I tried to give a little laugh.

"No," Liam said, "but being marked isn't a thing to take lightly. I've told you before, being near a trueborn can be dangerous."

I laid my hand on his cheek, reveling in the feel of his stubble beneath my fingers. "I've never been afraid of danger. And some things are worth any price."

Liam pressed my palm to his cheek. "The next part hurts a bit." He let go and reached into his pocket.

"Is this the bit where I bleed?"

"Only a little. I've got to give you your mark." He pulled what looked nearly like a pen from his pocket, but instead of a metal nib, a piece of deep blue stone sat at the tip.

"Oh." I stared at the glistening stone. "That does look a bit painful. Should I just take off my top?" I reached for the laces on my bodice.

"Just pull your shift up so I can get to your ribs." He turned to face the canvas.

"Who in camp is marked?" I loosened my laces and pulled my bodice over my head, trying not to think of how many tents Liam and his stone pen had visited.

"We have four now."

"Only four?" I froze with my shift pulled half out of my skirt. "But they all follow you. They're all here."

"By giving you my mark, I am accepting everything you do amongst the Black Bloods as my responsibility. If the Clans Council should whip you, they'd whip me, too. If they execute you—"

"We both swing together." My mouth went dry. "I'll have to be on my best behavior."

"If I found out you had betrayed me, it would be my duty to execute you."

"Crushed by the stones of the mountain?" I pulled my shift free of my skirt, clutching the length of it in my hands. "I'm ready."

Liam turned to face me. "There's a reason the mark is drawn on the ribs and made with a stone from the heart of the mountains. The pattern leaves a bit of the rock behind, too small to matter to any other trueborn, but my magic will have placed it there. A trueborn can use the tiny pieces and—"

"Ram them through my heart and lungs?" I took a deep breath, feeling my lungs fill without any hint of magic tainting them. "This is what the Brien require? Are all of their people marked? Do they all live knowing their trueborn could kill them without a moment's notice?"

"Everyone who is allowed to leave their stronghold hidden far belowground."

I let out a long breath. "I'm glad it wasn't a Brien who saved me."

He gave another faint smile. "Are you really sure you want to do this?"

"If you're willing to have me." My heart froze for a moment as I waited for him to say he wouldn't give me his mark. That he didn't want to have any sort of a connection to me, let alone one deemed sacred by his people.

"It's best if you lie down."

"Right." I lay on my side on my cot, feeling foolish as I tucked my arm under my head.

Liam took the stump seat and placed it beside me. "I really am sorry for the pain. If I could change it, I would."

"I believe you."

I held my breath as he lifted the edge of my shift, exposing the side of my ribs.

He ran his fingers along my skin.

"I never thought I'd have any sort of a mark," I said. "Let alone mountains."

"It won't be mountains." He placed his palm over the curve of my side. "There are a shocking number of rules as to how marks are given. In the Duwead Clan, no mark can be repeated by the same trueborn."

"That seems like a lot of pressure." I gave a little laugh.

"Try not to move." He lifted the tip of the stone pen and placed it on my flesh.

A strange pain cut into my ribs, as though I could feel the stone magic funneling into my bones where it would lurk, waiting for me to commit an offense worthy of execution.

"You don't see common folk with marks in Ilbrea." I forced my words to stay steady as the pen cut a white hot line down my side. "Only the paun with their Guild marks."

"They use the same sort of magic." Liam moved his left hand up, lifting my shift out of his way, exposing the side of my breast. His fingertips sent fire flying through my skin that made me forget the pain of the pen. "I'd like to believe they stole it from us, but I don't think there's really a way to know where the legend came from, or if the paun's version came first."

"What legend?"

He paused, lifting his hands away. The pain doubled in the absence of his touch.

"I should have told you first," Liam said. "I've never even considered giving a mark to a person who didn't know. I'm sorry."

"Don't be." I touched his knee. "This wasn't your idea in the first place."

"It has to do with the descendants of the mountain's child returning home." Liam started his work again, and heat burned through my side. "The mountain wanted the blood of her child brought home. She called to the descendants, luring them back into her embrace. But the mountain didn't understand the ways of men."

He placed his left hand back on my side.

I fought the urge to lean into his touch.

He didn't seem to notice what skin his thumb grazed as he tipped his head, his brow furrowing as he focused on his work.

"The mountain's child had gotten married and had children. Those children had gotten married and had children. The blood of the mountain spread to each new generation but not to the spouses chosen by the offspring."

I gasped as a new, sharp pain dug all the way into my lung.

"I'm sorry," Liam said.

"What happened to the spouses?" I said. "Did the children leave them behind?"

"Some did. Others tried to bring them into the mountain's embrace. But the mountain wouldn't accept them, and many were killed."

"That's horrible."

"The mountain had spent a long time keeping outsiders away,

and her stone couldn't tell the difference between enemies and those loved by the descendants."

"What happened?"

"Some fled, refusing to believe the mountain hadn't turned to evil. Some took their own lives, unable to bear the pain of their loss. But some were still determined to return to their home. There was a girl with stone in her blood who loved a man from Ilbrea with all her heart. She wanted to go to the mountain where she could live her life in peace but would not be parted from her mate.

"They say she begged the mountain for a path that would allow her love to live. Spent weeks kneeling in front of a great cliff, pleading for the mountain's mercy, until the rocks beneath her opened up and swallowed her whole. Her love mourned for her, begging the mountain to return his heart to him. The girl and the mountain both heard the man's pleas. So the mountain made a pact with the girl. If she would claim the man as her own, tie her fate to his by the magic in her blood, the mountain would let the man pass.

"The girl pledged her life in return for her love's safety, giving her vow to claim any pain caused by her mate as done by her own hand. Claiming every step he took as her own. The mountain returned her to the surface, and she grabbed a sharp stone to carve the mark of her devotion into her love's side. The mountain accepted her child's mate, and both were allowed to pass through to the safety of the land beyond Ilbrea's reach."

Liam fell silent.

The fiddlers in the clearing played a happy song with a bounding rhythm that didn't seem to fit the tale of the girl pledging her life for her love's passage.

"What happened to them?" I asked.

"I don't know. I'd like to think they lived long lives and died at peace. But making a vow to take responsibility for another is no easy task. I'm not sure what end they met."

"I suppose that would depend on what sort of people they were before they begged the mountain for mercy. It would be easy to claim a good man's deeds."

"Even good men do awful things when the world pushes them to it."

"I don't think I've ever believed in the existence of enough good men to think any of them turned into the evil slitches who torment the tilk."

"Even the paun aren't born evil." Liam twisted in his seat, leaning closer to me. "It's the Guilds that do it. They're our only real enemy. We fight against the soldiers and try to stop the sorcerers, but at the root of it all lies the Guilds."

"Are we going to stop them? The Guilds, I mean."

"I want to." Liam lifted his pen and pressed his palm to the painful spot on my ribs. Sparks tingled through my flesh. "But the elders in Lygan Hall don't think we can. Without their support, we've no hope of rallying enough fighters to make a real dent. I could spend a decade trying to recruit Ilbreans to stand with me, but I don't think I'd gather enough to make it past the gates of Ilara."

A scene of blood and men falling at soldiers' feet sent sour soaring into my throat.

"You're wrong." I hissed as he lifted his palm and touched the pen to my skin again. "It's not the Black Bloods' fight. Not as it is Emmet's and mine, anyway. It's easy to put off facing an enemy that may never come. It's harder not to fight when they're burning your house down."

"Watching a house burn and doing nothing to help is nearly as bad as setting the fire yourself."

"So," I said, "are *we* going to destroy the Guilds?"

Liam froze.

"I'm one of your band of brothers now, and I don't mind running into the flames if I can drag the paun with me."

20

Liam worked on my side until long after the music in the clearing fell silent. By the time he finished, I'd gone numb to the pain. My ribs had lost their ability to feel the bits of magic drifting into my body.

When he finally stood to leave, dark circles had formed under his eyes, as though the work had cost him more than a sleepless night. He warned me not to touch the raw skin and slipped out of my tent.

I drifted to sleep, though it wasn't the pure blackness I'd become accustomed to.

I stood at the bottom of a cliff, my palms pressed against the cool rock, waiting for something. I didn't know what it was exactly, only that I was willing to wait forever rather than give up hope.

A tapping on my tent pole woke me.

"Ena, its Finn," he whispered.

"Yes." I sat up. A dull throb reminded me of the pain in my side.

"I've brought a bandage." Finn popped his head into the tent. "You'll need to careful while we ride."

"Right." I rubbed my hands over my face and stood. "How soon are we leaving?"

"As soon as you're ready." Finn held a rolled bandage out to me. "It's a chivving long journey."

"I'll be out soon." I took the bandage, watching the tent flap flutter as Finn disappeared.

I lifted my shift, holding it up with my teeth.

The skin on my side was red and angry, but it wasn't the sting as I touched it that took my breath away.

A raven.

That was the mark Liam had chosen for me. A beautiful bird with its wings spread wide.

I laid my palm on the image as he had done hours before. I tried to feel for any of the magic that was now housed beneath my flesh, ready to kill me should I commit a horrible enough offense.

I couldn't feel it. No hum or heat. Like my body had absorbed the stone and destroyed its magnificence, turning it into something completely ordinary.

Gritting my teeth against the ache, I wrapped the bandage around my ribs, tucked my shift back into my skirt, tied on my bodice a little looser than usual, and pulled on my coat. It only took me a minute to toss the few things I would have carried if I'd been venturing into Ilbrea into a pack. Then I stepped out into the early morning mist.

It seemed strange that no one darted out of their tent to stare at me as I passed down the long row. The camp was filled with people who had been born Black Bloods, and now I was one of only five who bore Liam's mark.

The thought of it brought a bubble of pride into my chest. Then I remembered he hadn't wanted to give his mark to me, had only done it to stop the Brien from murdering sorci children, and the pride gave way to a dull itching in my side.

Liam and Finn waited by the paddock where three horses had

been saddled. All three beasts shifted their weight, as though Tirra had told them we were going to see the Brien and none of them were pleased to be making the journey.

"Where's Tirra?" I asked when I reached the others.

"Making sure no one decides to go on an early morning stroll around the camp." Finn lifted my pack from my back.

I gritted my teeth as the strap brushed against my side. "Who do we not want knowing we're leaving?"

Finn kept his gaze firmly away from me as he tied my pack to the back of a sturdy bay horse.

"Liam," I said, "who isn't supposed to know we're leaving?"

Liam shook his head before speaking. "Marta. Cati will tell her once we're well out of camp, but I don't think any of us want to face Marta's wrath this early in the morning."

"Right." I didn't take the hand Finn offered me as I climbed onto the bay. "Why would Marta be so angry?"

Finn's eyes grew wide, but he stayed silent and mounted his own horse.

"Liam, why would Marta be angry?" I asked again.

He rubbed his hand over his face. His skin was pale, like he hadn't even managed to steal a few hours' sleep.

"Am I not allowed to ask?" I said. "Is this part of being sworn to you? I'm just supposed to ride into the forest and not ask questions?"

"No." Liam mounted his horse.

"You should think about adding it in," Finn said.

Liam turned to Finn, a wrinkle forming between his eyebrows.

"Should the occasion for another marking ever arise." Finn shrugged.

Liam kicked his horse and led us south. He didn't say anything until we'd passed through the boulders that protected the camp.

"Marta is not going to be happy when she finds out I've given you a mark," Liam said. "When she finds out I've taken you to meet the Brien—"

"She'll have a chivving fit." Finn spoke from behind me.

"Cati is going to tell her?" I asked.

"Yes," Liam said.

"Don't worry," Finn said. "I'm sure Cati will go into the meeting well-armed."

I tried not to picture Cati and Marta squaring off to murder each other on the training field. Then I tried not to wonder what Marta was going to say to me when we came back from meeting the Brien.

A few solid hours passed with me trying to think as little as possible.

The cheerful green of the leaves overhead offered a bit of distraction. Listening to the different calls of the dozens of types of birds managed to keep me from asking why Marta would care so much about me getting a mark or leaving camp.

I had been going into Ilbrea on sorci runs for months. And if she was peeved about me being marked by Liam...

She and Liam can commiserate.

Counting the number of plants that could be used to kill a person lasted me until the sun was high.

Liam led us east into the rougher part of the mountain range, where solid ground gave way to scree that shifted under the horses' hooves.

The gait of the bay I rode rocked me from side to side so it felt like I might fall down the barren slope. I waited for Liam to hop off his horse and lead her the rest of the way to the rise above us. But he kept riding silently on, his gaze fixed forward.

My horse's hoof struck a stone, sending the rock tumbling down toward Finn.

His mount grumbled its response.

"Should we walk?" I gripped my reins.

"The horses are used to it," Finn said. "Honestly, I think it might offend the poor animals if we hopped off. Might make them doubt their own abilities."

I managed to muster a bit of a laugh.

"That and I don't fancy walking all the way to meet the Brien," Finn said. "Not that I mind a good wander through the woods, but a fellow has his limits."

"You've yet to tell me how far away the Brien actually are." I squeezed my mount with my thighs as she took a few quick steps to the top of the rise.

The expanse of the eastern mountain range stretched out before us.

My breath hitched in my chest as the feeling of being so small I barely existed pressed down on my shoulders. Summits peaked up on the horizon, the shimmering white snow resting on their tops giving the only real hint to their true height.

The vast field of mountains reached so far, it was nigh on impossible to believe anything could exist beyond the eastern edges.

"The Guilds could never conquer this land," I said. "It's too big. They'd never have enough soldiers to patrol it."

"They wouldn't have to patrol to conquer the mountains," Liam said. "They'd only have to kill all the Black Bloods."

I never feared the eastern mountains, not as the others in Harane did. I knew the woods on the western slopes, and the trees were my sanctuary.

I joined the Black Bloods, and the mountains became my home. I was never fool enough to believe I could understand the ways of the mountains as a born Black Blood does, but I loved them. I cherished the towering trees. The power deep within the stones grew a storm of longing in my chest.

It wasn't until the third day of riding behind Liam on our way to the Brien that I actually began to understand the depths of the mountains' mystery. What I learned gave me no comfort.

The rain poured down, creating a thick curtain of water that blocked our shelter from the rest of the world.

Finn paced at the very back of the cave, tucked behind the horses, humming a tune I'd often heard in the clearing at camp.

Liam sat, leaning against the side of the cave, staring out into the rain.

I sat opposite him, trying to convince my fingers they didn't want to trail along the hard lines of his jaw.

"We should just keep going," Finn said.

Liam waited a moment before speaking. "The path is dangerous in the rain."

"Danger lies in front of us no matter the weather," Finn said.

I untied my hair and shook it free of its braid, trying to occupy my fingers with working the sodden strands into a reasonable order.

"The Brien won't like us being late." Finn knelt and dug into his pack.

A minute stretched past before Liam spoke again. "The meeting isn't going to go well. Being late won't make it worse."

"You don't have to fake being cheery on my account," I said.

Liam fixed his dark gaze on me.

I wove my hair back into a braid, trying to ignore the longing in my fingers and the terrible itching on the side of my ribs.

"I don't want to risk it in the rain." Liam looked back toward the solid sheet of water that blocked us in.

I finished braiding my hair and shook it loose again. I needed something to do with my hands to keep from scratching the chivving mark on my side.

Thunder shook the rocks over our heads.

"Could you ask the mountain for a path?" I asked.

Finn stopped mid-step.

"No," Liam said. "The mountain offers us pathways, but only when she chooses and to where she chooses. It wouldn't be wise to ask a favor of the mountain so close to another clan's territory."

"Besides," Finn said, "you'll get plenty of walking through stone before we get back to camp."

Emmet's going to murder them both.

"Now that I've vowed to let Liam kill me if he wants," I said, "will the mountain see me as a real Black Blood?"

"How do you mean?" Liam asked.

Finn stepped around the horses to join us in the front of the cave.

"Will I get to open the secret tunnels?" I began weaving my hair into a more intricate, time-consuming braid.

"That part of the legend is just a story." A smile curved one corner of Liam's mouth.

"Pity," I said. "It would make sorci runs a bit easier."

"Are you trying to get rid of me?" Finn stopped chewing on his scrap of dried meat.

"Never, my love." I winked at him.

The smile left Liam's lips. "I don't think you should go on sorci runs anymore."

"Do you have more important things for me to do?" I asked. "Or do you think the Brien will trap me and never let me go?"

Neither of them laughed.

"We've lost too many," Liam said. "It doesn't feel right."

"No, it doesn't." Finn sank down beside me.

My heart skittered in my chest. There was a weight to their words that seemed too private, like I should find myself some pretty roots to play with and let them speak in peace, but there wasn't anywhere for me to go.

"Three in two weeks," Liam said. "We've had failed runs before, but not like this. Not with the Guilds just waiting to catch us. We stole the sailors' manifest in Frason's Glenn so I'd have a chivving shot at knowing where the soldiers were going to be moving over the summer. I've kept my runners well clear of the soldiers' encampments, but the paun keep finding them."

I stopped fiddling with my hair and slowly lowered my arms, trying not to break whatever spell had tricked them into speaking in front of me.

"They have to know where we're going," Finn said. "Ena and I had two run-ins with soldiers. Even if they were trying to find the same sorci as us, we shouldn't be cutting it that close."

"It doesn't make sense." Liam ran his hands over his face. "Do you think someone in camp has betrayed us?" He looked to me.

"Do I think one of the Black Bloods has been telling the Guilds where you're sending people on sorci runs?" I waited for Liam to look away or ask me to step out into the rain so he and Finn could have a nice chat about important business.

"People are dying under my command," Liam said. "If one of my own people—"

"How could they do it?" I leaned forward. "Every time Finn and I have gone on a sorci run, we've left the morning after you were told where the child was. Is it that way for everyone?"

"Yes," Liam said. "Word comes to me that the children are

ready to be moved, and then I send two from camp to collect them."

"Are there any other trueborn hiding in camp?" I asked. "Anyone else who can send a fancy message in the neck of a pretty stone bird?"

"No," Liam said. "The Duwead only have two trueborn, and I'm the only one at the camp."

"Then your problem isn't with any of the people there," I said. "They'd have no chance of getting word to the Guilds before the runners you sent after the sorci were well out of danger."

I reached to scratch my side before stopping myself.

"Smack it," Finn said. "A sharp slap dulls the itch."

"I don't think it's our trackers planted in Ilbrea," Liam said. "The ones watching for signs of magic have been there longer than I've been allowed out of Lygan Hall."

"Could they have gotten tired of the righteous path?" I asked. "Decided gold from the Guilds was worth more than innocent lives?"

Finn's forehead wrinkled as he looked to Liam. "I've never even met any of the trackers. Ena could be right. It could be one of them."

Liam gripped his hands together. If he had been a proper sorcerer, his anger might have exploded in a wave of fire large enough to engulf the cave. "The trackers aren't under my command."

I could hear my own breath as I waited for one of them to speak.

"Then on Orla's head be it," Finn said.

He snaked his arm through mine and took my hand.

"I..." My unsaid words pressed hard against my chest.

Don't be a coward.

"I don't know if a Black Blood has betrayed you," I said. "I don't know who Orla is, or if the trackers can be trusted. But the Sorcerers Guild, they are cruel and powerful. If they want a child with magic, if they know there is quarry hidden in a town, they will find it. I don't know if you should doubt your own people, but do not doubt the Guilds' will to slaughter everyone who stands in their way."

Finn squeezed my hand.

"Talk to Emmet when he gets back," I said. "He knows almost as much as I do when it comes to the wrath of the Guilds. Let him say if it's worth tearing through your own people or if the Guilds are just enjoying murder."

The horses scuffed their hooves as a fresh round of thunder shook the walls.

"Is this the sort of thing you usually chat about without me?" I asked.

"Yes," Finn said.

"You're bound to me now." Liam looked up to the stone above us, as though begging the gods for aid. "It would be wrong of me to keep information from you. If we burn, we burn together."

"The Brien had better be reasonable and willing to accept a polite *no*," I said. "Either that, or I've got the weight of potential betrayal and an awful itch in my side for nothing."

Finn lifted my arms and smacked my ribs, right on the raven mark. "You'll thank me when you stop seeing stars."

"Thanks." I swallowed the bile that rose in my throat.

You did not understand. You did not understand.

The thought kept rattling through my mind as my horse carried me along the spine of a mountain.

I had thought I could see the expanse of the eastern mountains from Harane. Then I truly believed I had seen the scope of the range from inside the mountains themselves. But as we traveled farther south, there was no hint as to where the mountains might end.

Finn was the first to stop his horse.

"There we are." Finn soothed his mount.

I looked behind me and watched him jump to the sodden ground before I pulled on the reins of the bay I rode. "Are you all right?"

"We can ride a bit farther." Liam stopped his horse but didn't dismount.

"You can also live through being stabbed," Finn said, "but I don't fancy trying that, either."

Liam kicked his leg over his horse and jumped to the ground.

The silty scent in the air filled my lungs as I waited for him to move or give some sort of an order.

To the east of us, there was nothing but a rocky slope that even our mountain-trained horses couldn't have survived.

To the west, the slope had a gentler feel. If Death had come flying toward me, I would have run that direction, seeking refuge in the woods far below.

Along the ridge in front of us rose a peak the horses would have had no chance of climbing. I wasn't even sure I'd be able to reach the summit.

Liam stared at that peak for a long while.

"We're here, Liam," Finn said. "We can't turn around."

I kicked my leg over my horse's back, willing my stiff limbs to stay steady as I dropped to my feet.

Liam still stared at the peak. I let go of my horse's reins and walked to his side.

"Liam." I touched his shoulder. A foolish tingle ran up my arm.

"I shouldn't have told you," Liam said. "About the letter, about any of it."

"I've known darkness, and I am not afraid."

He laid his hand over mine. "You are stronger than any of us."

I began to say *no*, but I heard the echo of Lily's voice in my mind. "I am as strong as I have had to be to survive."

A crack shook the rocks, sending loose dirt tumbling down the slope to the east.

The horses stamped their fear into the ground.

"I will do everything in my power to protect you." Liam held my hand for one more moment before starting toward the southern peak. "Leave your lae stone hidden. Duwead magic can't be used in Brien territory."

I waited for another crack to sound or for the earth beneath our feet to crumble entirely away.

My bay nudged me with her nose, offering her reins.

I looped the leather around my hand and followed Liam.

I kept waiting for the mountain to devour us as I listened to the dirt crunching beneath our feet. Or for a hundred Brien to leap out of hiding to slaughter us. Anything to explain why my gut had twisted up as though Death himself blew the breeze that tickled the back of my neck.

Liam stopped in front of the rocks. He didn't look back before disappearing into the stone.

I kept my gaze fixed on the swishing tail of his horse as I followed. The stone swallowed the horse, and I held my breath as I stepped into the darkness.

I had expected pitch black, but as the outside world disappeared, the blue gleam of two dozen lae stones surrounded us, leading us toward a dark tunnel.

The sounds of footsteps approaching sent my heart leaping into my throat, and the rasp of a blade clearing its sheath turned my nerves to steel.

"I am Liam Duwead"—he kept walking forward, leading his horse farther down the dark stone passage—"trueborn of the Duwead Clan. I have come at the request of the Trueborn Brien."

Another rasp of a weapon being drawn carried from the shadows.

I peered into the dark patches between the lae stones, trying to find where an attacker might be hiding. I could see nothing but black.

"I have come to request transport to the Brien enclave, for myself and the two who travel with me," Liam said.

The passage narrowed in front of us, leaving barely enough room for the horses to fit.

"Will you grant us passage?" Liam stepped in front of his horse and walked into the tighter tunnel.

I couldn't see him past the bulk of his mount. I wanted to shout for him to stop.

A clack of rocks carried from the darkness ahead.

"Liam." My voice bounced off the tunnel walls.

The lae stone beside me flickered out.

"Keep walking," Finn said in a steadying tone.

A dozen more of the lae stones went dark, leaving only enough light to cast foreboding shadows around us.

I stepped into the narrow tunnel where there was no light at all. Penned between two horses, the animal that had carried me for days now seemed like an instrument of my enemy.

I wished I had a weapon in my hand. Something to give me a chance of taking whatever ghoul lurked in the shadows to the grave with me.

The knife in my boot pressed against my ankle, begging me to free its blade with every step I took down the darkening corridor.

"We ask for passage," Liam said. "We are Black Bloods called to the Brien enclave by your trueborn."

A low grinding of stone came from overhead. I looked up to the ceiling and found only darkness.

These are the people I gave Riesa to.

A dim anger replaced my fear.

May the gods forgive me.

All light vanished.

"I travel with Ena Ryeland," Liam said, "and Finn Duwead. I am a trueborn Black Blood, and I demand passage."

A scraping carried through the pitch black.

The crunch of boots came toward me.

I reached down, pulling my knife from my boot.

The sounds of footfalls surrounded me.

"Do not touch me." I spoke into the darkness. "Your trueborn has asked to see me, and I've come. Let us pass, or let us leave. But if you touch me, I will kill you."

A low laugh sounded by my shoulder.

My horse stomped her displeasure.

The footsteps shifted around me. If there had been any light, I would have thought the people were examining me.

It sounded like three, maybe five people. And there were more moving through the darkness near Finn and Liam.

I gripped the hilt of my blade and kept my breathing steady. I'd no hope of fighting anyone in the dark, but I had been threatened by worse monsters and would not allow these fiends the pleasure of seeing me cower.

All at once, the footsteps stopped.

My heartbeat thundered in my ears.

"You may pass." A whisper surrounded me.

I turned, trying to find where the person had spoken from, but the words had seemed to come from everywhere at once.

A dull crack sounded from my left, and a weak blue glimmer fought through a slit in the wall.

"Thank you." Liam guided his horse toward the light.

Keeping my knife gripped in my hand, I followed.

I could still feel them, the people lurking just out of sight, staring at me. I didn't search for them. I kept my gaze fixed on the blue glow in front of us.

The light didn't come from specific points as the gleam of the lae stones had, but seemed to grow in a vast sheet in front of us.

I squinted at the glow, trying to figure out what trap the people in the dark had laid for us. Then Liam's horse stepped through the gap and out of the way, giving me a full view of the space beyond.

Water.

A glowing lake so vast, I could not see its far bank.

Are we to swim?

The question balanced on my tongue. I didn't dare speak in case my fear should sound in my voice.

I followed Liam away from the gap in the stone and onto the rocky bank surrounding the lake.

Large metal rings had been set into the stone wall, and a boat waited on the water.

The craft was large enough for the three of us to fit, but there was no hope of bringing any of our horses.

Liam tied his reins to one of the metal rings and lifted his pack off his horse's back.

I took a slow breath before speaking. "Are we just going to leave them here? In the dark?"

"They'll be cared for," Liam said. "And waiting when we come back."

I tied my bay to the wall and kissed her nose. "If they try to hurt you, stomp them." I stroked the soft hair on her neck and untied my pack.

The boat gave a soft thump as Liam climbed in. He settled his pack in the bow before reaching for my hand.

He held on to me as I lifted my skirt high enough to step into the boat, which swayed beneath me.

I leaned close to him, pressing my lips to his ear. "Should we trust them?"

"We don't have a choice." He squeezed my hand and helped me over the wide bench in the center of the boat and to the narrow seat up front.

Finn waited until I'd tucked my knife back into my boot before giving the boat a shove and leaping into the back.

The glowing water smacked against the hull as we drifted out onto the lake.

A numb fear pinched my spine as we floated away from land, away from any hope of defending ourselves against the people who lurked in the darkness.

Two oars were attached to the sides of the boat. I waited for Liam or Finn to take charge of them, but both of the men just sat.

The boat slowed and rocked to a stop twenty feet from the shore.

"Should I row?" I asked. "I haven't done it before, but I don't mind."

"The mountain isn't ready for us yet," Liam said.

"Right." I twisted in my seat, scanning the water around us, waiting for darkness to fall again.

Nothing happened.

There were no waves to lap against our boat, no current to carry us—only the faint blue glow coming up from the water.

I tried to listen for any hint of movement. There was nothing beyond the shifting of the horses onshore.

I dug my nails into my palms, trying to be patient instead of letting panic make monsters out of shadows.

"There." Finn pointed into the distance.

A gleam of light streaked toward us, not through the air, but through the water, as though some giant fish were swimming right for Liam.

I gripped the sides of the boat, waiting for a crash to capsize us.

As the light came closer, I still couldn't see what was forming or leading the glow. Then, a sparkling gleam surrounded our boat.

It was beautiful.

Pure, blue light shone all around us, like the fire trapped inside the lae stones had been set free.

I had never seen anything so exquisite.

My breath caught in my chest, and I reached for the water.

Liam grabbed my hand. "Best not to tempt what lies beneath."

His fingers lingered on top of a mine for a moment, as though he too longed to touch the dazzling blue.

"I'll take the first turn at the oars." Liam sat on the wide bench and twisted the oars out over the water.

"I would fight you for it, but I'm sure I'll have plenty of time to get a fine set of blisters." Finn sat in the bottom of the back of the boat, rubbing his palm against the red scruff on his chin.

Liam rowed us along the path left by the light. I waited for the glow to fade into the dull gleam that filled the rest of the water, but the bright shimmering did not cease.

"How long will we be in the boat?" I asked when we were far enough from shore I didn't think anyone would be able to hear us.

"I don't know," Liam said. "It's like the path the mountain gives us to reach camp. It's different every time she offers us safe passage."

"Will they feed the horses?" I asked.

"They'll be brushed, fed, and rested," Finn said. "Strange as it seems, protecting the animals is one point of kindness the Brien have never faltered on."

"Should I take comfort in that, or be worried I'm not a horse?" I leaned out over the water, wondering what creatures lurked below that the Brien might consider worthy of protecting.

It took a few hours for Liam to finally allow Finn to row us along the glowing path.

The beauty of the light hadn't faded, but being trapped on the water for so long had begun to wear on my nerves.

Before Finn had started to show signs of fatigue, I made him give up his spot so I could have something to occupy myself with besides waiting for something terrible to happen.

As I rowed, I stared at the trail of light, waiting to catch a glimpse of the shore. It took me a long time to realize I wasn't seeing the end of our watery path, only the end of what was in view.

When my strokes shortened from the fatigue in my arms, Liam took the oars, and I curled up in the back of the boat, trying to lure myself into sleep.

The boat rocked gently beneath me. I wished the motion were soothing.

"I haven't had a massive set of blisters in ages," Finn said. "It'll be refreshing to be in pain every time I move my fingers."

"It's not that bad," Liam said. "Just think of the sympathy you'll get back at camp."

"Treat them properly, and they'll be gone before we get back," I said.

"Do you happen to have any wonders in your bag?" Finn asked.

"Of course." I sat up and leaned against the back of the boat. "Best to wait until you're done rowing, though. No point in putting a salve on just to rub it off on the oars."

"I adore you, Ena Ryeland," Finn said. "You do know that, right?"

"I am aware," I said, "but it is always nice to hear you confess your love."

Finn laughed. The sound seemed strange against the soft slopping of the oars.

"Suppose this lake goes on forever," Finn said. "How long do you think it would take us to starve to death?"

"That depends." I gave a deep sigh. "Are you in charge of our rations, or am I?"

"I'm going to starve to death." Finn leaned against the bow of the boat.

We all slipped into silence for a long while.

The sound of the oars lulled me into a stupor. All I could do was stare at the place where the light disappeared in the distance and wait for the end to come closer.

My eyes drifted shut, and the peace of sleep surrounded me.

"Ena." A warm weight pressed on my shoulder. "Ena."

I opened my eyes to find Liam looking down at me. The blue glow of the water had faded, leaving deep shadows on his face.

"What's happened?" I sat up quickly, setting the boat to rocking.

The shimmering trail we'd been following had faded in front of us. Terror gripped my ribs as the horror of being stranded in the dark shot through me. Then I spotted the dark outline of a rocky shore.

"Thank the gods." I sank back down in the boat. "Are there going to be more people hiding in the dark to taunt us?"

"There shouldn't be." Liam furrowed his brow. "We shouldn't meet anyone else until we near the enclave."

"But?" I checked the knife in my boot under the pretense of tightening my laces.

"The Brien are protective of their territory," Liam said. "If the thought of traitors has plagued me, I can't imagine how far down that dark path the trueborn Brien's mind has journeyed."

"Good thing none of us are traitors, then," Finn said.

Liam gave two powerful strokes with the oars, and the tip of our boat scraped up onto the shore.

Finn hopped out and towed the boat farther onto the rocks.

I listened past the noise of wood grinding against stone, trying to hear any hint of people lurking in the shadows.

Finn grabbed my pack out of the boat before offering me his hand.

As I stepped onto the rocks, the air around me seemed to change. A chill breeze blew across my skin as though the first fall storm were sweeping down upon us.

"I'm not ready for this," I said.

"Ena—"

"I'm not." I gripped Finn's hand. "I don't know about magic, or the clans, or how a lake this large can fit under a mountain."

Finn wrapped his arms around me and pressed his lips to the top of my head. "Knowing won't make it better. Do you trust me?"

"You know I do." I held Finn tight.

"I came on this chivving trip to keep you safe," Finn said. "Everything else is just stone and nonsense."

I laughed and felt Finn's ribs shake as he joined me.

"Right." I stepped away and lifted my pack onto my back. "Into the stone and nonsense, then."

"Into the stone and nonsense." Finn nodded.

Liam stepped in front of us and toward the wall of darkness that bordered the shore.

"Still no lae stones?" I whispered.

"No." Liam's voice bounced off the rocks. "It's against the treaty between clans to use magic while in another's territory."

"Makes sense, I suppose." I put my hands in my pockets, trying to dry the sweat on my palms. My skin stung where rowing had rubbed it raw.

The breeze picked up, setting goose bumps on my arms.

Liam headed left, toward the source of the wind.

A slit cut through the dark stone. The crack reached high up, above the dim light still glowing from the surface of the lake.

Liam ran his hands along the sides of the opening. "It'll be a tight fit."

"Good thing I haven't had a proper dinner," Finn said.

Liam took off his pack and held it to his side as he slid into the crack.

You will not break. Blood has not shattered you, and neither will darkness.

I shrugged back out of my pack and balanced it on my hip as I had done with Riesa. Feeling the rough stone with my free hand, I stepped sideways into the gap.

I could hear Liam moving in front of me, slowly sidestepping as though wanting to be sure he didn't get too far ahead.

Finn stepped into the crack and blocked most of the light from the lake.

I closed my eyes, making my own darkness rather than waiting for the tunnel to steal the light from me.

Did Riesa have to travel through a place like this? Did the Brien trap her in darkness as I did?

I sent a silent plea up to the stars that Riesa might forgive me. Still, I couldn't regret ferrying her from her home.

Even knowing the Brien would be willing to murder children

rather than let the Sorcerers Guild have them, I couldn't think of any Black Bloods as more villainous than the Guilds.

I will make them protect you.

A rumbling carried through the tunnel up ahead.

I pressed my palm to the stone, feeling for any sign that the mountain had finally decided to tumble down upon me.

The rumbling grew to a growl.

My leg ran into Liam's bag.

The noise stopped.

I heard Liam take a deep breath before he started moving again.

A trickle of light silhouetted Liam as the tunnel twisted and widened. The light wasn't the blue of a lae stone, but the dull gray of twilight.

A breeze rushed toward us, filling the air with the smell of leaves, and fertile earth, and life.

Liam took another deep breath, as though scenting the magic of the mountains, and stepped out into the open.

I'm not sure what exactly I had expected to find on the other side of the mountain, but the woods I stepped into were beyond my ability to imagine.

Trees, whose trunks were as big around as a wagon, dripped with leaves the size of my head. In the dull light of dusk, the rich colors of the flowers surrounding my feet seemed thick and dense, like something out of a painting. A stream ran down the mountainside behind us, filling a pool with water so clear it reflected the gray hue of the sky.

We had stepped into a forest created for a fairy story.

The growl came again.

I spun toward the sound and caught a glimpse of a black tail swishing between the branches of a berry-laden bush.

"He won't attack," Liam said. "The animals know people aren't food."

"What a relief," I said.

The great cat gave another rumble.

Liam turned in a slow circle, examining the canopy of trees before nodding and leading us forward.

I put my pack back on, wincing as the weight bumped against

my mark, and trotted after him.

We were high up in the mountains. We had to be. We'd never traveled down. But it didn't seem as though the forest had been told.

As Liam weaved his way deeper into the woods, different sorts of trees began to dot our path.

The bright white bark of birch trees stood out in shockingly pale veins against the deep needles of evergreens. Tree limbs hung heavy with jewel-colored fruit. Tiny animals scampered through the branches, darting from feast to feast. Birds warbled as they settled into their nests for the night.

I've fallen into a fairy story.

I couldn't shake the feeling as a new form of beauty appeared with every twist in our path.

I wished the sun wouldn't set. I wanted to see the true colors of the bushes laden with berries and the deep hue of the moss growing alongside the bubbling stream.

A bright light flickered up ahead. I squinted toward the gleam as Liam slowed his pace.

I held my breath, waiting for something wonderful or terrifying to happen, but it was only a torch planted in the ground.

Liam stopped beside the torch, staring down at its flame.

Finn stepped up next to him. "No point in delaying."

Liam stayed frozen for a long moment before nodding. "I wish it didn't have to be this way."

"Old traditions." Finn took off his pack and shrugged out of his coat. "Centuries of mistrust." He pulled his shirt over his head. "A bunch of men worried about assassination attempts." He kicked off his boots. "And the lot us still too afraid of destroying the treaty to object." He yanked off his socks. "Put all those things together, and you have naked Black Bloods tramping through the woods." He dropped his pants around his ankles.

I looked up to the stars just beginning to show through the darkening sky.

"I've gone first," Finn said. "Now you two strip down so we can get this over with."

I tried to think of something witty to say as I turned away from the others to undress.

I set down my pack and bent to unlace my boots. I held my knife in my hands for a moment before opening the top of my pack and tucking it away.

"You know," I said while I untied my bodice and slipped it over my head, "when you said Emmet was going to be furious with you for bringing me here, I didn't think it would be for this."

"I'm only moderately terrified of Emmet," Finn said. "And I'm a faster runner than he is, so I might survive the coming wrath."

"Perhaps he'll finally give up." I dropped my skirt and pulled my shift over my head.

"How do you mean give up?" Finn asked.

"He could either call me a lost cause and wash his hands of me, or realize I can live my own life without him shouting about it." I folded my clothes and set them next to my boots. "Either way. I'm not picky."

You will not blush.

I took a breath and turned back toward the men.

"Not so bad right?" Finn said. "A good breeze around your nethers to keep you awake."

"Thank the gods it's warm." I kept my gaze locked on Finn's face.

"You've got to leave that, too." Finn pointed to the pendant hanging between my breasts.

"Right." I wrapped my fingers around the smooth black stone. "Forgot it was even there."

I lifted the leather cord over my head and waited for months' worth of nightmares to come flooding into my mind to destroy me.

You have to protect the children. It's just a stone, and you have to protect the children.

I tucked the necklace into my bag. Without the stone touching my skin, it felt as though my flesh had been torn away. I was worse than naked. I was utterly exposed to the world.

"We should go," Liam said. "Regan has never been patient."

"Is that a trait of all trueborn?" I asked.

"Yes," Finn said.

"This way," Liam said.

I waited until I heard him walking to look in his direction.

He'd pulled the torch from the ground and kept his gaze locked on the path in front of him.

He'd seen me naked before, he'd touched my bare flesh. But the fact that Finn now knew I'd been anywhere near Liam without my clothes on brought heat to my cheeks.

Don't be a chivving idiot.

I made myself breathe. I touched the place on my chest where the pedant had rested. The patch of skin felt cold.

The flickering light of the torch sent shadows dancing across Liam's back. The ridges of his muscles left tempting valleys. I wanted to memorize the feel of them. But there was more than the beautiful strength to be seen.

A foot-long scar marked his right shoulder, and another left a raised line on the back of his right thigh. Whatever had made those marks had been brutal. Wounds that large would not have healed on their own.

Someone had tended to him. Someone knew why he had been made to bleed so badly. And that someone was not me.

I looked up to the stars, wrapping layers of fire around the emptiness that dug into my chest.

Creatures moved through the shadows beyond the torchlight, and the woods lost their wonder in the darkness. The forest floor stayed soft beneath my bare feet, but there was no other hint of hospitality to be found as we wandered naked through the woods.

I was only a foot behind Liam when I realized he'd slowed his pace. I tucked my hands behind my back and let him get a few steps in front of me.

He swept the torch from side to side, scanning the shadows. "I've come at the request of the trueborn Brien. I have traveled across the mountains to speak to a fellow child of stone. Grant me safety at your hearth."

With a rustle of branches, a woman jumped down from a tree. Her long, light-gray braid seemed somehow out of place against the dark colors of her clothes. She tipped her head to the side as she walked closer to us, squinting in the torchlight to examine each of us in turn.

I balled my hands into fists as her gaze lingered on my face.

"Is that the one?" the woman asked.

The muscles in Liam's back tensed. "She is."

"Huh," the woman said. "I thought she would be older."

"I'm sorry to disappoint." I dug my nails into my palms. "If I'm not what you're after, I'd be more than happy to go home."

The woman wrinkled her forehead. "That, I expected." She gave a whistle.

The crackling and swishing of people moving through the darkness surrounded us.

"Arms up," the woman said.

Liam raised his arms to be straight out to his sides.

My arms tensed behind my back as the certainty that raising them would somehow place me in greater danger overwhelmed my reason.

Figures appeared in the darkness. The steel of their weapons glinted in the torchlight.

"It's all right," Finn said. "After this, we'll nearly be to the part where they give us a cloth to wrap up in. Raising your arms gets you closer to getting your clothes back."

Gritting my teeth, I lifted my arms.

The woman peered at my side, examining the bird Liam had drawn on my flesh.

"A fresh one," the woman laughed. "I'm sure Regan will be honored." She whistled, and the figures faded back into the trees.

"We weren't given much of a choice," Liam said.

"There's always a choice," the woman said. "Some people are just too blind to see it."

She started walking away, reaching the edge of Liam's light before beckoning us onward.

As we followed her, I kept as close to Liam's heels as I could, searching the trees for any glint of the weapons that had threatened us.

For a while, we weaved between the trees without any pattern I could see. Then she led us onto a path worn smooth by years of travel.

Great trees loomed up on either side of us, planted in long, straight rows with their branches arching over our heads, creating a living tunnel.

I stared up into the branches, marveling at the glimpses of stars I managed to catch through the thick leaves. Except it wasn't stars lighting our path. Tiny lae stones had been suspended from the branches, mimicking the night sky.

I wished I had my clothes. I wished there weren't people hiding in the shadows with weapons.

But I do not live in a fairy story. I do not receive beautiful things without pain.

Voices carried from the distance. Not the rough tones of warriors, but the sounds of everyday life lurking in an enchanted wood.

The lae stones hanging above us grew bigger and brighter as the path in front of us grew wider. Up ahead, where the voices waited, more lights glimmered, sitting on top of posts like torches made of stone magic.

The tone of the voices changed as the people noticed our party.

I waited for Liam's shoulders to tense or his pace to falter, but he walked toward the voices without any hint of fear or modesty. Before we had reached the end of the tree-lined path, two dozen people stood in front of us, watching our approach.

I couldn't press down the heat that flared in my face as the men and women whispered and stared. I looked to the structures behind the pack of gawkers, trying to pretend the people weren't there.

Wooden houses made of thin branches surrounded the clearing. They weren't like any homes I had ever seen. They all seemed too flimsy, too light to survive a proper storm, almost as though nesting birds had advised the Brien's builders.

A rock face rose in front of us, forming the back of the clearing. A small, wooden structure had been built right up against the stone. Swirls of light emanated from the door of the tiny building.

The people parted ways as we reached the end of the path, and the gray-haired woman led us toward the rock face.

"Duwead."

I heard the name whispered.

"She doesn't seem fit for it." The voice spoke louder.

I kept my gaze fixed on the tiny building up against the stone. The walls hadn't been built any more soundly than the houses, but someone had gone to great pains to ensure the structure would stand out amongst the others.

Giant lae stones hung from the front corners of the building, with smaller glowing orbs dripping beneath like water trickling downward. The door had been carved from a single piece of wood, and gleaming symbols had been painted along the edges. The blue that shone from the paint looked almost as though someone had split a lae stone in two and drawn with whatever magic lived inside.

I didn't know what the symbols meant, but I wanted to touch them, to see if they held any heat or were as cool as the stones that lit the camp I called home.

The gray-haired woman stopped in front of the building and just stood there, not knocking or reaching to open the door.

I waited behind Liam, trying to silence the battle in my mind that raged between my desire to reach out and touch the scar on his shoulder and my need to scream at all the people in the clearing to run away before I scratched their eyes out.

The markings on the wood glowed brighter, and the door swung aside. The woman stepped through, and Liam followed her. I didn't like the idea of entering such a small place.

You will not be broken.

I pressed my palms against my bare thighs as I stepped inside. A gasp pulled itself from my throat as I blinked at the space around me.

The little, wooden building was only the entryway to a cave larger than the Guilds' shining, white cathedral in Frason's Glenn.

Lae stones dotted the cavern, arcing high above us on the rock ceiling as though all the stars in the sky had come to peer down upon us.

Ten men with swords at their hips lined the sides of the great room. A gleaming blue stone shone from the hilt of each of their weapons.

The sounds of our bare feet against the smooth stone floor barely carried over the thumping of my heart in my ears as a woman stood up from the throne at the far end of the cavern.

She didn't wear plain brown or black as the people in the clearing had. Her deep violet gown, worthy of a princess, swished around her ankles as she strode toward us. Her long, golden hair flowed down her shoulders as she tipped her head to the side, considering Liam, then Finn, then me. She nodded to the gray-haired woman, who bowed and left us.

The door didn't make a sound as she closed us in.

"Trueborn Duwead," the blond smiled as she spoke, "I didn't imagine I'd see you in our enclave again so soon."

"Your letter didn't leave me much choice, Regan." Liam bowed, and Regan's smile grew broader.

"You." Regan pointed to Finn. "You, I've met before."

"Several times, in fact." Finn bowed. "Don't worry, I'm used to not being memorable."

Regan gave a laugh that didn't sound remotely real and turned to me. "You must be the one I've heard whispers about. Rumors of you flit in and out on the wind. A poor little girl who kills great monsters."

I bit the inside of my lips to keep from speaking.

"Quiet? That, I did not expect." Regan examined my face. "Arms up. Best to get this over with so you can get wrapped up."

Finn and I raised our arms, but Liam did not. He turned to face Finn.

Finn's jaw tensed as Liam curled his fingers through the air. The dark lines of the mountain marked on Finn's side shifted, as though a breeze had stirred the image.

A wrinkle formed on Liam's brow as he looked to me.

Breathe. He mouthed the word.

I took a deep breath as he swept his fingers through the air as though stroking the head of my raven mark.

A tingling ran through my ribs and burned my lungs as though thousands of miniature ants had bored their way into my flesh. Before I could decide if I was going to be ill on the floor or rip the skin from my own bones, the terrible sensation vanished.

"Hmm." Regan turned and walked back toward her throne. "I suppose I should be honored."

Finn lowered his arms, and I followed suit.

"Honored?" Liam said. "I don't know what you mean."

"Her mark is still raw." Regan turned back to us. "So much trouble to go through to visit me."

She waved her hand through the air, and a square of rock on the side of the wall slid open, creating a doorway where there had been nothing but solid stone.

"You didn't give me much choice," Liam said. "We have spent years protecting the sorcis together, and now you threaten to abandon them or worse."

"I have my people to think about," Regan said. "I must protect them, as you should yours."

Liam went still as stone.

People entered through the newly-formed door. Three men, all carrying bundles in their arms.

"Is that what we've come to?" Liam stepped toward her. "I ask the Brien for more men to aid me in Ilbrea, and I am told no. My people alone must bear the risk of venturing west of the mountains."

"Taking those children south is no small feat." Regan strode back toward us. Where Liam's face had turned to stone, fire danced in the blond trueborn's eyes.

"It is the risk you agreed to," Liam said. "We have a common cause, Regan."

The three men stopped in front of us, each holding out their bundle.

The man in front of me was thirty, maybe a bit older. He had wrinkles on his tan forehead, as though he had spent too much of his time despising the world. His eyes were gray-blue and his hair mousy brown. There was a tiny white scar on his top lip.

"I think you and I see the end of our journey differently, Liam," Regan said. "My aim is the survival of my people, my clan. That, I prize above all."

The man's gaze swept over my naked body as he unfurled his bundle, presenting a wide, black sheet.

"I have seen the power of the Guilds," Liam said. "I have seen the malice they hold. None of the Black Bloods will survive if we continue to allow their power to grow."

"I agree," Regan said. "We cannot allow them to gain an even stronger foothold in magic."

The man moved toward me, reaching to wrap the sheet around my body.

"And you would be willing to slaughter innocent children to keep them from the Sorcerers Guild?" Liam said.

A smile lifted the corners of the man's eyes as his fingers grazed my breast.

"Don't!" I leapt away from him, covering my chest.

"Ena." Finn ripped the sheet from the man's hands and wrapped it around me.

"Get them out." Liam stepped between the man and me, not bothering to cover himself.

"Go," Regan ordered.

The smile disappeared from around the man's gray-blue eyes. He stared at me for a long moment before following the other two through the door in the stone wall.

"We should get you settled." Regan strode back to her throne. "You've had a long journey. You need rest and food."

"Regan—" Liam said.

"We can discuss our partnership in the defense of all Black Bloods in the morning." Regan kept speaking like she hadn't even heard him.

"Do not make Ena a part of this," Liam said. "She has seen enough horror at the hands of the Guilds. Do not make the Black Bloods another terror she must endure."

"I will see that you all have places to rest comfortably." Regan gave me a smile that did not reach her eyes. "Everything but your weapons will be waiting for you."

"This way."

I looked toward the voice.

The gray-haired woman waited in the open doorway.

"The three of us will stay together," Finn said. "I don't care if we're all huddled on the cold ground."

He wrapped his arm around my waist, keeping me close to him as we followed the woman out of the cave.

My heart thundered in my chest, battering a rhythm I didn't recognize against my ribs. My flesh felt contaminated where the man had touched me, but there was something else. A scent in the air I couldn't name.

Liam stepped forward to flank me with Finn. He walked so close to me, his arm brushed against mine.

I looked to him, wanting his face to bring me comfort, but there was a shade of darkness in his eyes that made my heart scream in terror.

The woman stopped in front of one the wooden houses.

Up close, it was easy to believe the home had been built of twigs. We'd somehow fallen into a strange and magical land, and this was a house a child had built in the garden to lure in a tiny bit of magic.

I stared at the scar on Liam's shoulder as he pushed the door to the house open. Glittering wings did not sprout from his back.

He checked all the corners of the one room the house provided before beckoning Finn and me in.

Finn closed the door behind us, shutting out the fairy lights, and the man with the scar on his lip, and all the things I had thought I understood.

"No," Finn said as he slid the wooden bolt into place, locking the door. "No, no, no."

"Are you all right?" Liam took my face in his hands.

The feel of his fingers against my skin brought heat back into my body, cracking through the strange numbness of fear. "I'm fine. You shouldn't worry about me."

"He touched you." Finn paced the length of the room. "That chivving, slitching, cact of a letching—"

"I said I'm fine." I stepped away from Liam. "That was nowhere near the worst I've gotten from foul men."

Finn stopped pacing and sank down onto the only bed in the room. The things Liam had abandoned in the woods lay on top of the blankets.

"I don't know if Regan will be willing to take a *no* from me." I pulled the sheet tighter around my chest. "If she's really so eager to kill the sorci children, I don't know if anything we do will be able to stop her."

"We'll do what we can," Liam said.

I tipped my gaze to the ceiling as he pulled on his pants.

"Do you think you'll be able to convince her?" I asked. "I don't want murder on my hands, but I cannot let those children die because of me."

Knock, knock.

Liam darted to the door before I'd even turned to face it. He slid the lock aside.

Three women waited in the clearing. One held my things. Another, Finn's. The third held a tray of food.

"On the table." Liam stepped out of their way, extending his arm as they passed, as though creating a barricade between the women and me.

He stayed that way until the women left then locked the door behind them.

The scent of roasted meat and fresh baked bread wafted from the table in the center of the room.

Finn didn't run for the food. He just sat, his head in his hands, not even moving to get his clothes from the table.

"Is there anything we can say to her?" I asked. "Any bargain we make?"

Liam pulled his shirt over his head.

I hesitated for a moment before going to my pile of things. I dug into my pack, searching for the pendant. The smooth stone had lost none of its warmth in its time away from my skin. I gripped the pendant, waiting for it to soothe me, to quiet the fear that still thundered in my chest.

The calm did not come. I turned away from Liam as I slipped the leather cord around my neck.

"Can they grant us safe passage to the south?" I asked. "I would rather spend months leading the sorcis through the mountains myself than give Regan poison to use as she pleases."

Pulling my shift over my head did not calm my nerves.

"Or we can send the children to Lygan Hall, or out to sea," I said. "Maybe we could keep them in the mountains near the camp. You could use your magic to hollow out a cave big enough for them to survive the winter."

Neither Liam nor Finn spoke.

"We were only with her for a few minutes." I buttoned my skirt around my waist. "We traveled for days to get here. We can't just give up after a few minutes."

They both stayed silent.

"What?" I yanked my socks and boots back on. "What bit of Black Blood lore am I missing? Is the Brien trueborn's word law? Do women have more of a say in how things are decided than men?"

"He touched you," Liam said.

"I am quite aware." I stepped in front of Liam.

He kept staring over my head at the door.

"It wasn't a pleasant experience, but the lives of children are at stake," I said.

Liam closed his eyes. "There are laws we must uphold."

"What laws?" I asked. "The only ones I've ever known are those the Guilds use to ruin the lives of common folk."

"The Black Bloods have their own laws," Liam said. "Rules written into the treaty."

"What rules?" I looked between Finn and Liam. "Is there some law that says I'm obligated to help Regan?"

"No." Finn stood up. "But there are laws of safe harbor."

"What does that mean?" I asked.

"We came in good faith," Liam said. "We used no magic and hid no weapons. We came with honor to speak to the trueborn of the Brien Clan."

"And?" My heart crashed even harder against my ribs. "Is any of that wrong?"

"We committed no act against the agreement," Liam said. "And that man touched you. He violated your right to safety under the treaty."

I jumped as Finn slammed his fists on the table.

"There's a code to be followed," Liam said, "a way things must be done to maintain the peace between the clans."

My shift and skirt suddenly didn't seem like enough covering to protect me from the world. I snatched my bodice from the table, wishing it were a suit of armor.

"What does that mean?" I kept my voice steady. "What does the code say, and what has it got to do with me?"

Liam's face was still unreadable, set in stone as though the mountain in his blood had taken hold of him.

"Finn." I lifted his fists from the table. "What rules are there to follow?"

Finn wrapped his arms around me, holding me close. "Just breathe for a moment. It could be nothing. It could all come to nothing."

Knock. Knock.

Finn tightened his hold on me as Liam slid the lock aside.

The gray-haired woman had returned. "Three of our men witnessed the violation of the treaty. Justice is yours to be served. He will be waiting to the west." She took the door from Liam's grip and shut us inside.

"What is the Brien's justice?" I could feel my mouth form the words, but somehow they seemed to come from far away.

"Death." Liam didn't turn to face me. "The penalty for violating an envoy's safety is death."

"Death." The familiar word rattled in my mouth as I tried to discover some new meaning.

"The treaty between clans guarantees our safety." Finn didn't let go of me. "It's a part of the oldest pact. That man violated the agreement, and now he must pay the price."

"Pay the price." My legs lost their strength. I pushed away from Finn to sit at the table. "Death? The letch slides a hand along my breast, and the penalty is death?"

"Safety cannot be violated." Liam slid the bolt back into place, locking the Brien out of our house of twigs.

"Regan really will harm the children, won't she?" The table seemed to sway before me. "If she's so willing to execute one of her own, she won't hesitate to murder the sorcis."

"It's not about Regan," Finn said. "The treaty was created long before any of us were born. She has to follow it."

"So, she just hangs him and has a good night's sleep?" I asked.

"It's not her that's got to do it," Finn said.

My heart stopped. The thundering in my ears disappeared.

"If the one who was harmed is not dead, the treaty requires they carry out the sentence," Liam said.

Sound came crashing back into being.

"Me." My chair fell to the packed dirt floor as I stood. "They want me to execute him?"

"It's our law," Finn said.

"No. No, I won't do it."

Finn reached for me, but I stepped away and began pacing the maddeningly small room.

"Cut off his hand," I said, "that seems like a fair punishment for groping. Or whip him. Just tie him to a post and whip him."

I needed more space. I needed to run, to climb, to disappear from this false fairyland.

"It doesn't work that way," Finn said.

"Then cut off his bits!" I shouted. "Brand him. Lock him up. Shatter the bones in his feet. Or gouge out his eyes, then he'll never leer at any girl again."

"The treaty names death as the penalty for violating an envoy's safety," Finn said.

"I don't care what their rules are. I will not kill a man." My side burned, itching where Liam had drawn his mark. My steps slowed. "Our rules. I don't care what our rules are. I won't kill him."

"You don't have to," Liam said.

I turned to him. His face was still set like stone, and his eyes were still dark with danger.

"You are an envoy," Liam said. "You entered the enclave in good faith. They cannot force you to do anything against your will."

The pressure against my ribs didn't lessen. "So he'll be all right, then? They'll find some other punishment for him and we can speak to Regan tomorrow about the children?"

"Don't think any more of it," Liam said. "It's not what we came here—"

"You can't, Liam," Finn said. "I'm sorry, but you can't."

"Finn." Liam's voice held a note of warning.

"You have to do it, Ena," Finn said. "You have to follow the laws of the treaty."

"Stop—"

"Why?" I cut across Liam.

"If you don't follow the rules of the treaty and you let him live," Finn said, "you become responsible for his actions. If he violates another envoy, his crime would be on your head."

"I would protect her," Liam said. "I would never—"

Finn raised his voice to speak over Liam. "And not just your head. You swore an oath to a trueborn, and he accepted your fate as his."

"I command you to stop," Liam said.

"Then kill me." Finn spread his arms wide. "Use your magic and end my life. If that is my penalty, so be it. But you cannot lie to her. You want to protect her? Fine, but she deserves the honest truth."

"That isn't your decision to make!" Liam shouted.

"If you believe she can't take it, you don't know her half so well as you think." Finn looked to me. "If the letch gropes another woman, you and Liam would both be held accountable. Both of your executions would be ordered by the Clans Council."

I waited for my head to spin or to be sick on the floor. Neither happened.

"So, I kill him, or we wait for him to do something wrong and then they kill us." My voice sounded calm to my own ears.

"Yes," Finn said at the same moment Liam said, "No."

"There are ways around it." Liam stepped between Finn and me. "I can speak to Regan, remove the burden from your hands."

"At what cost?" Finn said.

"The price is mine to pay." Fire flickered in Liam's eyes. "I brought her to the Black Bloods, and I will not allow her place with us to harm her."

I wanted to believe he could make everything right. That

Liam could strike a bargain, give a handshake, and we'd be able to walk away as though nothing had happened.

I was not fool enough to believe Regan would be so kind.

"You didn't try to make me a Black Blood," I said. "You saved me, and I asked to stay. You wanted to send me away, find a place for me in Ilbrea, but I said no. It was me who suggested poisoning Drason, not you."

"It doesn't matter," Liam said.

"I won't allow you to be punished because I don't like the Black Bloods' laws." My chest had gone hollow. I couldn't understand where I was getting the air to speak. "I won't sacrifice your life to save a man who touched me. I won't let you make a bargain with Regan to protect me."

"Ena." Liam took my hand. "I don't want you to bear this burden."

"I'm strong enough. I haven't broken yet. If the Guilds haven't managed it, then one man's death won't be enough to shatter my soul."

I remember thinking that my hands should be shaking, or my legs should give out. That I should collapse to the ground or vomit in utter revulsion at the horrible acts survival demanded of me.

But I was calm as I squeezed Liam's hand then went to my bag to dig out my wooden comb.

"How is it to be done?" I asked.

Liam sank silently down onto the bed.

"They'll have him waiting," Finn said. "You'll just have to go and—"

"Kill him." My comb caught on the knots in my hair. "Do they care how it's done?"

"By the blade," Finn said. "It won't be quick."

"I doubt I was the first. He smiled at me before he touched me. I don't think he would have done that if he'd never been so bold before." I pulled my hair over my shoulder and wove the black strands into a braid. "Why would he risk it? If he knows the laws of the Black Bloods, why would he give his life to touch me?"

"He probably thought you'd be too afraid to react," Finn said. "That you'd let him get away with it rather than allow the treaty to be invoked."

"Should I have stayed quiet?" I asked. "Just let him touch me so Liam could convince Regan to help the children?"

"Men like that cannot be allowed to continue to hurt people," Finn said.

"No." I tied my string around the end of my braid. "But death is not the only punishment the world offers."

My knife had not been replaced in my bag. I felt naked without it. I stared at the ankles of my boots for a long time, just waiting for my weapon to appear.

"You don't have to be the one to do it," Liam said. "I can be the one to wield the knife."

"What would the punishment be for that?" I rolled the sleeves of my shift up as high as they could go.

"I don't care," Liam said.

I shut my eyes, willing the world to stop for just a moment.

"If you won't tell me, then it is more than I am willing to pay." I walked toward the door. "Where to the west am I to find him?"

"We can come with you," Finn said. "There is no law against that."

I froze with my fingers on the wooden bolt.

Better to let them watch your guilt, or to have them imagine it?

"We stay together," Liam said. "I don't care what the treaty says, we aren't trusting them with Ena's safety."

I pushed the bolt aside, grateful I hadn't had to choose if Finn and Liam would follow me.

The chill night air greeted me outside the little stick house. The air wasn't as cold as it should have been this far up in the mountains, but the wind swept around us as though trying to lure me into a dance.

All the people who had gawked at me before had disappeared, but the lights in the clearing hadn't faded. They gleamed around us as though, even in that dark moment, I was still supposed to find beauty in magic.

Someone had left a long knife lying on the ground outside our door. The hilt held a lae stone that shone with inordinate brightness. They had not left a sheath. The bare blade sparkled in the light.

I picked the weapon up, weighing its heft in my hand. This blade was larger than the one Cati had given me. The extra weight of it seemed right, like the knife knew it was going to end a life.

"You don't have to do this." Liam stepped in front of me.

I stared at his face, a face I had not bothered to find beautiful the first time we met. But now I would burn the world to protect his dark eyes. I would destroy the Guilds with my bare hands rather than let one more line of worry appear on his brow.

I reached out and trailed my fingers along the sharp angle of his chin.

A new pain appeared in his eyes.

I leaned in and pressed my lips to his cheek. "Where do we find him?"

"This way." Finn pointed to a path between the trees. He'd gone pale, leaving his freckles as the only color on his face.

Liam pressed my hand to his cheek.

"We should go." I slid my hand out from under his. "If the gods are thirsty for blood, we can't let them decide they would rather taste ours than his."

Liam nodded and started down the path.

I followed, and Finn stayed right behind me. We passed between the houses on the opposite side of the clearing and out into the trees.

I didn't let myself look at Liam as we walked. I was too busy searching the shadows, not for men hiding in the darkness seeking to slaughter us, but for any hint of my victim.

A tree crackled overhead as a large black cat prowled through its branches, but the birds had all gone silent. Even the wind stopped rustling through the leaves as we walked along the path with nothing but starlight to guide us.

I heard the man before I saw him. He screamed through the gag in his mouth, shouting words I could not understand.

Liam slowed his step and spread his arms to his sides as though trying to keep me from reaching the man whose life I was to end.

I ducked under his arm and kept walking up the path.

They hadn't hidden the man in a cave or even locked him in a cage. Perhaps the laws of the clans did not allow for such kindness.

The man stood between two trees, his arms tied out to his sides, the ropes so tight, they pulled at his wrists. His ankles had been tied as well, keeping his legs spread wide so the man could not shift his weight without pain.

They'd taken his clothes, leaving him naked and helpless in the darkness. They'd stuffed a black cloth into his mouth to stifle his screams. The cloth did not hide the scar on his top lip.

I stood before him, gripping the knife in my hand.

"What am I supposed to do?" I asked.

"I'll do it." Liam reached for the blade.

"And if they're watching?" I held the hilt tighter. "I wanted to join you. I will not let you suffer because of me."

Liam stepped closer to the man. The man screamed against his gag as tears fell from his gray-blue eyes.

I wanted to ask him why. Why had he been chivving foolish enough to touch me? What under all the gods and stars had stripped him of his senses and doomed us both to be in this dark forest?

"Where do they want me to stab him?" I moved closer to the poor naked beast left to die in the woods. "Am I supposed to strike him more than once?"

"A slice along the gut," Finn said. "Deep enough to cut through to his organs. Then leave him for the animals."

A pressure pinched around my lungs, threatening to suffocate me. "This is the treaty the Black Bloods agreed to?"

"It was forged a long time ago," Liam said. "The treaty has kept the Black Bloods alive."

"Am I only allowed one cut?" I asked. "Do I have to stick to his stomach?"

The man begged through his gag.

I couldn't understand his words, but I knew his desperation.

He was the beast who had broken the law, but I was the monster who had come for his blood.

"Am I allowed to cut him wherever I like?" I shouted over the man's screams.

A rustle of bird's wings carried from high up in the trees.

"Yes," Liam said.

I tightened my grip on the knife and stepped up in front of the man.

I wanted to say something. To beg forgiveness for taking his life or tell him he owed me a debt that could never be repaid. He had begun this horror, not me.

But my mouth had gone numb as my hand had gone numb.

I drew my arm back and stabbed.

The man's scream echoed in my ears.

I forced my knife down. His warm blood flowed over my hand.

I pulled the blade free and fought my instinct to throw the awful weapon aside.

In two quick moves, I cut a deep gash at the top of both of his thighs.

The knife tumbled from my grip, and I stepped away from the blood seeping into the dirt.

Holding my gore-coated hand in front of me, I walked back up the dark path to the clearing surrounded by fairy houses built of sticks.

29

My hands will never be clean again.

I had thought the very same thing many times before and had always been wrong. But somehow, as I scrubbed my hands in the bucket of cold water, it seemed like this time it might be true.

The door closed behind me, and the bolt scraped into place. I didn't turn to see who had come in. If they wanted to slit my throat, I was too tired to fight them.

Two sets of footfalls moved slowly behind me. A chair scratched across the dirt as it was pulled away from the table. Someone stopped beside me.

"I've brought soap." Liam held out a cracked brick of soap that smelled like fat boiled with rosemary.

"Thanks." Pink dripped from my fingers as I took the soap.

"Are..." Liam's voice faded. "Is there anything I can do to help you?"

"To help me wash my hands?" I shook my head. "No. I've washed plenty of blood off my hands before. Getting the red out from under your nails is the tricky bit, but I can manage."

"Ena—"

"Honestly, it was tidier than I expected." I dug my nails into the soap. "I even managed to keep my skirt clean. It's a wonder how much easier it is to avoid getting blood on you when you're the one who's causing the injury."

I rubbed the soap against my hands until my skin stung. "He should be dead by now." I rinsed my hands in the water one last time. "It doesn't seem like it should work that way, but one cut to the wrong part of the leg, and you'll bleed out. It happens much faster than dying of a gut wound, or an animal tearing through your flesh."

My breath caught in my chest. I stood and took the black cloth I'd been wrapped in from the table. If the man with the scar on his lip hadn't been assigned to bring me something to wrap up in, he would still have been alive.

And waiting to touch a girl who's too afraid to say no.

I dried my hands on the cloth, balled it up, and tossed it into the corner.

Then it was done. My hands were clean. The man had been killed. There was nothing more for me to do.

"We should eat." I looked to the table. The scent of the food sent my stomach rolling. "Or make a plan. What are we going to say to Regan? Do you know anywhere we can take the sorci children? Can you send a stone bird to Lygan Hall to ask for help?"

Liam took my hands in his.

"There has to be another place we can keep them safe," I said.

He kissed both of my palms.

"Liam." I should have pulled my hands away from him but couldn't find the strength. "We have to do something."

He gathered me into his arms and held me tight. "I'm sorry. I'm so sorry, Ena."

I laid my ear against his chest, listening to his heartbeat.

It thumped a steady rhythm. His blood stayed safely in his veins. He would not be killed in the woods because of one lecherous man's sin.

I could not regret the blood I had shed if it meant protecting Liam.

He pressed his lips to the top of my head, and I wrapped my arms around him, holding him close.

We stayed like that for a long time, until his scent replaced the stench of blood and foul soap.

"You need rest," Liam said.

"I don't deserve sleep." My own words chipped at the armor in my chest.

"You do." Liam led me to the bed. He moved his pack from on top of the blankets and set it on the floor.

"What are we going to say to Regan?" I didn't fight as he sat me down at the head of the bed and loosened the laces on my boots. "We have to plan. You have to know something about her or the clans that can help us."

Liam slid my boots off and pulled down the covers on the bed. "Sleep, Ena."

True terror welled in my chest as I stared at the pillow.

"I'll keep the nightmares away," Liam said.

I lay down on the bed, wishing the feather mattress would swallow me whole.

He pulled the blanket up over me.

Finn watched from his seat at the table. His face had lost even more color. Like I had killed him instead of the man and he had become one of the ghosts of the eastern mountains.

I rolled to face the wall, choosing to stare at the sticks rather than my friend's face.

"I'll keep you safe."

The bed shifted as Liam lay down behind me. He wrapped his arm around me and held me close, protecting me from every monster he could fight.

"Just sleep." His whispered words carried me into the blissful void of sleep.

30

The sun still hadn't risen when I woke up. I lay very still in bed, listening to Liam's steady breathing. Even through the blankets, his warmth wrapped around me like a cocoon. But I would not emerge from his embrace a beautiful butterfly.

I had killed a man. Not by passing a means of execution on to someone else. I had held the knife, and I had cut into his body, making sure he would die.

I remembered the warmth of his blood on my hand, yet somehow my part in his death didn't seem real. The whole thing was too quick, too absurd. As accustomed as I'd grown to the swift brutality the Guilds called justice, it was hard to make myself believe that I, Ena Ryeland, had ended up in a magical stronghold and been ordered to kill a man.

I nestled closer to Liam. He stirred and tightened his grip on my waist.

I had chosen to join this magic and madness. The Black Bloods had laws, and I had followed them. I would not plead innocence, and I could not regret my choice.

But there were innocent people left in the world. Children who had power running through their veins, magic they could not rid themselves of, that would see them locked up by the Sorcerers Guild if they were caught.

We needed a way to help the children escape that did not involve the Brien.

The gray light of sunrise filtered through the one window in the room.

There had to be a place we could keep the sorci children safe.

I had heard of lands beyond Ilbrea, across the Arion Sea or farther east than even the eastern mountains reached. But I had never seen those places. Even if I found a way to ferry the children to the kingless territories far to the south, I couldn't just pack the little ones up and send them to a place they might not be able to survive.

Wherever the Brien took them was supposed to be safe, Liam had promised me that much. If the Brien had found a safe place to take hundreds of magical children, surely we could as well.

But what if we couldn't? What if the children died because of me?

What if I gave Regan the poison and she caused a horror even worse than the Massacre of Marten?

There were no choices I could see that did not leave more death in my wake.

It all circled around and around in my head until Liam finally stirred behind me. He took a deep breath as he woke then shifted his head on the pillow.

I lay very still, hoping he would think I was sleeping and hold me for just a little while longer.

"Ena," Liam whispered, "did a nightmare wake you?"

"No, I don't have those anymore." I rolled over to face him.

The hard edges of his face had softened while he slept. His eyes held none of the fierce danger of the night before.

"I trust you, Liam," I said. "I have since you told me to run into the woods with you when Harane burned."

He brushed a hair away from my cheek.

"If you tell me to give Regan the poison, I will. But I don't trust her. She had me execute one of her own men."

"It's the law of the Black Bloods—"

I pressed my fingers over Liam's lips. "She smiled when she spoke of hurting the children. If she can do that so easily, will the life of one letch weigh on her conscience? If death is the justice she's used to, who would she be willing to kill with my aid? What if it isn't a monster but someone who simply refuses to do as she says? What if people die, from my poison, just because they're in her way?"

Liam lifted my fingers from his lips. "Then we tell her no. Refuse to give her anything."

"What about the children? We can't leave them out there waiting for the Sorcerers Guild to steal them, and we can't let Regan harm them."

"We'll figure something out."

"Or"—a shiver shook my shoulders. Liam drew me closer to him—"I can stay here. If Regan wants someone poisoned, I'll do it myself."

"No."

"That way, I'll know if the people killed by the brew I mix are guilty of a crime worthy of death."

"Absolutely not." Liam held me tighter still.

I lay my head against his chest, nestling under his chin, trying to memorize the feel of lying so intimately close to him.

"You will not stay here," Liam said. "I don't care what Regan demands. Your place is with the Duwead Clan. You swore an oath to me."

"But if it's stay here or—"

"No." Liam stood up, leaving the bed feeling too big without him lying beside me. "I am your trueborn, and my decision is final."

He pulled on his boots, slid the bolt aside, and stepped out into the dim morning light.

Follow him, a tiny voice called from the very back of my mind.

I wrapped the blankets tightly around my shoulders, trying to convince myself I wouldn't freeze without his warmth.

Finn lay on the floor with his back to me. I watched his side rise and fall.

"Do you agree with him?" I asked.

Finn kept breathing evenly.

"I've been sleeping next to you for months," I said. "I know you're not asleep."

"I don't know which of you is right." Finn rolled onto his back. "The Brien are powerful. They control the path south, have controlled the route for hundreds of years. You don't gain that kind of strength without being brutal."

"But?"

"I don't know if their kind of brutality would help our cause or make us worse than the monsters we're trying to fight."

I pressed my palm against the pillow. Liam's warmth still clung to the fabric. "If I stay, I can make sure helping them doesn't make things worse."

"You can't stay," Finn said. "It doesn't matter what either of us thinks. Your trueborn has made his decision."

"But if he hadn't, what would you think I should do?"

"It doesn't matter." Finn tossed his blankets aside and sat up.

"It does to me."

Finn stared at the wall for a moment, rubbing his fingers along the ginger scruff on his chin.

"I wouldn't have you stay," he said. "If we're the ones taking the risks in Ilbrea, then we should be the ones setting the rules. If we keep going on as we are now, we'll never move beyond saving sorcis. And as glad as I am to help the children, it's not enough to topple the Guilds."

"So it's better for Ilbrea if I refuse to help Regan at all?"

"I don't know." Finn stood and walked over to the bed. He took my hand in his as he sat down. "But I'm not going to lose you because the chivving Brien can't find a way to take care of their own chivving problems. You and I are partners, Ena. I would no more leave you behind with Regan than I would with the Soldiers Guild."

I kissed the back of Finn's hand. "I adore you. You know that, right?"

"Everyone adores me. It's impossible to resist my charm."

I ate the breakfast two women delivered without being ill. It seemed strange that my stomach should so cheerfully accept food when I'd gutted a man the night before.

The women didn't stare at me, didn't curse and call me a killer when they cleared away my empty plate.

I wished they had. It would have been easier to hear the word from someone else's lips than to listen to the constant echo of it in my own mind.

Finn chattered on as we waited in the stick house. Food, Lygan Hall, the people around our camp, the people of the Duwead Clan who hadn't come to the camp. He talked without pause for hours. It was almost as though he too could hear the word echoing in my head and wanted to drown it out.

"We should go look for him," I said for the fifth time when the sun had grown to full brightness outside our window.

"Better to wait here." Finn squeezed my hand. "Liam will come back when he needs us."

"What if he needs us now?"

"Then he would be here now," Finn said.

"Not if someone hurt him." I pushed away from the table to

pace the small, open patch of dirt. "What if someone wanted revenge for the letch's death? What if he's tied between two trees, bleeding?"

"He's not." Finn shifted to sit on top of the table. "He's probably out stomping through the forest, trying to convince himself not to level the mountain."

I made a sound somewhere between a whimper and a laugh.

"Either that, or he's decided it's better for him to speak to Regan on his own and they're already meeting inside the cavern."

"He wouldn't." I froze. "He can't."

"Of course he can. He's the trueborn. We are but his marked minions."

"No." I started for the door.

Finn leapt off the table and ran to block me.

"Finn, we have to make sure he isn't trying to meet with her on his own."

"We can't. It's not our place."

"Our place?" I shouted. "I'm the one who started this whole chivving mess. I'm the one who suggested poison. I'm the one who caused the Massacre of Marten. I will not be the one who leaves the sorci children to die!"

"You wouldn't be." Finn spoke in a low tone like I was a dog about to attack. "There are things in this world that are bigger than all of us, Ena. Only fools try to take the credit or blame for acts done by the gods."

"Get out of my way, Finn."

"Going out there will only make things worse."

Knock. Knock. Knock.

Both of us froze at the gentle knocking on the door.

I glanced to my bag before remembering I no longer had my knife.

"Come in." Finn stared into my eyes as the door opened.

Regan stood in the doorway.

"Good morning." She gave each of us a smile before crossing

the threshold. "I was waiting to be sure you were awake enough for company. I would find it rude to impose after such a trying evening."

"An evening you—"

"We slept quite well," Finn cut across me. "And breakfast was delicious. I'd never want to make anyone think badly of my own clan, but the food in our camp is nothing like what you have here in the enclave."

Regan laughed. "Call it a personal fault. I cannot feel like there is any safety in the world if I am being ill fed. The haven the mountain has granted us provides great bounty. I insist on that bounty being skillfully used. After all, what's life without a good meal?"

"Does it count as a good meal if there's poison in it?" I asked.

"Ena—"

"It just seems like a betrayal to taint the thing you love with death," I said.

Regan examined me.

I tipped my head to the side, mimicking her motion, and kept my face bland.

"Perhaps," Regan said, "but we marry for power, murder for justice, breed to honor the past. There are a great number of things that go against what we would do in a perfect world. It is the way we must behave to survive."

"Is that what you think?" I laughed. "There are some things you cannot compromise for survival. Better to die than live betraying everything worth living for."

"Do you really think yourself wise enough to educate me?" Regan stepped closer to me. The stiff skirt of her violet dress swished as she moved.

"Not wise," I said, "just experienced. I've lived in Ilbrea. With no enclave to hide in, no clans or magic to protect me. I've lost everyone I ever cared for. Twice. My story is not strange. Suffering, pain, loss—those are the realities of life for every tilk in

Ilbrea. And you would abandon the sorcis to the Guilds. You would allow children with magic in their blood to be locked up by the Sorcerers Guild."

"The Brien have spent years working to keep those children from the hands of the Sorcerers Guild. I have spent my life making sure they are ferried safely south."

"And now you would kill those same children?" I stepped toward her. "Is that the sacrifice you are willing to make? Is that what your laws and morals and chivving survival demand?"

"Yes." There was no hint of remorse in her tone.

"You shouldn't fear the Guilds invading the mountains. You are so much like the paun, you could become great friends. Slaughter everyone who displeases you and leave a river of blood in your wake."

Regan smiled.

I waited for men to come storming in to murder me, or for Regan herself to shoot a stone through my body and end my life.

"I see we will not be able to come to an agreement," she said. "Pity. Killing one of my people came so easily to you in the darkness, I had hoped by the brutal light of day you would see our situation as it truly is. I had hoped we would be able to continue saving those poor children."

A desperate fire flared in the center of my chest, blazing even brighter than my anger. "You want poison that badly? It's not even a hard thing to accomplish. Is there no one in your own clan you can order to brew something fatal?"

"Not with the subtlety you managed," Regan said. "I am perfectly capable of having a man killed. Ending his life without losing my allies is another matter."

The fire disappeared, replaced with an ice even more frightening.

"If it's only one," I said. "If you could promise you would keep the children safe. I could go and get the job—"

"I forbid it." Liam stepped into the house. Sweat coated his brow, and darkness filled his eyes.

"Forbid what?" Regan asked. "You, trueborn Duwead, do not hold that power in my enclave."

"I forbid Ena to brew poison for any purposes but my own," Liam said. "She shall not mix it, she shall not give instructions, she shall not work to kill by anyone's orders but my own."

A shiver shook my whole body as though the stone in my bones had recognized the command.

"That power I do hold here, Regan," Liam said.

I held my breath, once again waiting for Regan to rage or for her guards to come racing in to gut us.

"I'm impressed," Regan said. "I thought you were too soft for such a thing, Liam."

"I am not too soft to protect my own," Liam said.

"Then the sorci children must be dealt with." Regan brushed an imaginary speck of something off her perfect skirt. "I suppose it is time we stop risking so much to save children already tainted by Ilbrea."

"You won't be touching the children." Liam walked over to our line of packs by the wall. He picked mine up and thrust it into my hands. "Don't lie to yourself, Regan. Your people don't have the will or the resources to reach to the sorcis in Ilbrea without us. Don't bother sending your people into the woods to meet us. We won't be coming."

I slung my pack onto my back.

"And where will you take them, Duwead?" Regan said.

Liam tossed Finn his bag.

"It's nothing to do with you, trueborn Brien." Liam put on his own pack. "There's not a chivving rule in the treaty about a clan's right to give safe harbor to outsiders, so it's got nothing to do with you."

Liam stormed toward the door.

I kept close on his heels.

"What will Orla say?" Regan followed us out into the clearing. "Will she be generous? Will she accept the Ilbreans into her hall?"

Liam rounded on Regan. "To the Hall, across the Arion Sea, up to the white north itself. Whichever way we send them is none of your concern."

People appeared in the clearing, stepping out of their homes, emerging from the trees, surrounding us on all sides.

"You cannot make this decision for all Black Bloods," Regan said. "You are one tiny pebble born of the mountain. Do not think you are so mighty as to topple the summit."

"If the summit cracks, it will not be my doing," Liam said. "It will be the fault of those who forget the mountain granted shelter to a child."

He stormed up the long path of trees.

Finn took my arm, staying close to me as we followed behind him.

The forest around us held more magic during the daylight. The greens of the trees' leaves shifted from emerald to pine to mint. Birds with feathers of obscenely bright colors cooed as they flew overhead.

With the sunlight beaming down, I could see that we weren't in a valley as I had imagined, but in the hollowed-out summit of a mountain. Perhaps it was the gods themselves who dug out the top of a high peak to create a paradise for Regan to rule. Perhaps the mountains favored children born of the Brien line.

Either way, as I leapt over sparkling streams and dodged around brightly-hued wildflowers, I wanted nothing more than to return to the plainness of the camp. Featherbeds be damned, feed me slop all my days, I wanted to return to the camp as I had never craved a place in my life.

As I chased after Liam, I kept thinking that maybe I just didn't recognize our path through the woods since we were moving in the opposite direction by daylight, but when we reached a crevasse that dug deep enough into the ground to swallow the sunlight, I knew we had traveled a different trail.

I glanced up and down the fissure, searching for a way across, but the split in the earth reached as far as I could see in either direction.

Finn stepped up to the very edge of the crack, gazing down into the darkness below.

I waited for Liam to turn and follow another path, but he just stood beside Finn, staring into the black. Digging my nails into my palms, I stepped up between them.

The blackness below was not complete. It held shadows and textures that marked it as something different than a nightmare.

"It's not too late to go back," Finn said. "Ena could brew the poison and give it to me. I could feed it to the poor slitch Regan wants dead."

"I meant what I said." Liam knelt by the edge of the crevasse. "We've spent too long bowing to the other clans. Every sorci we deliver to Regan makes the Brien stronger. The more power we give them, the worse it will be for all of us if they start pushing down a path the Duweads cannot follow. The Brien will not gain one drop of poison made by Ena's hand."

"Where are we going to keep the children?" I asked.

Liam took my hand. "I swear to you, I will find them a safe place."

A bit of the pain in my chest ebbed away.

"I see them." Finn pointed farther along the crevasse.

I held on to Liam's hand as we followed Finn, not caring if I seemed like a frightened child.

Straining my ears, I listened for the sounds of a coming attack, waiting for an animal to leap out of the trees to devour us, or the Brien to charge out of the woods seeking vengeance for the blood on my hands.

"There." Finn stopped by the side of the rift, squinting into the darkness.

I followed his gaze, trying to find what might have caught his eye.

A thin staircase poked out of the rock wall, each step barely big enough to support a foot. The path led down into the pitch black below the reach of the sunlight.

"I suppose the mountain isn't feeling very generous today," Finn said.

"Any path out of here is a gift." Liam let go of my hand and stepped onto the first stair.

My heart leapt into my throat as sense told me he would plummet into the darkness and disappear forever.

Liam shifted his weight back and forth before moving to the next stair down. "We'll have to go slowly, but if the mountain wills it, we should make it to the bottom alive."

Finn waited until Liam's head had sunk below ground level before bowing me toward the steps.

"You don't want to go first?" I stepped up to the lip of the rift.

"Being marked by Liam won't make the mountain recognize you as one of her own," Finn said. "Better to have a Black Blood behind you so she doesn't decide the path is no longer needed."

"Thanks for that." I adjusted the pack on my back and stepped down.

I have never been a tiny waif of a creature, but my frame was still much smaller than Finn's or Liam's.

Even so, as we traveled down the rock staircase, it seemed like there wasn't enough width to the steps to keep me from toppling sideways and into the darkness. The shadows cast by the sun distorted the shape of the black rock below my feet. I tried to find the slanting shadows comforting, promising myself there was really more stone to the steps than I could see.

Then I placed my heel too close to the edge.

I swayed, and panic rushed through every nerve in my body.

"Ena!" Finn rammed his arm into my shoulder, slamming me against the solid wall.

"Are you all right?" Liam tried to look back but couldn't turn enough to see me.

"I'm fine." My voice came out too high. I took a deep a breath. "Wishing I had some decent light, that's all."

"We'll be out of here soon," Liam said.

"Good." My voice sounded stronger. "I've always loved to climb, but this is not the sort of challenge I crave."

Liam started down the steps again.

"I don't think any sane person would like these stairs." Finn lifted his arm away from me.

The shadows below seemed to taunt me, like they were waiting for me to slip again and fall into their terrible clutches.

I pressed my palm to the rock wall, wishing I could find even a hint of a handhold.

This is not the way your life ends, Ena Ryeland.

I steadied my nerves, taking slow breaths until my heart calmed. I kept my gaze locked on my feet as I stepped down.

"Is this always the way out of the enclave?" I asked.

"No," Liam said, "there are many paths in and out of the Brien's haven, but this was the only one that called to me today."

His voice soothed me almost as much as if he had been touching me.

I wanted him to keep speaking until I learned how to fill my body with the sound of his words.

"What's it like," I asked, "feeling the stone as you do?"

Liam didn't answer until I'd already opened my mouth to apologize for being too bold in asking.

"I don't really know how to describe it," Liam said.

The stone wall curved, leading us away from the shadows and into pitch black.

"Lovely," Finn said.

I felt for the next stair down with my toe.

"It's like a pull," Liam said. "Or an instinct, I suppose. I don't know if it's a scent, or magic, or the stone in my veins being pulled by the mountain itself. I can feel the stone around me. Some bits are dull and normal. Others call to me. When the mountain offers me a path, it burns bright."

"What about the boulders that protect the camp?" I kept feeling in the darkness for each new step. "Do they burn bright, too?"

"They're a part of me."

I could hear the smile in his voice. I wished there were light so I could see one side of his mouth arc up.

"It's my magic that creates the spell that protects us."

"It is?" I froze in the darkness.

"Why do you think the camp is run by a trueborn?" Finn said. "We've got to have one to work the stone magic to protect us. Liam wasn't chosen for his charm."

"Hmm." I couldn't think of a better thing to say.

"I can feel the boulders, though." Liam's voice sounded farther away.

I stepped as quickly as I dared to catch up.

"Returning to the camp feels like putting myself back together," Liam said. "And when the spell ends as the cold comes, it's like losing a slice of myself. It's not painful, but there are no more bits of me in the great stones. I am reduced to a being a normal man."

"Nonsense," Finn said. "You've scattered your magic in the little stones we use to protect ourselves outside the camp. You aren't normal, only small enough to travel in a pocket."

Liam and Finn both laughed.

I tried to join in, but the bouncing of my ribs jostled the pendant against my skin.

The warmth of the smooth stone sent heat soaring into my cheeks.

"Slow down," Liam warned.

I stopped with one foot in the air. My heart thundered in my ears as I listened for whatever danger lurked in the darkness.

A scratching and dull tapping carried from below.

My ankle itched as I longed for my knife.

The tapping carried out to my side and then behind me.

"We've reached the bottom," Liam said. "There's a tunnel for us to follow."

"Thank the gods," Finn said. "I try to be cheerful no matter how dark things get, but I don't think I could have climbed back up these chivving stairs with a smile on my face."

"Ena," Liam said.

Something brushed the side of my skirt.

"Take my hand. I'll help you the rest of the way."

I reached down and took Liam's hand. I had managed to climb down into the crevasse on my own, but knowing he waited for me in the darkness eased my fear of the black.

"Don't fuss over me," Finn said. "I can make it on my own."

"Last stair." Liam took my elbow as I stepped down onto the blissfully smooth ground. He guided me through the darkness to the side of the stairs.

"If I wasn't so eager to be out of Brien territory, I might suggest we take a bit of a rest," Finn said.

"I just want to reach the open air soon enough to put a fair bit of distance between us and the way out before it gets dark." Liam let go of my arm and placed my hand on a smooth wall of rock. "This way."

I stretched my other hand to the side, touching the opposite wall.

The tunnel was large enough for me to walk easily down, but the stone I trailed my fingers along sent shivers up my arms.

To my right, the rock was smooth, as though a mason had spent years meticulously grinding the surface.

To my left, the rock was cracked and uneven, as though the magic within the mountain had somehow missed this part of her stone.

I wanted to see what the ceiling looked like, to know if there was any design or reason as to why our path had been created this way. I settled for gratitude at being away from the stairs.

A rustling carried through the tunnel. I stopped, trying to hear details in the sound.

"Keep moving," Liam said.

"Of course." I tried to think through anything in my pack that might be used as a weapon. Beyond choking someone with my spare shift or smacking them with my comb, I had nothing but my fists, teeth, and utter will to survive to defend myself with.

The rustling came closer faster than we were moving. Another new sound joined the noise, flapping and squeaking.

"Liam!"

I barely managed to say his name before something heavy knocked me to the ground.

"Just hold still." Liam spoke close to my ear.

The rustling and flapping surrounded us.

Liam shifted to cover my head as a smack sounded right behind us.

"Chivving cact of a paun chivving, slitching—" Finn shouted. "I hate chivving bats."

My nails bit into my palms as the bats continued to surround us.

"Just hold still, and they'll give up," Liam said.

"I have never liked Regan." Finn's voice sounded muffled. "It's not that she never remembers my name. It's her chivving temper tantrums that drive me mad."

"It that what this is?" I spoke into the crook of Liam's shoulder.

"I knew she'd send a goodbye," Liam said. "At least she only chose bats."

The flapping faded away toward the terrible stairs.

"And this isn't against the treaty?" I asked.

"Not in any way that matters." Liam pushed himself off of me and took my hand, helping me to my feet. "There was no one here to witness it and no way to prove she sent her animal minions to scratch at us."

"Petty," Finn said. "That's what she is, plain petty."

"Come on," Liam said. "I'm tired of being down here."

"If either of you got cut, we'll have to clean the wounds," I said.

"Later," Liam said, "when we're free of Regan."

I strained my ears as we kept moving, listening for any more visitors in the darkness. But Regan had only been bold enough to scratch at us, not deliver a mortal wound.

We walked for a long while before a faint blue glimmered in the distance.

"Thank the gods," Finn muttered behind me.

The light grew brighter as we approached.

Soft sounds of movement carried from up ahead, but not the flapping of wings.

Leaning sideways, I peered around Liam.

We hadn't returned to the unground lake. A vast cavern, larger than even Regan's hall, waited for us.

Liam slowed as he reached the end of the tunnel, taking a moment to look around the cavern before letting me step into the open.

Our horses had been tethered to the cavern wall. A pile of our weapons lay nearby.

"Thank the gods." Finn's voice rang around the cavern.

The ride north through the mountains didn't hold the same dread as our journey to the Brien, but as the miles passed, a weight still hung over us.

Where will we send the children?

I didn't ask. Neither did Finn, but as Liam rode silently in front of us mile after mile, I knew Finn was wondering the same thing.

We made it all the way to the bit of the mountains we called home before any of us did anything but think.

It was the sharp scent of blood I noticed first, carrying past the earthy fragrance of the woods.

"Liam." I stopped my horse, sniffing the breeze.

The bay fidgeted beneath me, like she too could smell death on the wind.

"What is it?" Liam looked back over his shoulder at me, his face calm.

"There's something wrong." I slid down off my horse. "I think something's been killed."

"It's a forest, Ena," Finn said. "Things are killed in forests all the time. It's how the bigger creatures eat."

"I know that." I walked east, leading my mount behind me. The wind picked up, blowing a sweet and sickening stench of decay.

"Something has died." Finn jumped down from his horse and strode up beside me, covering his nose with his hand. "Do we really need to go near whatever is making that foul stink? Let the animal decay in peace."

I handed him my reins but didn't answer. I was too busy searching the trees for whatever had died.

I'm not sure why I needed to find the creature whose life had ended. Perhaps it was the familiar scent of blood that called to the bit of me that had been trained as a healer. Maybe the mountain was calling to me, begging to tell me her secret.

The mountain sloped down, cutting a gentle path around a place where the ground had collapsed, leaving a stream of boulders scattered between the trees.

Bile rolled into my throat as the wind carried a fresh wave of the stench.

"Ena." Liam thumped up behind me. "What are you looking for?"

"That." I pointed to the side of a moss-covered boulder.

A spray of blood had coated the green, dying it a putrid shade of black. The corpse of a deer lay on the ground, its stomach ripped open but the rest of its body intact, as though the scavengers of the forest had somehow been warned away from this feast. There wasn't even a fly buzzing around the rot.

But it wasn't the death that drew me forward. It was the long lines of claw marks sliced into the boulder, cutting through the moss. The same claw marks gouged the ground around the deer's body.

"It looks like the same beast who came after Finn and me." I picked my way around the corpse to get a better view of the claw marks. "It wasn't a bear that did this, Liam. There's no animal I know whose claws could cut so deep into stone."

"What did Orla tell you of the beast I warned you about?" Finn asked.

"Nothing." Liam turned away from the decay. "Only that she'd have to speak to the story keepers."

"Wonderful." Finn's mouth twisted as though he might be ill. "It's always nice when you have to refer to legends to gather information. Makes knowledge so reliable. And I was worried this summer was getting to be a bit dull." Finn climbed back up the slope, the horses outpacing him to the top.

"Could Regan have sent a beast after the camp?" I asked.

Liam frowned.

"She sent her bats to scratch at us," I said. "Maybe other animals with bigger claws obey her as well."

"I don't think she'd be foolish enough to send a beast into Duwead territory." He scrubbed his hands over his face.

"What are we supposed to do?" I backed away from the corpse, trying to rid myself of the fear that Death himself hid in the trees, watching me.

"We get back to camp," Liam said. "Make sure everyone there is safe, and see if any of the hunters have spotted anything."

I followed him up the slope, trying to convince my stomach I didn't need to be ill.

"Why are you being so calm about this?" I asked. "There's a monster in the woods. I've seen it, Finn's seen it, and it's close to camp."

"You don't run when you hear signs of danger," Liam said. "You don't flinch at the sight of blood."

"Of course not," I said. "I grew up in Harane living with an illegal healer. If got sick at the sight of blood, I wouldn't have made it this far."

"The legends of the mountains are in our blood," Liam said. "The creature you saw was only a bit bigger than a bear. It's killed a deer."

"But Regan—"

"Compared to the monsters that have roamed the eastern mountains, it's no worse than a wound that needs stitching," Liam finished.

I let out a great sigh and took my reins back from Finn. "Will I ever stop feeling like I'm stumbling through the dark?"

"If you can't tell there's sunlight, we have bigger problems than the beast." Finn mounted his horse.

"That's not what I mean," I said. "Every time I feel like perhaps I understand a bit about the Black Bloods, it all slips away in oaths, and marks, and bats, and monsters."

"If it makes you feel any better, I was born in Lygan Hall, and I still don't have a chivving clue what's going on half the time," Finn said. "Think of your confusion as a sign that you're accepting your life as a Black Blood."

"Thanks, Finn." My horse stomped her hoof as I climbed onto my saddle.

"I'll speak to the hunters as soon as we get back," Liam said. "Don't fret about the beast. The boundary will protect the camp."

"I'm sure it will." I urged my horse to follow Liam. "But I don't fancy meeting the monster on our next sorci run."

Liam's neck tensed.

"You said you'd gotten word about one we might need to rescue," I said. "We'll have to leave straight away if we want any chance of keeping them from the Sorcerers Guild. With how long it took us to find out we're truly on our own, we might already be too late."

"They'll have to hold on a bit longer," Liam said. "We have to prepare for them."

"Prepare for them how?" I asked.

"I still don't know," Liam said.

There was a sad resignation in his voice that I hated.

Self-loathing curdled in my gut. Liam could blame the clans and Regan, but it was me who had made the system begin to crumble. If those children were taken by the Sorcerers Guild, it would be because of the choices I'd made.

I placed my hand on my chest, pressing the stone pendant against my skin.

He stopped the nightmare. Liam can save the children, too.

The great stone boulders that surrounded our camp came into view, but the wonderful relief I'd expected didn't come.

The longing filled my chest, and hunger devoured my soul as we passed through the spell Liam had cast to protect the camp. I lingered between the stones for a breath, trying to feel a hint of him within the magic.

The longing threatened to shatter me.

"Liam," a man called from high up in the trees. Rothford dropped from the branches a moment later. "We've been hoping you'd be back soon."

There was something in the set of Rothford's jaw that replaced the longing with fear.

"Emmet's back. He's been pacing in front of your tent for two days now," Rothford said before Liam could speak. "Won't tell any of us what he's so fussed about, and no one fancies telling him he's got to stop."

"I'll go to him," Liam said.

"And a hunting party went out two days ago and hasn't come back. Neil's raving like it's a plot against him, and Marta's barely managed to keep the camp calm. She sent a search party out after the hunters, but we haven't heard back from them yet."

"Case," Finn said. "Where's Case?"

"Far as I know, he went out with the search party," Rothford said. "They didn't pass this way, so I'm not really sure who went."

Finn kicked his mount and raced toward the camp.

"I have to see Marta," Liam said. "We have to go after the rescue party."

He rode off as well.

"Why is he so worried about the rescue party?" Rothford

asked. "I'm more concerned about your brother tearing the camp apart."

"Have you seen any animals?" I said. "Monsters prowling beyond the stones?"

"Haven't seen much of anything as far as animals," Rothford said. "Why? What's going on?"

"Just keep a close watch."

Rothford grabbed the reins of my horse. "It's my chivving job to keep a close watch, and I'll continue doing my duty well. What are you going to do about your brother?"

"Liam can…" I shut my eyes, trying to sort through everything that needed to be done to find my place in the madness. "I'll take care of Emmet."

"Thank you." Rothford let go of my reins. "All of camp thanks you."

I kicked my horse and galloped off toward camp.

I'd never ridden through the paths around camp before. I leaned close to my horse's neck, ducking beneath the tree branches and trying to pretend I didn't notice the people staring at me.

Liam's horse was by the cook tent, but neither he nor Marta was anywhere in sight.

The usual people sitting scattered through the clearing started when I came charging through, and others peeked out of their tents as I slowed my horse right in front of my brother.

"Ena." Emmet looked up at me. He hadn't shaved in a while. The dark brown scruff on his face had nearly grown into a proper beard. Dark rings stood out against the pale skin under his eyes, which did not brighten as he looked at me. "Where have you been?"

"Did no one tell you?" I draped my hands over the front of my saddle.

"I was told you'd gone to speak to the trueborn Brien," Emmet said.

"Well then, why are you asking questions?" I tipped my head to the side, keeping a look of innocent ignorance on my face.

"You should not be speaking to the Brien." Emmet stepped closer to my horse.

The bay sighed her displeasure.

"Well, it's done." I stroked the horse's neck. "I'm back now, so there's no use fussing over it."

"The Brien trueborn shouldn't be trusted, let alone—"

"Are you pacing in front of Liam's tent waiting for me?" I cut across him.

Emmet's face darkened.

"If you are," I said, "you can stop now. What's past is past, so go get some rest. You look like a chivving corpse."

"I need to speak to Liam," Emmet said. "So you go get some rest. Quite frankly, you look like the gods have tried to take you as well."

"I can't rest. I have work to do."

"What work?" Emmet took hold of my horse's bridle.

"Do not try to pretend you have any control over me, Emmet." I kept my voice steady. "If you want to speak to Liam about whatever men you killed on your rampage of vengeance in Ilbrea, so be it. But as for my work, my seeing the Brien, anything to do with my life, leave it be."

Emmet kept his grip on the bridle as he stared at me. "Where's Liam?"

"He went to find Marta at the cook tent. I don't know where they went from there. There's a monster roaming the woods. We found a deer it had killed. He's worried about the hunters."

Emmet looked up to the sky.

"What did you need to tell him?" I asked. "If it wasn't about me, why would you spend two days pacing?"

He didn't say anything.

"I was fine with the Brien," I said. "They kept to the word of the treaty."

"You and I were not born Black Bloods, Ena." Emmet reached up and took my hand. A barely-healed wound marked his wrist. "We were born Ryelands. We are children of Ilbrea, not the mountain. We cannot trust their magic to protect us, and no one can trust their treaty."

"What's that supposed to mean?"

"You'll have to ask the one you swore yourself to." Emmet let go of my hand and the horse's bridle. "I don't care if you like me, Ena. But I hope you know I would never betray you."

I shut my eyes, pressing down the old hurts that flared in my chest. "Is there a traitor in the camp?"

"I don't know. I'm not sure who's betrayed us."

"Is the camp in danger?"

"The whole chivving world is about to burn."

I have never been one to trust easily. I'm not sure if I was born that way or if the Guilds stole that childlike habit when they stole my parents.

But in Harane, I had always known who I could not trust. Every paun was an enemy. There was no need to question, no need to guess. Anyone in a Guild uniform was out for our blood.

Standing in the clearing, I missed that simplicity.

"We only have a few hours until dark," Liam said. "I want you traveling in groups of three. Everyone is to be fully armed. If you find the beast, protect yourselves first, but if the opportunity comes, kill it. You have to be back inside the camp before dark. Do not add yourself as another person we have to save. It will only make our job in looking for the others more difficult. Go, all of you."

It didn't seem like Liam to dismiss everyone so abruptly, but then I'd never seen him address the whole camp before.

"This is chivving ridiculous." Finn checked the sword on his hip and arrows on his back. "I need a horse. And I can't come back before dark."

I took his face in my hands. "We will find Case. I promise you."

"You aren't going out there." Emmet spoke from behind my shoulder.

"Yes, I am." I rounded on my brother. "And as you are not the trueborn in charge of this camp, you really don't have a say in it."

Emmet glared at me for a long moment.

"We have to go. I can't waste time with the two of you bickering." Finn strode south.

"If you're so fussed, join us," I said. "I'm not letting Finn go out there without me."

"You should stay behind in case someone comes back injured," Emmet said. "Winnie may need help if anyone needs healing."

"I should go out there and find the ones who are too hurt to make it back to camp." I patted the bag at my hip. "I'm not wandering into the woods unprepared. There are people out there who might need my help."

"There's a lot of mountain around us. Do you really think you'll be the one to find them?"

I leaned close to whisper to Emmet. "If you really think someone in this camp may have betrayed the Black Bloods, I'm not sitting here alone waiting while everyone else leaves. And I am not letting Finn go out there without me. He's your friend, too, Emmet. Abandoning him when he's afraid is a betrayal, even if you don't see it."

I took off running, following Finn's bright red hair through the trees. I smiled without even meaning to as Emmet's boots thundered behind me.

"Where did you find the deer?" Emmet asked as soon as we reached Finn.

"About a mile south of the boundary," Finn said.

"There wasn't a sign of the monster, but the kill wasn't that old," I said.

"Ena!" Marta shouted.

We paused as she tore through the trees behind us.

"Ena, are you going out there?" Pink had crept into Marta's cheeks, and sweat beaded on her brow.

"Yes," I said. "This is our party of three."

"We have to go." Finn shot a glare at Marta before continuing his path south.

"The three of you are a group?" Marta glanced to Emmet. "Liam didn't mention you joining the search, Ena. I think he meant for you to stay behind."

"Did he give that order?" I asked.

"Well, no—"

"Is he still in camp?" I cut across her.

"He rode out with Tirra and Kerry," Marta said.

"Then I suppose it's too late for him to tell me to stay behind." I turned and headed south.

"Emmet," Marta said, "I could go as the third."

"Get back to camp," Emmet said. "I don't have time to wrestle my sister into reason."

I ducked under the drooping bows of a pine tree to catch up to Finn. "Case will be all right."

"The search party left at dawn," Finn said. "A beast with claws that large could have torn through all of them in a minute."

"We saw the beast at night," I said. "If it came after us at night, it's probably sleeping right now."

"Maybe," Finn said.

"So, we'll find Case and bring him back before dark." I gripped the hilts of the knives on my hips. It seemed strange, almost foolish, to have three knives on my person. What could I accomplish with three knives that I couldn't manage with two? But Cati had handed them to me, and the weight of them offered a strange comfort.

The boulders of the boundary loomed in front of us.

"We can go as a party of two." Emmet shoved aside a tree branch to walk next to me.

"Liam ordered groups of three," I said.

"I just got back from slipping in and out of an Ilbrean city on my own," Emmet said. "Finn and I will be fine."

"You haven't seen the monster," Finn said.

Dread settled like a stone in my stomach.

"Ena—" Emmet began.

"I thought you'd learned not to argue with me." I pulled one of my knives from its sheath as we stepped through Liam's spell.

Please stay safe. I sent the wish into his magic, hoping he could somehow hear me.

Finn didn't slow his pace as we headed straight for where we'd found the deer.

The stench had somehow worsened in the short time we'd been away from the carcass. The stink led us straight to the awful scene without even needing to think about retracing our steps.

Emmet strode around the body and straight to the gouge marks in the rock. "What under the stars…"

"It left the same scratch marks in the stone when it tried to attack us," I said.

"This thing tried to attack you?" Emmet spun toward me. If the stench bothered him, he showed no sign.

"On the way home from our last sorci run," I said. "We told Liam when we got back."

Finn examined the ground where the beast had left scratch marks in the dirt.

"We should track the monster," Emmet said. "If it's attacked the search party, we'll find them along his trail. If not, we still stand a chance of finding and killing the beast."

I searched the dirt around me for signs of tracks. There was lichen, and mushrooms, a bit of sweet grass. My eyes spotted all the things I'd trained myself to look for but no sign of animal prints.

"Did it leave a trail after it attacked you?" Emmet knelt between two trees.

"Not that I noticed," I said, "but I wasn't exactly looking."

Finn kicked a tree, cracking off a great chunk of bark. "Why? What legend spawned a monster that doesn't leave tracks?"

"We'll keep looking." I circled off through the trees, squinting at the earth, searching for any oddity left in the dirt.

"Ena, do not walk that far from me," Emmet said.

I pressed my palms to the sides of my head. "We need a plan. We need a search pattern or…"

We'd never had to search for anyone in Harane. If something horrible happened to one of the villagers, it was usually at the hands of the Guilds and done in full view so everyone could watch in powerless horror.

"Case!" Finn shouted, heading east down the slope. "Case, can you hear me?"

"Hello." I cupped my hands around my mouth and called into the trees. "Is anyone out there?"

It seemed foolish to make such a racket, like we were calling the ill will of the gods down upon us, but I followed Finn and shouted into the forest anyway.

I had spent enough time wandering through this part of the woods to recognize where we were.

My steps veered away from Finn's path.

"Ena, where are you going?" Emmet caught my arm.

"Toward the falls." I yanked free of his grip. "Animals, people, we all need water. If we're going to wander and shout, shouldn't we go toward something that might draw people in?"

"Finn," Emmet shouted, "come this way."

Finn didn't acknowledge that he'd heard Emmet, but he shifted his path to follow me toward the waterfall.

I gripped my knife tighter as the rushing of the water carried through the trees. At best, we might find the missing Black Bloods huddled by the bank. At worst, my sanctuary would be contaminated by death and blood.

"Case!" Finn shouted. "Can you hear me? Case!"

I held my breath as the falls came into view. There was no hint of blood or terrible scratch marks to be seen.

"Hello!" I called. "Is anyone there?"

"We can head back toward camp," Emmet said. "Cut a wide circle and see if we find anything else."

"Give me a minute." I lifted my bag off my shoulder and tossed it to Emmet.

"What are you doing?" Emmet asked.

"Getting a better view." I tucked my knife back into its sheath and wiped my palms on my skirt.

"I'll head farther south," Finn said.

"We stay together, Finn." I started climbing.

"Ena, don't be foolish," Emmet said.

"You'd rather risk missing something than trust me to complete a task?" I asked.

"Just…" Emmet paused. "Just be careful."

Climbing the rock face naked had been faster and easier, but even with having to move carefully to keep my skirt from wrapping around my ankles, it only took me a few minutes to reach the top.

"Case!" Finn shouted into the woods. "Case, please answer me!"

I dragged myself onto the ledge and rolled over to sit on the rocks. The wind sweeping through the trees held no hint of rot or blood. I squinted into the distance, following the path of the river through the forest. Birds flew from tree to tree, but there was no other movement in sight.

I stood and picked my way across the ledge, peering into every shadow below me.

"I don't see anything," I called. "We could follow the river. There might be something downstream I can't see from up here."

"We haven't got much longer before we have to head back," Emmet said.

"I'm not going back to camp," Finn said. "Not until we've found them."

"I know you want to find Case," Emmet said, "but Liam is right. Wandering through the dark would just leave more people who have to be found."

"Would you leave Ena out here?" Finn asked.

I looked away from them, not wanting to see my brother's face.

"We head back to camp and check in," Emmet said. "Make sure they haven't been found. We'll search a different path on the way back, and if there's still no word, we'll collect what we need to keep searching through the night."

"Thank you," Finn said.

I turned around to kneel at the edge of the rocks and begin my descent. I looked upstream, and my mind stopped.

I could not find a way to process the blood that stained the dirt by the banks, or the bones picked so clean they did not smell of death.

"Emmet." I pushed myself back to my feet. "How many Black Bloods were in the hunting party?"

"Two," Emmet called up, "and there were eight in the search party."

I couldn't feel my feet moving as I walked toward the bones.

They had been shattered and scattered across the bank.

"Ena?" Emmet called up. "Ena, what's going on up there?"

The sounds of him climbing came from behind me, but I couldn't find the words to answer.

I stopped between two crushed skulls. A nauseous grief rolled through me.

"I've found the hunters," I shouted.

"Just the hunters?" Finn called up. "Are they alive?"

Emmet laid a hand on my shoulder. "We need to get back to camp."

"Are they alive?" Finn shouted.

"No," Emmet said.

"What should we do with the bones?" I asked. "I don't know what Black Bloods do with their dead."

"We'll come back for them in the morning," Emmet said. "We don't have a way to carry…"

"All the pieces?" I nodded and headed back to the cliff. "What if an animal scavenges the bones?"

"It won't matter to them," Emmet said. "They're already dead."

It didn't take us long to get back to camp. We made it well before dark.

The watcher wasn't hiding up in the trees. She stood in the open, her bow drawn as we approached.

"We found the hunters," Emmet said before she could ask. "Tell anyone else who comes in this way."

A gasp caught in her throat, but she nodded just the same.

I wasn't sure who she cared so much for or if she would have grieved that fiercely for anyone from the camp who was lost to the monster in the woods.

I didn't even know who the hunters had been, and now that I'd seen their shattered bones, I didn't want to know.

Neil was in the cook tent as we passed, laboring on his own to provide an evening meal. No one waited in line to eat.

The silence inside the camp prickled against my neck. I'd never noticed all the little sounds the Black Bloods created just in living their lives. Without the voices and footsteps filtering through the trees, the woods felt like a tomb.

Only four people waited in the clearing.

Marta paced a long line down the center of the packed earth, and three others sat together, their shoulders hunched and voices silent.

"Marta," Emmet said.

Her gaze whipped toward us at the sound of his voice. Her eyes brightened for a moment before her face went paler than its usual porcelain.

"What did you find?" Marta's voice didn't waver.

"The hunters are dead," Emmet said. "Ena found them."

"Is the search party back?" Finn asked.

"Not yet," Marta said, "but you're early. There's time before dark, and most will look till the last moment, the search party included."

"Then we should go back out," Finn said. "We should keep trying to help."

"We wait until dark," Emmet said. "Find out where everyone else has searched."

"We can't—"

"Think through it." Emmet took Finn's shoulders. "Actually think through what I'm saying and tell me running through the woods without any information will be better for Case? This isn't about you feeling better because you're doing something. It's about finding him alive."

Finn let out a shuddering breath and nodded.

"You should eat," Marta said. "If you're going to go against Liam and run into the forest, you can't do it hungry. I'll go fetch you some food."

Finn looked like he might argue for a moment before he nodded and sat on a bench.

"I'll help," I said.

"No, you rest." Marta shooed me toward a bench. "If you're going to be running back out there—"

"Ena won't be coming with us," Emmet said. "And I will not to be swayed on it."

"That's not—"

"Food first," Marta cut me off and grabbed my hand. "No point in arguing about anything. The search parties will back soon."

I let her lead me toward the kitchen tent.

"Do you really think I should let Finn and Emmet run through the woods on their own?" I asked as soon we were out of the clearing.

"Of course not," Marta said. "The two of them are excellent fighters, but it only gives them confidence they shouldn't have. A beast has leapt straight out of a legend and come to terrorize our camp. Neither of them should go back out there tonight."

"Then why are we fetching them food?" I stopped in the middle of the path.

Marta looped back around, took my arm, and dragged me toward the kitchen tent. "Because if I told them they couldn't do it, I would have to spend the next hour standing in the clearing, fighting with two pigheaded fools, neither of whom is capable of seeing reason when they're riled up. Better to feed them and keep them calm while we wait for the others to return."

"But what if they haven't found the search party?"

"Then we make Liam order Finn not to go." Marta furrowed her brow.

"And Emmet?" I asked. "Will Liam order him to stay in camp as well?"

We stopped outside the kitchen tent.

"Emmet has never taken kindly to orders," Marta said, "but we'll do whatever we can to convince him. And if that doesn't work, I'll knock him over the chivving head and tie him up until morning."

She strode into the tent, leaving me staring at her with an open mouth.

"They're all going to complain." Neil slopped stew into bowls. "They'll come back tired and hungry, and all of them will complain."

"And I'll tell them to be grateful for what they have or there will be no more ale this summer." Marta passed me two wooden bowls and tucked two spoons into my pocket. "You're feeding the entire camp on your own tonight. Anyone who isn't thankful is a fool." She patted Neil on the shoulder before taking two more bowls and nodding me out of the tent.

"You're good at that, you know," I said as we followed the path back toward the clearing.

"I do know," Marta said. "My grandmother had five children and twenty-three grandchildren. Who knows? There could be even more of us by the time we get back to Lygan Hall this fall. I learned how to handle a pack of rowdy children from her. Minding the camp is honestly the same thing. The only difference being the ones who whine around here are more likely to cheer up if I offer them a mug of ale rather than a sweet."

I laughed without meaning to.

"There you are." Marta shot me a dimpled smile. "A bit of food and you'll be ready to face whatever the gods send us next."

"Thank you, Marta."

Voices carried from the clearing, and more than just the five we'd left behind.

Marta and I picked up our pace, moving as quickly as we could without spilling the stew.

A pack of people had gathered in the center of the clearing.

I headed for the bench where I'd left the boys, but Finn wasn't sitting beside my brother. "Where's Finn?"

Emmet pointed to the middle of the group where Finn held Case tightly in his arms.

Case's dark hair wasn't as carefully-combed as usual. Dirt covered his clothes, but he bore no sign of injury.

"Did the whole search party make it back?" I pressed a bowl of stew into Emmet's hand.

"All eight," Emmet said.

"Did they see anything?" I sat beside Emmet.

"Not the beast you and Finn spoke of, but they did find a wolf den. The whole pack had been slaughtered and left to rot." Emmet began eating his stew.

We sat together, waiting for the rest of the camp to return.

Finn broke the news to the others that the hunters had been killed. I suppose it was right. He was truly one of them. He shared the grief of the people who cried at his words more thoroughly than Emmet or I could.

Since the groups of three returned in stages, the cycle repeated over and over.

Three would return. They would see the original search party, and joy would light their faces. They would see the grief around them, and questions would begin.

I wished the guards would tell the returners. But most of the guards probably didn't know. I pitied the person who would have to circle the boundary of the camp, delivering the horrible news over and over again.

Marta moved quietly around the clearing, taking a tally of who had returned, sending people to get their dinner and warning them to be kind to Neil.

Someone hung the lae stones as true night began to fall. As the blue glow cast shadows across the clearing, the mood shifted again.

I left my empty bowl beside Emmet and crossed calmly to

Marta, trying not to spook any of the grieving people. I took her arm and leaned close to her ear, careful to keep my face placid.

"How many still aren't back?" I whispered.

Marta's arm tensed beneath my touch. "Six."

"Where's Liam?"

"I don't know." Her breath shook as she inhaled. "He'll be fine, he's a trueborn. He rode out too far searching, and now he's on his way back."

"We have to find him." I moved to step away, but Marta caught my arm in an iron grip.

"It is dark, and there is a monster out there," Marta whispered. "We cannot have people charging madly through the woods."

"I'm not going to go charging anywhere," I said. "I am going to get a light and Finn's bag of magic stones, and then I will calmly find Liam."

"No, you won't."

"Then knock me over the head and tie me up until morning." I wrenched my arm free. "I will not leave Liam out there."

"Ena," Marta whispered after me as I walked away. "Ena."

I weaved through the crowd to where Finn and Case sat gripping each other's hands.

I knelt in front of Finn. "Liam's not back."

Finn looked around the clearing as though I had somehow missed Liam in the pack of people.

"He's out there, Finn," I said. "I have to do something."

"Do what?" Case asked. "We got back from our search to find that a beast killed Dillon and Pierce—"

"Pierce?" A ringing filled my ears. "Pierce was one of the hunters?"

"Ena." Finn took my hand, lacing his fingers through mine, anchoring me to the world.

"Those bones belonged to Pierce, and I didn't know it?" A

burning hot panic rose in my chest. "I should have known. I should have asked who was out there."

"What's wrong?" Emmet knelt beside me.

"She didn't—"

"Liam's still out there." I swallowed the sick in my throat. "We have to find him."

Emmet closed his eyes and curled his fingers into tight fists. The scars on his hands shone in the light of the lae stones.

"He is the trueborn of this camp," Finn said. "Even if he was a chivving slitch, it would still be our duty to protect him."

"Finn," Case said, "think through this, please."

"We should find some others to go with us," Emmet said. "See if we can figure out which direction they rode."

"We can ask if anyone ran into them in the woods," I offered.

"Marta might know," Finn said.

"She doesn't want to cause a panic," I said.

"Everyone will panic," Case said.

A scream cut through the woods, carrying toward the clearing.

"Liam." I sprang to my feet and ran to the bench where I'd left my bag.

"Ena." Emmet chased after me.

"Someone is hurt." I dodged around him, racing toward the sound.

"You don't know that." He sprinted along beside me. "The camp could be under attack."

"It doesn't matter." My heart lurched into my throat as another scream pierced the darkness. "I know that sound, someone is in pain. I didn't get to escape Harane for Nantic when I was a child. I know what agony sounds like, and I will not ignore it."

We passed the cook tent where Neil stood facing the screams, a kitchen knife clutched in each hand.

A lower shout joined the screaming, but I couldn't understand the words.

I raced toward the low voice, running so fast Emmet fell behind.

Liam.

He knelt on the ground. Blood covered his hands, but he was alert and moving.

"We need help." Liam spoke to a gray-haired man. "Go find Winnie. Find Ena."

"I'm here," I panted as I dodged around Tirra and three terrified horses to reach Liam's side.

I started to ask where he'd been hurt, but the woman lying in front of him screamed.

"She's in so much pain," Liam said. "Ena, please help her."

I tore my gaze from Liam's face to look at the woman on the ground. I'd never seen her before. Her clothes looked closer to what was worn in the cities in Ilbrea than the plain colors the Black Bloods in camp favored. Sweat glistened on her pale face, and deep red splotches marked her cheeks and neck.

A gash sliced into her right arm, but there was more blood on her skirt around her thigh.

"Hello," I said, my voice calm even as the woman screamed again, "my name is Ena. I know you're in pain, but I need you to breathe."

She gave a whimpering cry.

"I have to lift your skirt to look at your legs." I took my bag off my shoulder and opened the flap before folding up the woman's skirt. A blood-stained bandage had been wrapped around the woman's leg.

"Did you put this on?" I asked Liam as I pulled a little bottle of liquor and a clean cloth from my bag.

"No," Liam said. "She was already hurt when we found her in the woods. She must have bandaged it herself."

"That was very brave of you." I glanced at the woman's sweat-slicked face. She didn't seem to have heard me. I opened the bottle, and lifted her arm. "I'm sorry about how much this will sting."

She screamed as I poured the liquor onto the cut.

I pressed a cloth over the wound. "Liam, hold this right here, and don't move. It'll need stitches later, but some good pressure will do for now."

The woman whimpered as Liam pressed down on the deep cut.

"I'm going to unwrap your leg." I pulled my knife from its sheath. "I'll get a look at what's happened, and then we'll get you patched up."

She hadn't used a proper bandage to dress her wound. The bloody fabric I sliced through looked to be bits of a shawl she'd torn into strips.

A shiver shook her shoulders as I gently peeled the bandage away.

Her flesh had been torn by sharp teeth. The jaw of whatever had bitten her had been massive, large enough to clamp around her thigh. Lines of indigo blue wound through the broken skin, standing out even through the red of the blood.

"Ena," Liam said.

"Where's Winnie?" I folded the bandage back into place. "Emmet, find Winnie."

My brother tore away through the trees without question.

"What bit you?" I leaned over the woman.

Her glassy eyes didn't find my face.

"Look at me." I patted her uninjured hand. "I just need you to tell me what bit you."

"I think it was the beast you and Finn saw," Liam said. "She mumbled something about the animal's claws, but we couldn't get her to tell us much. She didn't seem to hear all our questions. She kept talking about the children."

"Children?" I looked out to the darkness beyond our boundary. "Are there children out there?"

"She's a tracker from Ilbrea." Liam's voice grew raspy. "She was trying to bring a message about a sorci. She must have been attacked on her way to camp."

"I'm coming!" Winnie's high-pitched voice cut through the trees. She toddled on her bad hip, moving as fast as I'd ever seen her manage.

Emmet kept by her side, both arms extended and ready to catch her.

"I need help." I moved my bag out of the way before Winnie even reached us. "The cut on her arm can be stitched, but she's got a bad bite on her leg. I've never seen anything like it."

Emmet took Winnie's elbow and helped her to the ground. Her hands were steady as she lifted away the bloody fabric.

"By the gods," Emmet breathed.

"I didn't want cleaning it with the liquor to make it worse," I whispered. "I don't know how to treat that kind of infection."

Winnie's hands shook as she covered the wound. "It's not an infection. It's a venom."

"What?" Liam said.

"How do we help her?" I asked.

Winnie picked up the bottle of liquor and handed it to me. "Feed this to her."

"Will it help?" I jumped over the woman and knelt on her other side, carefully lifting her head to drizzle the liquor into her mouth.

"It might dull the pain." Winnie winced as she shifted to sit in the dirt.

"Should we get her back to camp?" I asked.

"We'll wait here with her," Winnie said. "Moving her will only cause pain, and it shouldn't be too long now that she's gone quiet."

I looked down at the woman's face. I hadn't noticed that her screaming had stopped in the rushing of my own fear.

"What kind of animal with teeth like that has venom?" Emmet said.

"No idea." Winnie furrowed her brow, adding extra depth to all the lines on her weathered face.

"It's got to be the beast," Liam said. "At least I hope it is. I pray the gods haven't set two monsters on this mountain at once."

The woman's breathing slowed. The red had swallowed her whole face.

"The hunters," Liam asked, "were they found?"

A sharp pain dug into the center of my chest.

"They were killed," Emmet said.

Liam's face crumpled.

"We found their bones." Emmet placed a hand on Liam's shoulder. "We can gather them in the morning."

"Did everyone else make it back?" Liam asked.

"We were still missing a group of three when I heard the screaming," I said. "Marta was counting everyone."

"I should go to her," Liam said.

"You don't have to hold the wound," Winnie said. "It might be kinder if you didn't."

Liam didn't move.

"What was her message?" I asked. "About the child?"

"It doesn't matter," Liam said.

"Yes, it does," I said. "She climbed through the mountains and faced a monster to deliver it. Her message matters."

"The Sorcerers Guild is circling the sorci she's been watching. She was trying to find out why we hadn't come to rescue the child."

I have seen Death too many times.

He is a constant shadow that follows me on whatever path I tread. I see the shape of him lurking in places where there should be only light. I see him mirroring my every movement like a child taunting me.

I have tried to save the people I love from that dark embrace, but I am not that mighty. I have tried to offer myself in place of those Death seeks, yet I am spared.

I will never be stronger than Death, but I have never been reasonable enough to stop fighting against him.

Perhaps Death is not lurking behind me. Perhaps he is pinned to my soul, and all the suffering I have seen has been caused by my own hand.

The last three returned an hour after darkness had fallen. None of them had met the monster in the woods.

There was no music in the clearing that night, but most of the camp was still there, sitting on the benches and stools, unwilling to leave the comfort of their fellows. Neil built the fire in the corner up to be twice as large as normal. The blaze sent a flickering light dancing through the shadows. It should have been beautiful.

I couldn't find any comfort in the fire. I couldn't manage much of anything but trying not to stare at Liam's empty chair as I wondered what had been done to the tracker's body and if Pierce's bones had been carried away by a scavenger.

"Can I sit?"

I looked up to find Emmet towering over me.

I didn't have the energy to tell him to leave me alone. I patted the empty bench beside me.

"I brought you a drink." Emmet passed me a mug of ale. "I've heard you like the stuff."

His gaze slipped toward the barrel in the corner where Marta stood beside Neil.

"Not really." I took a sip, trying not to wince at the pungent, floral taste.

"You don't have to drink it then." Emmet sipped from his own mug.

"I know, but at least it gives me something to do with my hands."

Emmet nodded.

We sat quietly for a moment. Everyone in the clearing spoke in hushed tones. I wasn't sure if the whispers were born of grief or fear of the monster roaming in the dark.

"Marta told me you and Pierce were friends," Emmet said.

I gripped my mug and waited for him to start raging about my having run into the woods with a man.

"I'm glad you're making friends here," Emmet said, "and I'm sorry you lost one."

"We weren't friends. Not really. But he was a good man."

"I didn't hate him."

I took another drink. The ale tasted like Pierce's lips. I couldn't tell if the pain in my stomach was grief or utter revulsion.

"I didn't know," I said. "When I found the bones, I didn't know he was one of the missing hunters. I know it's absurd…"

The image of his blond hair and bright blue eyes pounded through my mind.

I took a long drink of my ale.

"I feel like I should have recognized him," I said. "There was no way for me to tell, but I knew him. He shouldn't have seemed like a stranger in death."

"It was bones, Ena." Emmet laid a hand over my mug as I moved to take another drink. "His own mother wouldn't have known him. At least you found him. Because of you, we don't have to put any more lives at risk searching the woods. I'll lead a party out to collect the bones in the morning. Pierce will have a proper burial because of you. His family won't have to wonder what became of him because of you. That is a true gift to give a fallen friend."

I lifted his hand off my mug. "Thanks, Emmet."

"Sure." Emmet downed the rest of his ale. "You should get some rest. You look terrible, and the stars have already tormented you enough for one day."

"You don't look much better, you know."

For a moment, I almost believed I caught a hint of a smile on my brother's face. "Some of us deserve more torment than others." He gave me a nod and went back toward the barrel of ale.

I watched him as he was bowed to the front of the line for a drink. Neil didn't argue as he filled Emmet's mug. My brother crossed the clearing to sit on a stump by himself, and all the people he passed nodded to him.

They didn't approach him or try to bend his ear, but they were all aware of Emmet. I didn't know if their attitude came from deference or fear. It didn't matter either way.

I sat alone as I finished the rest of my ale.

Finn and Case were on a bench by themselves, deep in a whispered conversation. Cati sat with the last group that had returned. Those four didn't talk much.

When I finished my drink, I sat for a few more minutes, waiting for something to happen. For the gods to send a miracle or for the world to burn around us. The stars did not send a sign to block my path.

I stood up, returned my mug to Neil, and walked down the path toward the tents.

A blue light glowed through the canvas of Liam's tent.

I knocked on the pole without letting myself hesitate.

"Yes?" Liam's voice still had the same gravelly texture to it as when we'd been kneeling beside the tracker.

"It's Ena." I forced my shoulders to relax. "I need to speak to you."

"Come in."

My fingers froze on the flap of his tent.

Time will not make this easier.

I stepped into Liam's home.

Someone had brought him food and drink. He hadn't touched either. The scent of stale root stew filled the space.

Liam sat at the table, his face drawn and pale. Sheets of pressed paper, a pen, and a tub of black ink waited in front of him.

"What do you need?" Liam said. "Has the beast been sighted by the guards?"

"Not that I've heard of." I started for the other chair at the table and froze.

This could be the end for you.

I shoved the what-ifs, grief, and regret aside and sat at the table. "How are you?"

"Alive," Liam said. "Which doesn't seem fair as I've lost three people under my command in the past two days."

"Did they know it was dangerous?"

"What?" A wrinkle creased the center of Liam's brow.

I wanted so badly to soothe away the worries that plagued him.

"Coming with you to camp, ferrying the sorcis, daring to breathe without the blessing of the Guilds—did they know what they were doing was dangerous?"

Liam looked up to the steep angle at the top of the tent.

"You made it abundantly clear to me when I wanted to join," I said. "I know being here is dangerous. I know helping the sorcis is dangerous. Do you think any of the fallen weren't smart enough to have figured that out?"

"No. They knew. They all knew."

"Then do not give yourself credit for their deaths." I leaned across the table. "They chose to risk their lives for something they believed in. The sacrifice was theirs to make. You do them a disservice by thinking your place in their end was more powerful than their own bravery."

"I should have warned people about the beast," Liam said. "I should have forbidden everyone from leaving camp. Sent out parties to kill the monster—"

"You couldn't kill the monster while keeping everyone trapped in camp."

"I should have found a way." He banged his fist on the table. The cold stew sloshed onto the corner of his papers. He didn't notice.

"How many monsters and legends have you seen in these mountains?" I lifted the papers away from the spill. "Liam, how many?"

"I don't know. Between the ghosts in the Blood Valley, the creatures that lurk below, and the odd things roaming through the mountains, it's enough for a century's worth of stories, but I've never seen anything like it this far west."

I dried the papers on my skirt. "Have any of the other creatures attacked like this?"

"Not here," Liam said. "Not this far from the heart of the mountain. Our camp is settled between the land of myths and the power of Ilbrea. We stay here because it's the thin strip of sanity between two worlds."

"And you've no idea what the beast might be or how easy it would be to kill it?"

"I know absolutely nothing." Liam dug his fingers through his hair. "I sent another stone bird to Orla, but I'm not sure how long it will take her to answer or what she might say. I should have done something sooner."

I set the papers down and leaned across the table, lifting Liam's hands away from his head. "You exist in a world of shadows. When you live in a realm of flickering shades, it's hard to tell which darkness might be a demon. What's done is done, Liam. The important thing is what we do now."

"I'll have to talk to the others." Liam kept his hands locked with mine. "There must be a way to set a trap for the beast. I don't like the idea of luring it close to camp, but I don't want anyone straying away from the boundary, either."

"I'm going into Ilbrea." The words rushed out of my mouth.

"What?" Liam tightened his grip on my hands.

"I'm going after the sorci the tracker was watching. I'm leaving first thing in the morning."

"You can't," Liam said. "You don't even know where the child is."

"I know, but you'll tell me."

"No, I won't." Liam stood and began pacing the worn patch of dirt in his tent. "There is a monster out there, Ena."

"There are worse monsters in Ilbrea. And there is a child who will be snatched up by them if we don't get there first."

"We can't save anyone if we're all dead. We have to protect ourselves. No one can go back out there until we've stopped the monster."

"It'll be too late by then." I laid my hands flat on the table, begging my body not to betray my fear. "We can't afford to wait another day, let alone long enough to stop the beast."

"It's killed three people."

"I've seen all three bodies."

Liam froze.

"I've seen the monster, too, and I am not afraid of it. You promised me we would find a way to save those children, and I'm going to do it."

He covered his face with his hands. "You can't. You can't go out there, I won't let you."

"Will you send someone in my place?" I stood and crossed slowly to him, testing every step for a crack that would shatter and devour us both. "Will you use the magic in my mark to kill me?"

He looked at me. A deep pain filled his dark eyes.

"Just tell me how to find the child and where to take them," I said. "That's all I want from you. The rest is my choice, and the consequences lay on my shoulders."

"There is nowhere to hide the child."

"Then I will put them on my back and swim them across the Arion Sea. I am brave, and I am capable. I am strong, Liam. But sitting in this camp, knowing that an innocent child is going to have their freedom stolen from them…I am not strong enough to survive that."

Liam reached out. His fingers brushed my cheek before he laid his hand on my shoulder.

"If you make me stay here, I will suffocate."

"You'll be safe."

"I will drown." I laid my hands on his chest. "Please, Liam. Let me do this."

We stood in silence for a long moment. Without the normal music coming from the clearing, I could hear his breath shaking in his chest.

"There won't be a horse and cart waiting for you," Liam said.

A spark of the fire in my chest broke free of its shroud. "I don't care. I'll find a way."

"The mountain won't open for you."

"Then I will walk the long way."

"I should go with you." Liam laid his hands over mine, pressing them against his chest. "I have to go with you."

"You have to protect the camp. Your people are in danger, you have to stay here."

"Please don't do this, Ena."

I slipped my hands out from beneath his. I traced the worried creases by the corners of his eyes and took his face in my hands.

"I have to go," I whispered. "I won't be able to survive if I don't."

He pressed his lips to my forehead.

I took a deep breath, reveling in his scent of fresh wind and reckless freedom.

"The child is in the Lir Valley." Liam pulled a blood-stained paper from his pocket. "This is all the information I have."

"Then I will make it be enough." I took the paper and felt the weight of another's soul sink onto my shoulders.

"You can't go alone," Liam said.

"I can't ask anyone to come with me." I tucked the paper into my pocket. "I'll be fine. I can find my way through the mountains on my own. I'll go as soon as the sun's up. You can tell Emmet I snuck out if you like. You shouldn't have to face his wrath because of me."

"I won't lie to him."

"Then at least give me a good head start." I managed a small smile. "However this ends, I am choosing to go. My path is of my own making. I'll find the child and a safe place for them to hide. There are lands outside Ilbrea. There's got to be a place in this world for a sorci child that isn't controlled by the Brien or the Guilds, even if I haven't heard of it yet."

"You would go that far? You would leave everything you know behind?"

"I have to."

"Bring the child here." Liam stared at the lae stone hanging from the top of the tent. "I'll get rid of the monster before you come back."

"But Orla doesn't want—"

"This is your home now, Ena. You've got to promise me you'll come home."

I turned his face to make him look at me and leaned in to kiss his cheek.

He wrapped his arms around me, holding me close to his chest.

"Don't pack up the camp for winter without me," I said. "I don't know how to get all the way to Lygan Hall."

Stepping away from him tore a hole in my lungs. It felt as though I may never be able to breathe properly again.

But I gave him another smile and walked out of his tent, unable to promise myself I would ever see Liam again.

39

I didn't really sleep that night. I had to pack my clothes, then sneak the long way around to steal food from Neil's supplies. When I got back to my tent, I found a little leather bag on my cot. Six black stones waited inside. By the time I'd stuffed the rocks and all my pilfered food into my pack, there were only a few hours left until sunrise.

I lay on my bed, trying to convince myself to sleep. I'd need the rest. Without the mountain providing me a path, it would take days to reach Ilbrea. Then I would have to find the Lir Valley and the child.

I closed my eyes and gripped the pendant around my neck. I trusted Liam. Emmet would tell him about the Black Bloods being betrayed. It was better that the news had been lost in tragedies caused by the monster, and right of me not to mention it. Liam couldn't know until I was gone. I hadn't a prayer of him agreeing to my leaving camp if he thought a traitor might sell me to the Guilds.

Pulling my blankets up to my chin didn't slow the racing of my mind.

The camp would be fine. Emmet and Liam would find the

traitor. The monster would be slain. There was nothing I could do in camp to protect the people I cared about.

"The decision's already been made, you fool. Now rest so you can run from the beast."

I squeezed my eyes shut and forced my body to relax, focusing on the weight of the stone pendant against my skin.

"Oy, you."

My eyes sprang open as someone poked my cheek.

"Sun's almost up." Finn leaned over me in the darkness. "If we want to slip out at dawn, we should start moving."

"What?" I pushed my blankets back as I sat up, running my fingers through my hair to get the strands away from my face. "What are you talking about?"

"Have you changed your mind?" Finn handed me my boots. "Are you not going to nab the sorci?"

"How do you know about that?" I tugged my shoes on.

"Does it matter?"

"Yes." I slipped my sheath and knife into my boot.

"You didn't think he'd let you go alone, did you?"

"He had no right to do that." I glared through the darkness toward Liam's bed, swallowing the urge to shout through the canvas at him.

"He has every right." Finn held out my coat. "You swore an oath to him."

"You can't come with me. It's too dangerous."

"And you'd be safer alone?"

"No, but you'd be safer here." I snatched my coat and shrugged on the chill fabric. "Risking my life to go after the child is one thing. I can't ask you to risk yours. I'm going alone."

"Ena"—Finn took my hands and pressed his lips to my palms—"you are my friend. You are choosing to risk your neck to help a child. I'm choosing to risk mine for you. Is my choice any less worthy than yours?"

My anger crumpled at the edges. "No, it's not. But Liam still shouldn't have told you."

"At least he didn't tell Emmet." Finn shrugged.

"I don't like it when you're logical." I swung my pack onto my back. "It makes it more difficult to be angry."

Finn held open the tent flap.

"Do you have a plan for sneaking past the guards?" Finn asked.

"I was going to creep up behind them, then run like the Guilds were at my heels and hope they were too frightened of the monster to follow."

Finn gave a low laugh and waved me down the side path toward the training field.

"I take it you have a better plan?" I glanced back toward the tents. The silhouette of Liam's home stood out against the night.

You've chosen your path, now follow it.

"Where are we going?" I whispered.

"There are blind spots in the guards," Finn said. "The perimeter is too large to have eyes on every inch. If you know where the posts are, it's easy to slip in and out. We don't have to fuss about people getting in since we've got the boundary stones protecting us against anyone Liam doesn't want entering camp. But if you want to slip out unseen, you've got to know where the guards are spread wide enough."

"I've gone outside foraging before. I never thought much of the guards not saying anything as I came and went."

"And this, Ena, is why I am useful." Finn bowed.

It seemed wrong to be laughing as we snuck out of camp, but that was how things were with Finn. Easy, light, like there were people in the world who weren't scarred beyond redemption.

The gray of dawn began as we reached the training field. The strange emptiness of the clearing laid a deep chill across my neck.

I kept waiting for Cati to stride out of the trees and ask where we thought we were going. Or worse, for Marta or Emmet to come storming after us. But we didn't meet anyone on our way to the ring of great black boulders.

We stopped just within the boundary. The sky had yet to turn the golden orange of true daybreak.

Neither of us spoke as we watched the eastern sky, waiting for the sun to touch the horizon.

A faint hint of red kissed the treetops.

I looked to the woods beyond the boulders. There was no trace of living creatures moving through the shadows.

"You should go back," I said.

"So should you."

The orange glow blossomed over the sky.

I took a deep breath and walked out through the barrier.

The longing pulled at my chest. For a moment, I thought the wanting would devour the fire that drove me to risk my life fighting against monsters and vicious men. But the soul-consuming desire nurtured the flames, setting my heart to blazing with an inferno that could devour cities and level mountains.

I will fight to come home.

I sent my silent promise into the stones and turned my path east.

The rasp of Finn's sword clearing its sheath seemed to echo through the trees.

I pulled my own knife from my boot. For the first time, the weight of the blade seemed flimsy and worthless in my hand. I'd seen the monster's claws—what hope did I have battling against the beast with a knife?

Finn and I stayed side by side as we moved through the woods. Neither of us spoke. When Finn wanted to alter our course, he'd give me a wave, and we'd shift our path.

I tried to listen beyond the thumping of my own heart to hear the noises of the forest. The birds had begun to wake for the day. Their chirping held its usual cheer as they swooped between trees. But the forest floor had gone silent. No rustling through the low brush, no chittering of small animals.

What has the monster done to our woods?

An hour passed, then another.

The quiet wore on my nerves, making the sound of every footstep seem as loud as a scream.

Does the beast hunt during the day?

There had been no trace of a camp where I'd found Pierce and Dillon. No hint that they'd been planning on spending the night outside the safety of our stone boundary.

I gripped my knife so hard my hand hurt as I searched the shadows for a flash of deadly claws.

As though the mountain had heard my thoughts, a foul stench drifted on the wind. I turned toward the north where the stink carried from.

Finn tapped my arm and pointed east.

I nodded and kept to our path. What good would seeing another dead animal do anyway?

Crack.

The sound carried through the trees to the north.

Finn doubled his pace, still heading due east.

Crack.

I glanced north but couldn't see anything between the trees.

The ground in front of us dropped away in a steep slope. Finn pushed me in front of him, making me run down the hill first.

I leapt over the deep gouges carved into the earth, slipping on the loose dirt where the mountainside had collapsed.

A crashing carried from behind us.

Rocks had taken over the ground below me. I was too afraid of tripping to look back.

A roar shook my lungs and froze my heart.

I'm sorry, Liam. This was my choice. Please remember.

The ground flattened out near a giant boulder that had a crack straight down the middle.

I dared to glance behind as the pounding of massive paws shook the earth.

The monster stood at the top of the slope, his bare head smeared with dried blood, his massive claws glinting in the sunlight.

I scanned the trees around us, searching for one sturdy enough for me to climb out of reach of the beast's deadly bite.

Debris tumbled down the slope as the monster chased us, his mouth wide and his eyes locked on me.

"Finn, we have to—"

Pain shot through my shoulder as something yanked on my arm.

I raised my knife, ready to slash into the monster. The blade glinted in the early morning light as I brought it down in a wide arc.

"Ena!"

I barely managed to stop my swing from cutting off Finn's hand as he jerked me toward him.

A guttural roar shook the trees, claws swiped at my face, and everything went black.

The roar disappeared. The wind vanished.

If it weren't for Finn's hand squeezing my arm, I would have believed the monster had given me a mercifully swift death.

"Did it touch you?" Finn's voice shook. "Did it bite you?"

"Close, but I'm fine." My words trembled just as much as Finn's. "It didn't get you either?"

"No." Finn pulled a lae stone from his pocket.

Our dark shelter was barely more than a hollow, only a few inches taller than Finn and just wide enough for the two of us to fit.

"My mother always told me the mountain plays favorites." Finn wiped the sweat from his forehead with the sleeve of his coat. "I never quite believed her. All children of the mountain, all loved the same. Except the trueborn, of course, but we can't hold ourselves to their chivving standards. But now"—Finn pressed his palm to the rock above us—"I am willing to believe the mountain may, in fact, love me above her normal child."

The sound of my faint laughter bounced around the tiny space.

"You, Finn, are most definitely favored by the mountain, or gods, or stars." I lay my hands against the cold stone. "Quite frankly, I don't care what force likes you so much. I'm just grateful for the shelter."

"Shall we then?"

"Shall we what?" I looked at the bit of rock Finn had pulled me through. "We're not going back out there. The beast will still be out there."

"You couldn't make me walk straight up to that beast unless I had Liam and Emmet by my side." Finn took off his pack. "Or just Cati. Honestly, I'd go hunting the beast just to see her in her full glory."

Finn knelt down in the back of the hollow where there was a bit of darkness that seemed deeper than the black of the stone.

"What is that?" I peered over Finn's shoulder.

"Our way forward." Finn stretched his arm out into an opening two feet high and barely wide enough for his shoulders. "Shall we allow the mountain to test our gratitude?"

I took off my pack. "I do believe we shall."

40

I have never been afraid of small places, but inching forward through the tunnel tested my nerves. I couldn't see Finn over my pack in front of me. It was only the sounds of him crawling forward that kept me from fearing I was utterly alone.

My body ached from the movement. Bruises covered my arms and legs. My hand cramped from clutching my lae stone as I slithered along. I wanted to stand up and stretch, but even my growing pain did not dull my gratitude for the mountain saving us from the beast.

My pack caught on a rock as I shoved it forward. I wriggled the fabric free and gritted my teeth as the very same rock dug into my ribs as I crawled over it on my forearms.

"Talk to me, Ena," Finn said.

"I'm still here if that's what you're worried about." My knee hit the same chivving rock. "If I find a lovely detour, I'll be sure to let you know."

"I know you're behind me. You keep dropping your pack on my feet."

"Sorry."

"Don't be. I find it comforting."

My laugh jostled the new set of bruises on my ribs.

"Just talk to me," Finn said. "Keep me from going mad."

"What do you want to talk about?" I shifted my pack as far forward as I could, making sure to drop it on Finn's feet.

"Tell me about life in Ilbrea."

"It's hell."

"All of it?" The sounds of Finn's movement stopped. "Is there nothing good out there?"

"You've seen more of Ilbrea than I have. Until I joined the Black Bloods, I'd only ever been to Harane and Nantic."

Finn didn't reply.

"Keep crawling, or we'll never get out."

He began moving forward again. "I've seen most of the cities. But I've never lived out there. Never had a home in Ilbrea."

"I suppose it wasn't all awful." I shifted my bag forward and kept crawling. "There were lots of terrible things. Death and pain and fear taint the corners of everything. But the farmland around Harane was beautiful.

"The men would bicker about whose cows were better and whose sheep kept breaking out of their pastures to harass other animals. But they never hated each other over it. Some of the women hated their husbands, and their husbands would hide at the tavern. Cal would tell me all about the things the husbands said when they were drunk."

"Cal?"

I froze. Rocks dug into my arms.

"A boy I knew. He was very good to me. I don't think I could have survived Harane without him."

"I'm sorry."

"What for?" I shoved my pack forward, trying to blame the ache in my chest on the tunnel.

"That he's not with you now. Do you think…"

"Think what?"

"That you'd still be with him—if the world were a less violent place?"

"I don't know." The truth of it made the ache grow until I could no longer ignore the pain. "He was good and kind, and gods he was handsome."

Finn laughed.

"But his family made their money catering to the Guilds. I couldn't live with that."

"But if the Guilds weren't in power?"

"If there were no Guilds, I would still have parents. My brother would be more to me than some stranger with a terrible chivving temper. My life would have been so different, I can't even begin to suppose who I might have been able to love. It would have been easier if I could have loved Cal, but that is not the life I was given."

"You didn't love him?"

A deeper, harsher pain throbbed through my lungs. "I'm too broken for that."

"I don't think that's true." Finn's voice shifted. "I used to think I was destined to spend my life as a hopeless rogue. Tried to convince myself to fall in love a dozen times, and it never worked. But I figured it out in the end."

"What did you do?"

"I found the right person to fall in love with. Mended my shattered heart."

"Ah, but did it make you any less of a rogue?"

My pack shifted out of my path, and Finn's grinning face appeared.

"No. But I do have a love to come home to, and that's a beautiful thing." Finn winked and held out a hand to me.

I scooted forward, toward the lip of the tunnel.

Finn took my hand, helping me balance as I pulled enough of my body out of the narrow space that I could get a foot on the ground in the chamber beyond.

"I'm going to have bruises from that for weeks." I stretched my arms toward the ceiling.

"Better than being torn to shreds." Finn handed me my pack.

"Much better." I gave Finn a smile.

The chamber the mountain had opened for us offered only one path forward. A tunnel with a mercifully high ceiling cut out of the back of the space and twisted out of sight.

Finn shouldered his own bag and led the way.

I trailed the fingers of my free hand along the stone wall. It wasn't jagged and shattered or perfectly smooth. The rock held a natural roughness to it. The coarse texture soothed me.

I tucked the old hurts away, not allowing myself to examine them before sending them back into the darkness hidden behind the flames.

"What was it like growing up in Lygan Hall?" I asked.

Finn let out a genuine laugh that echoed down the curving tunnel.

"Rowdy," Finn said. "Cold. Wearing. I think the strangest thing was how trapped I always felt when I was little. The Hall is a sanctuary in the middle of the mountains. But the land beyond is wild with untamed magic and legendary beasts. It's like the magic from the heart of the great mountain somehow leaked to the surface and caused chaos."

"Chaos made you feel trapped?"

The tunnel twisted sharply and began sloping down.

"Not being allowed out into the chaos was what trapped me," Finn said. "I could stand on top of the summit above Lygan Hall and stare out into the great wilderness beyond. I could see the epic possibilities for adventure, but I wasn't allowed to get to any of them. I just ended up wreaking havoc in the Hall, causing as much chaos as I could, since they wouldn't let me out. I almost wasn't allowed to venture west with Liam."

"Really?" I tried to picture the camp without Finn. I couldn't do it.

"Orla thought I was too wild to be trusted to Liam's cause. I had to beg and make a hundred promises to be assigned to his camp."

"I'm glad she agreed in the end."

"I'm pretty sure she thought I'd get myself killed right off and then I wouldn't be anyone's problem anymore."

"Finn." I smacked him on the shoulder.

He caught my wrist and kissed the back of my hand.

"I don't blame Orla. I was a terror," Finn said. "But I made myself useful, didn't die, and swore the oath to Liam. So the leader of the Duwead Clan now despises me just a little bit less."

"What does she think of Emmet? Is she grateful for the ruin he leaves in his wake?"

Finn stopped and turned to face me. "We don't tell Orla everything. Only the bits of our work that she really needs to know. Since Emmet saved Liam's life, she thinks he's a bit of a hero, and we choose to allow her belief to continue."

"How did Emmet save Liam's life?"

"You'll have to ask them." Finn started down the tunnel again.

"Why will no one tell me stories about Emmet? If he's done such wonderful things to save people, I'd like to know what they are. It would be nice to have something good to think about him."

The slope of the tunnel pitched even more steeply. The floor didn't have the same rough texture as the walls but was as smooth as polished glass beneath my feet.

I steadied myself with my hand against the wall as my boots slid with each step.

"As much as it shames me to say it"—Finn slipped, tottered, and caught his balance—"I don't actually know how Emmet saved Liam's life." He turned sideways and inched his way forward.

I followed him, sidling my way along.

"All I know," Finn said, "is that Liam went down into Ilbrea, and when he came back, his face was purple, his back had been sliced open, and he'd brought an angry tilk up the mountain with him."

"Hmm."

"Emmet is probably the only one who can give you an accurate account of what he's gotten himself into and how under the stars he's survived. You should ask him."

"No, thank you. I've finally managed to speak to him without wanting to scratch his eyes from his face. Best not to push."

"Fair." Finn stopped moving. "Chivving tunnels."

I leaned away from the wall to peer around him.

The slope of the tunnel became even steeper, beyond our ability to stay on our feet as we traveled.

"I am grateful," Finn shouted to the ceiling. "Dubious of my ability to survive this, but still chivving grateful!"

"What do you suggest we do?" I peered as far into the darkness as I could. All I could see was the slope traveling down at a frightening angle.

"Pray to the gods, and hope they're willing to protect a pair of fools." Finn shook out his shoulders and sat on the ground.

"Are you really just going to slide down there?" I grabbed his shoulder.

"Do you have a better idea?"

I gripped my lae stone in my hand for a moment, savoring the light it provided, and then rolled the stone down the slope. It clacked along as its glow disappeared.

"Shall I fetch?" Finn pushed himself off and began sliding downward.

"It's to light the bottom!" I shouted after Finn. "And give you a warning—"

"It's not that bad!" Finn's voice and light faded away.

Darkness surrounded me.

I sat on the ground and tucked my skirt carefully beneath me.

"This is a terrible idea."

I pushed off as hard as I could and began sliding forward. In the black, I couldn't tell how fast I was going. It didn't seem like an absurd speed, and letting the mountain do the work for me was better than crawling through the tiny tunnel on my stomach.

"Ahh!" A scream carried from far below.

"Finn! Are you all right? Finn!"

I shot my hands out to my sides, trying to grip the wall to stop my descent, but there were no walls for me to touch.

"Finn!"

I leaned farther to the right, trying to find something to catch hold of. The tilt of my body made me spin sideways.

The angle of the tunnel shifted again.

My speed tripled.

I fought to right my body as the tunnel hooked around a bend, banging me into a wall.

Pain shot through my shoulder, but I didn't have time to scream as the tunnel whipped the other way, hurling me into a tight spiral.

I squeezed my hands to my chest, trying to keep my bones from shattering as the tunnel shot me around and around and around.

"Ahh!"

"Finn!" I shouted as loud as I could. "Finn, are you all right?"

I couldn't hear his reply over my own scream as the ground disappeared.

41

Blue light glowed around me, and before I could try to see what sort of place my shattered body would lie in, I hit the ground.

Pain flared through my bottom, my teeth bashed together, and I was still.

"Oh," I groaned.

"I'm glad I managed to roll out of the way in time."

I looked to my right where Finn lay spread eagle on his stomach.

"Still better than the monster," Finn said.

I began laughing, but pain shot through my ribs. "Ow, ow, ow."

"You all right?" Finn pushed himself to his hands and knees.

I made myself sit up. I wiggled my fingers and toes, bent my knees and my elbows. "Maybe a bruised rib, but nothing I won't survive. You?"

"I'll be fine." Finn got to his feet. "As long as no one asks me to sit for the next week."

"Don't make me laugh." I stood up. "Laughing is now a horrible idea."

"Right. No humor from me."

I looked around the space the mountain had chosen to spit us into. Another tunnel continued to our right.

I gritted my teeth as I bent to pick up my lae stone. I checked the crystal-like surface for cracks, but the stone, unlike Finn and I, had been undamaged by the fall.

"Shall we?" Finn grimaced as he bowed me toward the tunnel.

I bowed back and let Finn go first.

"Once we get into Ilbrea," I said, "I'll find us some nice roots and herbs for a balm. Make the journey to the Lir Valley a little less painful."

"Have you ever been to the Lir Valley?"

"No," I said. "I think it's in the northern part of Ilbrea. Closer to Ilara than I've ever traveled."

"I've never been on a sorci run without a map and a plan before."

"Neither have I."

We walked in silence for a long while. I spent the time trying not to think through all the things I wished I knew and how many ways our journey could go terribly wrong. I don't know what busied Finn's mind.

I tried to focus on the child.

In my mind, it was boy. Young with fair hair. He didn't know how to control his magic, and he was terrified. I pictured him hiding, tears coursing down his cheeks, as he wondered why the gods had cursed him with magic.

Then I didn't mind that our work could go terribly wrong. The imaginary child was worth the danger and pain. I would risk my life to keep him from being locked up by a lady wearing purple robes.

"Please." Finn slowed his pace. "Oh, please, please let this be it."

A wall blocked our path.

Finn laid his palms on the wall and pressed his forehead to the stone.

"We are going out into Ilbrea to rescue a child. A little one with magic in their blood. Let us help them find shelter. Please."

I held my breath, half-expecting the mountain to speak.

In a way, I suppose she did.

A rumbling carried from beneath my feet, and Finn stepped back as the wall before us crumbled to dust.

"Thank you," I whispered to the mountain, though I had no hope she would hear one who did not carry stone in her blood.

The full brightness of a summer afternoon waited for us beyond the rock.

I took a breath of the forest air and turned to look back at the tunnel.

The mountain had already healed itself. A flat rock face that seemed as old as the stone around it blocked the path we had traveled.

"It would be wrong to linger, wouldn't it?" Finn said. "We don't know how far we've traveled, and the monster could be on us at any moment."

"Hold still." I dug a packet of dried meat and a waterskin out of Finn's pack. "Eat as you walk. It'll be good for the soreness."

Finn took the food, sighed, and headed down the mountain.

I walked beside him as we tramped through the woods. The fear I'd felt early in the morning didn't return. There was something about this part of the forest, a lightness to it, that the woods around the camp didn't hold. I tried to think back to the spring when I'd first arrived at the Black Bloods' summer home.

It had seemed like such a vibrant and perfect place. A nest of safety hidden away from the world. But when we'd walked away, that air of peace had been gone.

A knot twisted in my gut.

I didn't know when that feeling of sanctuary had disappeared. If it had slipped away so slowly I hadn't noticed the fading, or if it had vanished all at once when death found the Black Bloods.

The mountain had been kind to us. Finn and I made it to the

edge of the woods before dark. We climbed back up a bit, away from the mountain road, and found a place to shelter for the night.

Finn set out his six black stones to protect us.

I laid out our bedrolls and climbed beneath my blanket, grateful for the weight of the pendant against my chest.

I drifted into the darkness of sleep, and no monster came to find me in the night.

42

Having kohl drawn around my eyes to walk down the mountain road seemed like a foolish thing to do—the kind of vanity that would have driven Lily absolutely mad, and I myself would have laughed at, before I had a healthy fear of soldiers recognizing me and wanting me hanged.

But the men driving the caravan of wagons heavy with barrels of chamb didn't seem to think the paint and powder I wore was foolish when they offered us a ride north.

I pushed aside the fear that nibbled at my chest and gratefully accepted the ride, careful to keep the men in sight even though Finn sat by my side.

One of the men had a map of Ilbrea and let Finn and me study the roads we'd need to take to reach the Lir Valley.

The path he showed us did not ease my worry.

Liam had given Finn a bag of coins, which allowed us a hot meal to satisfy Finn, and a comfortable bed in a tavern to please me.

The next day, we traveled on foot, leaving the mountain road to head northeast. Finn did not take so kindly to the tavern fare on our second night.

The third day, Finn bought us a ride in a cart carrying a dead body to its funeral. The scent of the corpse did not seem worth saving my feet from the road. But at least the carcass kept the soldiers lurking around the town from asking any questions. We snuck into a barn to sleep that night and slipped out before the sun rose in the morning.

But, somehow, none of it seemed real until we reached a signpost driven into the dirt at a crossroad in the middle of a forest. The sign was not weathered and worn like those I'd seen on my other journeys with Finn. The words on the wood were untainted by the weather and carved in a neat script.

One slat read *Lir Valley*, the other, *Ilara*.

"How long do you think it would take us to reach the capital?" I asked.

"Two more days," Finn said, "maybe three. Why? Do you want to go and burn the place?"

"Do you think we could manage it?"

"Probably not." Finn grinned. "But that doesn't mean I'm not willing to try."

I stared down the road to Ilara. It seemed wrong that a path leading to a city of murderers should look so plain.

"The poor sorci has been living a few days' walk from the Sorcerers Tower. How has the child not died of terror or run far away?"

"Maybe they aren't afraid of the Sorcerers Guild," Finn said. "They could want to join them, you know."

"Then we'd have nearly been killed by a monster for nothing."

"Not nothing." Finn started walking down the road to the Lir Valley. "We'll give the child a choice. An offer of freedom means the world, even if the person you're trying to save would rather stay in their cage."

"I know." I tore my gaze from the path to Ilara and followed Finn. "But I hope none of the children who choose to join the Sorcerers Guild regret it too late."

"I'm sure some of them do." Finn took my hand.

"That's horrible."

"It is, but at least they know there are people in the world who want them to be free."

"Do you think that helps?"

"I hope so."

The road to the Lir Valley wound through the woods, cutting up and down hillsides.

We'd started climbing a high hill when the low rumble of water carried through the trees.

I stopped at the crest of the hill, looking down at the long wooden bridge stretching over a rushing river. I barely breathed as we crossed the planks, for fear the whole thing might collapse beneath me.

A small part of me was almost angry it held. I hated the Guilds and didn't want any of their endeavors to succeed, even if their work was only carrying people safely across the water.

On the far side of the bridge, on the western bank of the river, a wide boat was tethered to a large dock that reached out into the water. Three merchant carts waited nearby.

The men around the carts stared at me as we passed. A tall man with ash blond hair whistled at me.

I kept my pace even and my gaze fixed on the road ahead.

"A pretty thing like you shouldn't be walking."

I forced my hands to stay relaxed, not allowing my fingers to betray my rage by balling into fists.

"If the ginger can't provide a proper ride for you, maybe you should set your sights on a real man," the ash blond called.

The men around the merchant carts laughed.

"Too afraid to look?" the man said. "Don't want to know what you're missing?"

"She's not missing anything," Finn said. "She knows plenty of what a real man should be. She doesn't need to spare a glance down your pants to know you don't qualify."

"Why you cacting little chiv"—footfalls thumped up behind us—"of a cow chivving slitch."

"Language, sir," Finn said. "My darling has tender ears."

"Your petal whore should learn the consequences of lingering with a foulmouthed letch."

"Would you like to have a fight with me?" Finn asked. "Honestly, I've been plodding along for days, and I could really use a bit of a diversion."

My heart hitched up into my throat as Finn drew the two knives that lived at his hips.

"Oh, you've brought weapons?" The ash blond's voice didn't lose any of its dripping bravado.

"Yes." Finn smiled. "And I'd be chivving thrilled to use them."

The men around the wagons began shifting toward us.

"I'll tear you to shreds and toss you in the river," the blond said.

"No." I pulled my knife from my boot. "You won't. You'll either climb up onto your carts where you can sit like lazy laxe scum with your pretty cargo boat, or Finn and I will kill you. And we won't bother dumping your bodies into the river. I'll carve your eyes out and drop them on the ground for the ants to eat. Then I'll chop off your tiny, limp pricks and leave them on the road for the carrion eaters."

"You brazen—"

"Now you've worked your way up to being gutted." I pointed my blade at his stomach. "So go back to your carts or pray to the gods that mercy may find you in death."

The men laughed.

"Finn, make the slitch hurt," I said.

Finn threw one of his knives. The blade sank into the blond man's foot.

The man screamed.

His fellows back away.

"Get them," the blond shouted. "Thrash them!"

"Have a lovely day, fellows." Finn nodded to the men as they climbed up onto their carts.

"You're going to be sorry for this," the blond growled.

"No, he won't," I laughed. "Now give him back his knife."

"What?" Sweat beaded on the man's brow.

"Bring him his knife, or he'll sink one into your other foot," I said.

The man stared at me.

"Careful when you pull the blade out," I said. "It's going to hurt."

"Do it." Finn tossed his second knife from hand to hand.

The man reached down and wrenched the knife from his own foot with a whimper.

"Now bring it nicely over here," I said.

The man limped toward us, the tip of the blade pointing toward Finn.

"Careful there," Finn said, "or I might hit your heart instead of your foot."

The man flipped the knife around and presented Finn with the hilt.

Finn wiped the blood from the blade onto the man's shirt before slipping the knife back into its sheath.

"A word of warning," I said. "Keep that cut clean. Dump some strong liquor on it and bandage the wound well. If it won't stop bleeding, you might need to find a healer. An infection in your foot could steal your life if you aren't careful."

"Enjoy your day." Finn bowed to the men in the carts. "Come along, my love. All this excitement is making me hungry."

"You are a ravenous beast at the best of times." I looped my arm through Finn's, and we strode up the road.

I listened for signs of them following even as Finn and I chatted while we walked out of sight.

"Into the trees then?" Finn said as soon as we'd rounded the bend. He led me south of the road and into the woods, cutting deep enough that the trees nearly blocked the path from view.

"We could have just kept walking." I let go of Finn to lift my skirt over the tangle of branches littering the forest floor.

"Sure," Finn said. "But then they would have gnawed on the next pretty girl to cross their path, and she might not have had anyone to defend her."

I stopped for a moment, listening for any hint of the men following us. "I just hope none of them end up being related to the sorci we're trying to find."

"They're laxe. If they spotted a sorci, they'd sell them to the Guilds straight off."

"A lot of common folk would do the same." The certainty that I was right rolled sickeningly through my stomach. "It's amazing we get any of the children out."

"Cheer up, love." Finn took my hand, dramatically helping me over a narrow log on the ground. "What we do may only be the work of birds pecking at a giant's head, but better that than to wait on the ground pretending we aren't about to be stomped."

"Fair." I pushed away my growing urge to flee.

"And who knows? One of the tiny wounds we make from pecking at the giant's head could get infected."

I laughed, and the rest of my worry shook free.

"I'm not joking." Finn poked me in the arm. "The giant may not have someone as brilliant as you warning him to tend to his wounds. He doesn't pour liquor on the peck marks to clean them, and the tyrant falls down dead with blood poisoning."

"I don't think Emmet told me that story when we were young." I wrinkled my nose.

"That's because we're writing it, dear Ena." Finn stopped and turned to me. "What if future generations sing songs of our heroic deeds and all they know about me is how much I eat? What if instead of being the rogue with the red hair, I just tromp through the ballads eating? Should I stop eating in front of people? Protect my legacy?"

"No, keep eating." I took Finn's chin in my hand. "Eat the most absurd things. When they sing of you, they'll say you ate an entire goat for lunch then defeated the King himself. All the children will love your song best, and tales of your glory will be sung by every scabby-kneed littleling in the land. Ilbrea needs a hero like you, Finn."

"And what of you?" Finn kissed my forehead. "What will your story be?"

"I won't have one. I'm a Ryeland. Apparently, our stories aren't allowed to be told."

Finn laughed, then I laughed, and the woods around us became bright and beautiful. I didn't know what lay ahead, and the mystery of it lured me on through the trees.

We didn't forget the men from the river as we walked arm in arm through the forest. We listened and watched, but there was no hint of any menace in the afternoon shadows.

The reality of the dangers we faced slipped further and further away as we tromped through the woods, until the fact that Finn had stabbed a man's foot seemed like nothing more than a bit of a children's song.

We heard the Lir Valley before we saw it.

The mooing and braying of livestock carried into the forest, followed quickly by the scent of their dung. Voices cut through the sounds, and every once in a while a dog would bark, setting the other animals off into a round of calls.

"I didn't think the Lir Valley was farmland," Finn said.

"It's not what it looked like on the paper." I hesitated before reaching into my pocket. My fingers felt cold as they found the bloodstained parchment. I bit the insides of my cheeks as I pulled out the little map and opened it.

A roughly-drawn image took up most of the folded page. One thick line formed a strange shape that seemed to be the outline of the valley. Another thick line, which I assumed to be the road, cut in on one side and ran to the center of the page.

Two circles, one much larger than the other, had been marked in the top left corner. Inside the smaller circle, the tracker had written one word.

Death.

Tiny v's clustered together on the far left side of the page, though I couldn't begin to reason through what exactly they might mean.

At the bottom of the page, a big dot had three little squares leading up to it like stepping-stones.

Near the end of the road, in the center of the page, a set of lines weaved through each other in a pattern I couldn't understand.

"Not the best map I've ever seen," Finn said.

"She must've thought she'd get a chance to explain it."

I tipped the paper into the light, reading the words along the border of the page. The letters had been smeared by her blood in places, but enough was legible that at least the meaning of her writing was clear.

The death is not natural. The people of the valley know something is wrong. The lies began long before. Started in winter. Father must know. Find him for the names.

"Should we start for hunting for the *death* now?" Finn pointed to the word on the page. "Or should we find a place to stay and wait for morning?"

"I say we find a tavern. Can't be caught prowling about at night. We don't want the locals suspicious before we even know what child we're looking for."

"Too true." Finn cut north, toward the road we'd been walking alongside.

I folded the paper back up and tucked it into my pocket.

I won't fail you. I pressed my hand against the map. *I won't let your death be in vain.*

When we reached the last of the trees, we peered up and down the road. There was nothing in sight save some dents in the dirt large enough to wrench a wheel off a cart.

I stepped out onto the road and looked into the Lir Valley.

It was not a sad patch of farmland at all.

The road wound down the slope of the hill, past pastures and fields, then into a proper town at the base of the valley. A web of streets curved as they weaved between stone buildings, with not a straight line among them.

A massive home, grand enough to be a palace, loomed over the hill opposite us.

Large houses, big enough to fit a dozen families, dotted the hill to the south of the fancy estate. In the north, where the circles had been drawn on the map, two little ponds sparkled in the late afternoon sun. To the south, a giant, black hole marred the earth.

"What is it?" I asked Finn.

"Mining." Finn placed my hand on his elbow as he led me down the road and into the valley.

"What are they mining for?" I squinted toward the dark patch but couldn't see enough to guess what lurked below the ground that men might find valuable.

"I've no idea," Finn said. "But I'm sure there will be someone at the tavern complaining about it."

The road down into the valley was longer than seemed possible from the top. We passed herders coming in for the night, travelers on horseback, and a few carts heavy with goods.

My feet ached, and my stomach craved food. But, I smiled pleasantly at everyone who went by, careful to keep my face placid as I studied the fields we passed, searching for both enemies and signs of magic.

By the time we reached the outskirts of the town, twilight had nearly arrived.

The dimming sky gave the dark gray stone of the houses a foreboding feel, even though they all seemed to be well-kept.

"Out of the way," someone shouted. "Everyone get out of the way!"

I leapt off the street, yanking Finn with me as a man in red robes tore around the corner on horseback.

The horse's hooves pounded against the dirt as the healer raced east.

"Huh." Finn stared after the horse.

"What?" I peered around the corner of the stone house, checking for anyone else who might trample us.

"Do you think the healer might be going to look after a foot injury?" Finn whispered.

I turned to look up the road, watching the healer travel toward the river.

"Well," I said, "how clean do you keep your knives?"

"I'm not sure." Finn frowned. "I wipe them."

"I did warn him to tend to the wound. And it may not be the laxe at all."

"I don't know," Finn said. "I'm too well acquainted with our luck."

I pulled Finn around the corner and onto the main street of the town.

Someone had taken the time to pack in the ruts in this road, at least on the bit I could see. Beyond the first five houses, the road twisted, blocking the next portion of the street from view.

Little flowerbeds had been planted in front of each of the homes. Pink, blue, purple, and yellow blooms grew from the miniature gardens.

I stepped out of the way of a hay cart and bent to sniff a flower with lavender petals and a scarlet disk in the center. I smiled as the sweet scent filled my lungs.

"Those are pretty," Finn said.

"Lily used to grow them in our garden."

I studied the house the garden belonged to. Built of the same stone as all the others, the house bore no mark of being special. Even the shutters and door were painted a plain, dark green.

"I suppose you don't have to know what a flower can be used for to be able to appreciate its beauty." I breathed in the scent of the bloom again before stepping back out onto the road.

As we wound down the path toward the heart of the town, we

passed a young man with a long lamplighter's pole. He carried the flame high, humming a tune I didn't recognize.

We rounded another bend and came upon the first of the shops.

I stopped and looked back up the road behind us.

The boy moved from lamp to lamp, going about his duty with a leisure that seemed to imply a complete lack of fear. The shutters of the homes hadn't been closed against the coming dark. Most houses had their windows thrown wide open, welcoming in the evening chill.

"What are you looking at?" Finn asked.

"They're not scared. We have a map with the word *death* marked on it, and the people in the town aren't afraid."

The color drained from Finn's face. "Are we too late? Did the Sorcerers Guild already claim the child?"

"I don't know." I gripped Finn's hand. "But we'll find out. Until then, we've got to act like someone still needs us."

"Right." Finn nodded. "We'll find out at the tavern. Someone there will know if the sorcerers have been through."

The jingle of a horse's bridle came from the around the bend in the road. Finn and I stepped to the side.

A man with a beautiful black horse to match his shining black cart and slicked back black hair came around the corner.

"Excuse me." I waved to the man. "I'm sorry to bother you, sir."

The man wrinkled his brow as he stopped his cart. He looked from me to Finn and back again. "How can I help you?"

"We're looking for a room for the night," I said. "I'm afraid the winding streets have us a bit confused."

"Ah." The man's face brightened. "Follow this road until you see the dress shop with the red door. Turn right there. Keep going until you reach the open square, then take a left at the far end. You'll pass a public stable, then take another right, and you'll find the tavern."

"Thank you." I gave a careful nod, trying not to shake the directions out of my head.

"You'll probably get lost at least once," the man said. "Don't worry. The people around here are used to confused outsiders. Just keep asking, and you'll find your way eventually."

"Right." I gave the man a smile. "Thank you."

"Best of luck." The man clicked his tongue, and his horse trotted on without pause.

"I'm starting to think I might have judged the tracker's map making skills a bit too harshly." Finn sighed. "I suppose the tavern won't be out of food even if it takes us a while to find."

The man in the fancy cart had been right. It took us nearly an hour and asking three people for help before we found the tavern.

All of the people we spoke to were kind. All of the homes had light peering out through their windows. All of the houses and shops were built of the same stone. The empty square we passed through had a sign marking which days there would be a market, but there was no hint of rubbish or rotting food trampled into the mud.

By the time we stood on the steps of the tavern, a worry had begun tickling the back of my neck. I couldn't name the unease that breathed on my skin, but I knew something lurked in the shadows and feared it might be vile enough to drag me into the darkness.

"In we go, my love." Finn opened the tavern door for me. "After today's journey, I think some food and rest are well in order."

The scents of ale, roasted meat, and fresh baked bread filled the dining room of the tavern. Lanterns hung from the ceiling and along the walls, casting the whole room in a cheery glow.

"Hello there." The man behind the bar waved us toward him. "Can I help you folks?"

I let my gaze slide around the room as we weaved through the two dozen tables. Most of the seats were filled. The people chatted to their fellows, but the place held neither the raucous noise of the places Finn favored, nor the familiar, sad comradery of the tavern in Harane.

"Hopefully," Finn said. "We're looking for a hot meal and a room for the night."

"Oh." The man furrowed his brow and drummed his fingers on top of his balding head. "I'm sorry to have to ask, but are you two married?"

"We are," Finn said. "Though most people don't believe I managed to catch such a pretty wife."

"Good," the man sighed. "Not allowed to let unmarried folks share rooms. The fuss some outsiders make about it."

"No fuss from us." Finn laughed.

The man stepped out from behind his bar, waving for us to follow with his clean white cloth.

"We'll get you a seat over here." The barkeep pulled out a chair for me. "I'll make sure a room is ready for you by the time you're fed."

"Thank you." Finn gave the man a small bow. "After a long journey, your establishment is just what we need."

44

We took our time with our meal and ordered two rounds of ale. The barkeep chatted with the people he served, but there was no one patron who seemed eager to befriend travelers.

"We should get some sleep." I downed the rest of my ale, grateful the hint of honey in the brew made the flavor a little more bearable than the stuff in camp. "We can poke around in the morning."

"I'm not ready to pack it in," Finn said.

"Are you going to waltz up to the bar and ask if he has any interesting stories of death and magic?"

"Probably not the best idea," Finn said, "but I won't be able to sleep if we don't do something."

"I'll go get you another ale then."

"Do you really think you'll be able to flirt answers out of the man who checks to see if his patrons are married?" Finn raised one ginger eyebrow at me.

"I'm more than just a pretty face, Finn." I flicked his ear.

"You also have magnificent breasts, but I really don't want to get kicked out. Or hanged."

"You should have more faith in me." I lifted his mug from his hand.

"I have infinite faith in you." Finn frowned. "It's the men of this sad world I can't bring myself to believe in."

"One more ale and then to bed." I kissed Finn's cheek and headed to the bar.

The patrons in the room had rotated. A fresh batch of people had entered the tavern, but the place hadn't emptied at all. A gray-haired woman had joined the man behind the bar, working the taps and bustling back and forth from the kitchen with trays of food.

I headed toward her and smiled when I caught the woman's eye.

She frowned and went back into the kitchen.

"Right," I murmured. "Not her." I moved down the bar to where the barkeep chatted with a pack of men as he poured glasses of frie.

"It'll be an early winter this year," the barkeep said. "I'm sure of it. You can tell by the way the wert grass grows."

"You'll bring the ice back just by speaking of it," one of the men said. "Keep quiet about your grass."

"The wert grass doesn't lie." The barkeep wagged a finger. "From the mine to the estate, we'll all be covered in ice well before winter should begin."

The men laughed.

"Sorry," I said as soon as the sound began to die.

All the men turned toward me. I gave each of them a smile before looking to the barkeep. "Could I get one more ale for my husband?"

The barkeep rubbed his chin. "Do you think it's a good idea, or will you have a rowdy lout on your hands?"

"Give the girl the ale." One of the men pounded the bar.

"Yes, please," I said. "Truth be told, it's the only thing I've found that keeps him from snoring."

The men laughed again.

"All right, then." The barkeep took both mugs from my hands and led me away from the men to the far set of taps. "One more ale."

"Thanks," I said. "We've had a long day on the road, and a good night's sleep will be welcome."

"We aim to provide a nice place to rest."

"The Lir Valley is much better than I imagined it would be." I leaned closer to the bar. "I don't mean any offense, but from the rumors I'd heard of this place, I wasn't sure I dared to come."

"The Valley is a wonderful place." The barkeep poured the ale. "Anyone who says otherwise is either blind or a fool."

"I wonder where the awful rumors started." I frowned. "The town is so pretty. The valley, too. Why would anyone say that death haunts such a lovely bit of land?"

"I try not to waste my mind on such gossip."

"Isn't it bad for business, though? To have rumors about evil magic scaring travelers away?"

The barkeep's face paled a shade. "It is a bit. I do my best to run a fine establishment. The whole town does everything we can to keep the place clean and respectable. It's hard with the mine lurking at our back door, but we do our best."

"I feel a bit foolish, but what do they mine here?"

"Minerals." He set Finn's mug on the counter. "The Lir family mine digs rocks up from the ground. They built the mine, they built the town, and the estate. Makes it hard to complain about the mine being here, since there wouldn't be anything else in the valley without it."

"But..." I took a moment, trying to find the right words to ask my question. "But why would a mine start stories of evil magic? I was told death had swept through the valley and that a sorcerer came from Ilara, trying to find the one who'd caused it."

The man's face grew paler still. "Bad things happen in all sorts of nice places. The fact that some choose to blame magic instead of accepting tragedy as the gods' will is foolishness that has never made any sense to me. But if you find the one spreading such rumors, tell them we've had plenty of sorcerers come through town and none of them have ever made a fuss about evil magic. This valley is a nice place, and you won't find a soul here who will say otherwise."

"You're right." I picked up the mug. "By the Guilds, it's just not right that fine people like you should suffer because a few fools got bored and decided to make up frightening tales about Death himself taking over a pond."

The barkeep's face shifted to gray.

"Thank you for the ale." I gave him a smile. "My husband will sleep much better now."

45

I woke long before Finn the next morning. I'd slept through the night without any terror chasing behind me, but as soon as I opened my eyes, awful images gnawed at the corners of my mind. I lay by Finn's side, trying to keep still as I battled my own thoughts.

Memories of Harane, of the horror I had abandoned my home to, were better off banished to the deepest corners of the blackness where I tucked the things I was not strong enough to remember. I didn't want the images of Lily hanging from the tree to make my hands tremble, but I could not purge the picture from my mind.

What did people say of Lily? What did travelers whisper to each other of the terror of Harane?

The soldiers had slaughtered our people and burned our homes. Had the villagers tried to erase those horrors? Did they pretend it had never happened and lie to anyone passing through who bothered to ask why charred frames of houses loomed on the sides of the road?

Did Cal's mother flap her bar rag in the face of anyone who dared mention the horrors inflicted on Harane and warn them not to spread dark stories about a lovely place?

"Are you all right?"

I gasped when Finn spoke.

"Ena?"

"Of course I'm not all right. You just scared me, you slitch." I pressed a hand to my chest as though the weight could somehow slow the racing of my heart.

"I meant before I said anything." Finn propped himself up on his elbow.

"I'm fine." I curled closer to his warmth.

"You're not." Finn stroked my hair and tucked a stray strand behind my ear. "I don't think you could be, not after all the world has taken from you."

"I'm strong enough to bear it."

"That's why I adore you, Ena Ryeland. But that doesn't mean you're not allowed to crumple a bit around the edges."

Finn stared at me, waiting for me to say something.

I wanted to tell him to mind his own chivving business and let anger coat everything else I could possibly feel. But Finn kept patiently waiting for me to speak, and I couldn't bring myself to rage at him.

"Ena," Finn whispered, "you're allowed to be afraid."

"It's not that." I gripped the pendant around my neck. "Something horrible happened here. Somewhere in this valley is a child who's got to be scared out of their mind. If they worked enough magic for *death* to be written on the map, they've got to be petrified of themselves and the Guilds and everyone around them.

"I know what it's like to have your whole world collapse around you in a flood of terror and blood and fire. I've lived through it. If Liam had been an hour slower in reaching Harane, I'd…" I let out a slow breath, forcing all the tendrils of fear that crept through my body back behind the rage that burned in my chest. "I'm not a hero, Finn. I'm an inker from Harane who's good at stitching people back together and knows a bit about poison. That poor child deserves someone better coming to their rescue."

"Am I worth nothing?" Finn furrowed his brow.

"You're worth everything. But you should have Cati with you, or Emmet."

"Oh gods, not Emmet." Finn winced. "I'd rather have my mad inker by my side than any of the others. You were the only person bold enough to even suggest leaving camp. And the rest of it, that's just flashy sword work and bravado."

"Is it?" I felt a smile curving my lips against my will.

"Of course." Finn held me tight. "Just act brave, and people think you're a warrior. Swing your sword around a bit, and half of them will run straight off."

"I wish Cati had taught me that trick months ago. It would have saved me a few hundred bruises."

"I'll be sure to tell Cati to update her training methods as soon as we get back to camp." Finn kissed my forehead. "You are exactly what the sorci needs, because we're the only ones who bothered to show up. Now come on, my little mad woman. Let's go be heroes."

I forgot my fear as we dressed for the day and I painted my face to an acceptable hue.

It seemed strange to be leaving our packs behind as we walked out of the tavern, sweet buns in hand, and headed north toward the circle on the map marked *death*.

The people on the streets were cheerful in the fresh morning air. They talked and laughed without any trace of the worry or dragging pain that marked the towns I'd visited with Finn before.

I smiled at the people we passed, trying to look as happy as they did to be out on a fine summer morning. But there was something about their airy nature I couldn't seem to match.

We found the northern edge of the town without too much fuss and from there could easily see the narrow road winding north toward the ponds.

I looped my arm through Finn's and tipped my face up to the sun.

There was an untamed freedom in the way the wind blew about us, as though the land had no idea that anyone had mastered its terrain.

As we moved farther north, the road changed from a wide path, to a narrow trail, to a strip of dirt running through the high grass.

Finn shifted to walk in front of me when the way forward became too narrow for us to move side by side. The grass grabbed at the fabric of my skirt, pulling me back with every step.

"This isn't right." I studied the plants around me, searching for a hint of poison or a predator waiting to pounce.

"It is," Finn said. "The blob of water up ahead is definitely the thing marked *death* on the map."

"I know that." I grabbed Finn's sleeve, stopping his loping stride. "There's a whole town's worth of people back there, and this trail is barely worn. If there had been a pond like this anywhere near Harane, there would have been a pack of children racing to the water on a day this fine. There should be marks in the dirt where carts have been hauling picnics back and forth. What happened in that pond to scare a whole town away?"

The bright sunlight still warmed my face, but fear muted the joy of it. I took a deep breath, trying to catch a hint of decay carrying on the wind.

"Maybe no one's taught the children how to swim." Finn took my hand, pulling me behind him. "Maybe they banned visiting the pond because too many unmarried couples were fraternizing by the water's edge."

"Do you really think either of those things could be true?"

"No. But I'd rather let myself enjoy the morning just a little while longer."

I kept scanning the tall grass as we walked. There were no

paths trampled through it by animals come to drink their fill or patches eaten away by hungry livestock.

The ground grew softer under our feet as we neared the water's edge. My boots squished with every step, the sound joining the swishing of the grass against my skirt.

"Finn." I pulled on his hand, but he kept moving forward. "Stop."

He reached for the knife at his waist as he looked around. "What?"

"There are no birds." I froze, listening for any hint of a chitter or caw.

"What under the stars happened here?"

I reached down, freeing my own knife from the sheath tucked into the ankle of my boot. The weight of the blade didn't bring me any more comfort than it had when we'd been chased through the mountains by a monster.

The water came into view, glistening in the morning light. I wished there would be some hint of menace in its beauty, anything to explain the utter dread that curled through my stomach.

A band of barren dirt surrounded the pond. I squinted at the brown, trying to catch sight of any paw prints a thirsty animal might have left behind.

I stepped up to the very edge of the pond, where the water kissed the toes of my boots.

"We could ask in town," Finn said. "Tell the barkeep we fancy a swim, and see what he has to say."

A gentle wind blew around us, and the grass sighed as it swayed. The breeze dipped tiny waves into the surface of the water, giving it a texture that lent depth to the shadows below the surface.

"Finn, look down there." My voice was calm as I spoke. Almost too calm, as though my mind had slowed my words to give my eyes time to understand the submerged shapes.

A man riding a horse, sat at the bottom of the pond. The man wore a dark coat and a white shirt that somehow worsened the pallor of his skin. His head was barely below the surface of the water. He held one hand in front of his face as though trying to protect himself from an attack.

The wind blew again, harder this time.

The water stirred. The very top of the man's head emerged for a moment. His brown hair fluttered in the breeze. Then the wind died down. The water settled, and he was back below the surface. A human statue, carved by a master and dumped into a pond.

"Come on." Finn took my arm, pulling me back down the path.

"It's not right." I kept my gaze fixed on the man, squinting through the sunlight reflecting off the still water.

"Clearly."

"Bodies float. If that's a real man, he should be floating." I paused at the edge of the grass, unwilling to stop staring at the drowned figure.

"If he were killed by natural causes, then I would agree with you. Come on, Ena."

"Come where?" I shut my eyes tight, making white spots dance in front of them.

"Away from the death pond seems like a reasonable start. From there, I would be willing to negotiate."

"We need to see the other pond." I took Finn's hand and started blazing my own trail through the tall grass. The rib-high blades scratched at my bare hands.

"Do we really need to see how many corpses can fit in the big pond?"

"Is he even dead?" My steps faltered. I looked back toward the water, but the grass hid the pond from view. "Is he just frozen, should we help him?"

"I don't have any magic in my blood." Finn stepped in front

of me, leading me on a wider path around the water. "I don't claim to be an expert on magic, but I did grow up in Lygan Hall. I have seen my fair share of enchantments and curses, and I can promise you with absolute certainty there is no chance under the stars we could haul that man out of the water and save him.

"I can also say with relative certainty that if we were to try such a chivving foolish thing, we'd probably die. If you want to go see the other pond and check for more death, fine. But we are not touching that chivving water."

"No touching." I nodded, even though Finn wasn't looking at me.

The ground squished beneath my boots, and a shiver shook my spine.

"The people in the town have got to know," I said. "There's no way they could have just always hated that pond and not noticed the man at the bottom."

"I don't think either of us is that lucky."

The second pond came into view. It was larger than the first, at least three times as wide, and surrounded by a similar band of plain dirt.

I held my breath as I stared down into the water, searching for a frozen massacre lurking beneath the surface.

Movement caught the corner of my eye.

"This way." I started around the side of the pond, careful to keep my feet out of the water.

A cluster of reeds grew along the western bank. Flashes of movement darted through the stalks.

"Fish." I leaned over the water.

Finn wrapped an arm around my waist, pulling me back.

"This pond has fish, and the other has a dead man." I stepped away from the water and into the grass, which suddenly felt safer than being in the open. "It doesn't make sense. If there were something wrong with the water, it should be bad in both ponds.

They're so close together, a big enough storm would flood it all into one."

"We should go to the squiggles on the map," Finn said. "The tracker was right about the death pond. Maybe whatever she found on the western hill will make a bit more sense."

"We can hope."

I didn't pull the map back out of my pocket as I began leading Finn up the hillside and away from the water. I had a sense of something watching me, following me, and I didn't want it to know about the bloodstained piece of paper in my pocket.

The map was private, sacred. A woman had given her life for the information she'd tried to pass on in those squiggled lines. I would not allow my failure to betray her.

Sweat had begun to bead on my back by the time we made it free of the tall grass. There was no fence, or rocky soil, or any other hint as to why the wild grass that had so determinedly wrapped around my ankles suddenly gave way to low greenery and wildflowers that all seemed to have been recently chewed on by hungry livestock.

A field mouse darted through the grass and down into a hole. The sight of the tiny creature brought me an absurd amount of relief.

"The animals know there's something wrong with that chivving pond." Finn stared at the place where the rodent had disappeared.

"Finn, you know I despise the Guilds." I cut south along the open field. "You know I loathe them with every ounce of my being."

"I do know." Finn tucked his knife back into its sheath.

"I would have sent for them." I knelt, hiding my own weapon away. "If there were a man trapped in a pond and a place even the animals feared, I would have sent for the Sorcerers Guild."

"You wouldn't," Finn said. "You would have thought about it and decided you'd rather be killed by an evil curse."

"At the very least, I wouldn't have hated the one who sent for a sorcerer's aid." I stood up and looked to the pair of ponds below us. From a distance, they seemed innocent. I couldn't see the shape of the man at all. "If the people of the Lir Valley know what's under the water, why have none of them sent for help?"

A hundred birds perched on the ground. Some of their heads tipped at different angles. A few had spread their wings as though preparing to fly. No two birds were identical, but they were all made of stone.

Is this how Liam's bird was made?

Even as I thought the horrible question, I knew it couldn't be true.

Liam's bird was stone brought to life by his magic.

The birds on the barren hillside were living creatures cursed to become stone.

"What sort of sorcerer could even manage a thing like this?" I knelt beside a bird, studying the prefect outlines of the feathers on its wings.

"I know a few. But none of them are children, and all have spent years training," Finn said.

I balled my hands into fists, resisting the temptation to touch the bird and feel the texture of its stone feathers.

"Either we're here chasing a frighteningly powerful child or an adult who's managed to live in Ilbrea and avoid being taken by the Sorcerers Guild," Finn said. "The trouble is, I don't know which is more terrifying."

I stood and brushed the dirt off my skirt.

The hillside where the birds had met their untimely end was pretty, with a sweeping slope and a wide view of the town below. Farther up, toward the top of the valley, the castle-like estate stared down at everything below.

From this angle, I could just make out a dirt road leading to a giant barn hidden behind the massive stone structure. I tried to think through how many people could live in the castle and how many it would take to maintain it. Even just the people living on the estate could leave us with a dozen possibilities for a child that could be hiding magic.

I dug my fingers into my hair, pulling at the roots. "How do the trackers manage it? How do they find the sorcis for us to save?"

"I'm starting to think they might be using a strange form of sorcery of their own," Finn said. "Either that or a combination of luck and intervention by the gods."

I closed my eyes and tipped my face up to the sky. "How charming are you feeling this morning?"

"Why, my love? Are you considering leaving me for another man?"

"No"—I wrinkled my nose as I looked to Finn—"but I am considering doing something very foolish and may need your charm to save my neck."

"Then point me in the right direction, and I will prove to the world exactly why my mother never chucked me out of the house, no matter how close I came to burning the whole place down."

"Perfect." I turned toward the estate. "Aren't the homes made of stone in Lygan Hall?"

"They are." Finn offered me his arm.

"You almost burnt down a stone home?"

"The stone would have stayed standing." Finn laughed as we strode farther up the hill. "But everything in it—furniture, clothes, my mother's prized collection of books—they would have all gone up in flames."

"Your poor mother."

"Don't be too hard on me." Finn nudged me with his elbow. "It's shocking how flammable bedding can be."

"Poor you."

We chatted all the way up the hill. Finn would take over every time I ran out of cheery things to say. I would respond and laugh, prompt another tale of him angering his mother. But no matter how funny his stories were, I couldn't shake the feeling of something watching me.

I hated that feeling. The powerless knowledge that some unknown thing could see me, but no matter how many times I stopped to take in the view of the valley, carefully searching the open ground around me for a hint of anyone following, I couldn't find whatever it was that had set the chill on the back of my neck.

I stopped one final time as we reached a flowerbed that seemed to mark the beginning of the estate proper. Holding my breath, I searched the valley below for any flicker of movement or wisp of a shadow that could be trailing in my wake.

Nothing.

"Come on." I tugged on Finn's arm, leading him around the flowerbed.

The blooms had been planted in a twisting pattern, with deep black rocks nestled between the rows. The design held a certain beauty, but the plants themselves were the same sort that grew in the little gardens in front of the homes in town.

The castle itself was built of the same stone as the houses and shops far below, though the rocks were where the similarities stopped.

I could only see one entrance cutting through the thick wall of the massive structure, and the lowest set of windows didn't even begin until ten feet off the ground. Even then, all the panes had heavy bars across them, as though whoever had built the place was expecting to be attacked at any moment.

We passed another flowerbed. This one had been planted to bloom into an image of the sun with bright golden rays of light streaking through a field of deep blue.

I don't think anyone in Harane would have dreamt of trying to create such a thing, even if they'd had the time and land to plant so many flowers.

"Ena," Finn whispered, nodding toward the entrance of the castle.

A woman dressed all in black stepped onto the stone slab in front of the shadowed doorway and glared down at us.

"You did say you had a plan when you wanted to come up here?" Finn said.

"Close enough to a plan." I smiled and waved at the woman.

She did not smile back.

A very foolish part of me wanted to shout a hello to the woman just to see if she'd cringe.

But I kept my pace even and my smile bright as we walked toward the stone mouth of the castle. I didn't say anything at all until we were only twenty feet away from the door.

"Good morning." I gave the woman a nod. "It's a beautiful day out."

"The view from the Lir Estate is always lovely," the woman said. "That is why the Lirs have declared this private land."

"A wise decision," I said. "I can't imagine owning a castle only to end up with a town full of people picnicking at my doorstep."

The woman blinked at me for a moment before speaking again. "The Lir family values their privacy, as they always have in the century since this estate was built."

"Of course," I said, "and I wouldn't want to intrude upon the family. I was just hoping someone here might be able to answer a question or two for me."

"You'll have to forgive my wife." Finn stepped around me, bowing to the woman. "She is exceptionally curious. We truly don't want to intrude, but I'll never hear the end of it if she doesn't get to ask."

"It'll only take a moment," I said. "I was just hoping to find out who created the little stone birds."

Finn's neck tensed as the woman's eyes widened.

"Do you know who made them?" I stepped up to Finn's side. "I was hoping you must since they're just down the hill from here."

"The birds are not on the grounds of the Lir family estate," the woman said.

"Right." I furrowed my brow. "I'll ask in town, then. I've never seen anything like them, and I've got to know who's responsible."

"You cannot pester people about the birds." The woman stepped toward me, her tone harsh and low.

"Why not?" I asked. "Do the birds belong to the Guilds? I don't know anyone but them who would have the right to say what I'm allowed to ask about."

"That will be quite enough," a man's voice carried from the shadows of the entryway. The man with the black hair we'd met the night before stepped out into the open. He looked to the woman. "Back to your work."

The woman gave me one final glare before bowing to the man and bustling back into the shadows and out of sight.

"You'll have to forgive her." The man smiled. The expression fit his face, like he had been born to live a life where joy was common. "Birgit means well, but she's overly protective of the grounds."

"I can see why she would be," I said. "The views from up here are lovely. They must be coveted by many people."

"They are by me, at least," the man said. "Though I can't say I have any interest in the stone birds."

"Really?" I said. "So, you don't know who put them there?"

The smile vanished from around the man's eyes, leaving a frightening darkness behind. "If I did, I would make sure the one who defaced my hillside understood the consequences of their actions."

"Can't you just take them down if you don't like them?" Finn asked.

"I will not give the vandal the satisfaction," the man said.

"That's a pity," I said. "I was hoping to find the sculptor. Do you think anyone in town might know?"

"You'll not find a murmur in town regarding the maker of the birds." The man's smile returned. "I'm sorry I can't be of more help."

"Please, don't be," I said. "I'm sorry someone left a flock of birds on your hill. Though I can't imagine anyone from the town would maliciously leave something on your land."

"That's very true," the man said. "Would you like my help in returning to town? I could have my cart ready in a few minutes' time."

"No." I looked out over the valley. "It's a perfect a day for a walk. We'll be off your hill in no time, I promise. Thank you for your help." I took a few steps away from the entrance before stopping. "Is there a child who should be playing around these grounds?" I looked back at the man.

Darkness flashed over his face again. "What do you mean?"

"It's just you prize your privacy so much, and you've had a problem with vandals." I shrugged. "I didn't know if they were supposed to be here."

"What did you see?" He stepped toward me.

Finn shifted his weight, easing his hand up toward the knife hidden at his waist.

"When we were coming up the hill," I said, "I saw a child. They were still for a while then sprinted away. I was never close enough to see much of them. It was a bit peculiar, though. If I see them on our way back to town, should I tell them off or have them come up here?"

"Neither." The man smiled again. This time the expression did not reach his eyes. "I'm sure they are far away by now."

"Ah well." I shrugged. "Have a lovely day."

I held my hand behind me, reaching for Finn, and walked down the hill without looking back. I twined my fingers through Finn's, trying to look like a couple in love as I hurried down the slope.

"Tell me you have a plan," Finn said. "Tell me we didn't just go waltzing up to a chivving castle to shout that we're looking for the maker of some magically frozen birds."

I moved a bit faster, walking as quickly as I could without actually running.

"Ena."

"I don't have a proper plan," I admitted. "But we do have the black-haired Lir very upset."

"Which is a bit of a problem since we're in a valley named after him."

"Oh, calm down." I stopped and turned Finn to face me. "I have to kiss you now."

I leaned in and gave Finn a slow kiss. I wrapped my arms around his neck and pressed my body against his. I pulled my lips from his and whispered in his ear. "Now we're going to run to the tall grass, and you're going to beam and laugh the whole way like you're about to get the best roll of your life."

I took Finn's hand and sprinted down the hill. I tossed my head back and laughed at the sky.

"Is this a part of your non-existent plan or have you finally given in to my charms?" Finn asked through his laughter.

"I have never been immune to your charms."

Sense told me to stop at the edge of the high grass, to stay out in the open and leave whatever the animals were afraid of to the shadows. But I charged into the grass, laughing like a mad woman and dragging Finn behind me.

We ran for a full minute before I glanced behind.

There was no sign of movement in the castle high up on the hill.

I dropped to the ground, yanking Finn down with me.

"Do you actually want me to roll you?" Finn asked. "I take our duty to protect the sorcis seriously, but I don't know if our friendship could survive my crawling up your skirt."

"Oh, hush and be still." I rolled onto my stomach. "We just need to hide here for a bit and watch."

"Watch for what?"

"A man who lives in a perfect castle, on top of a perfect hill, looking out over his perfect town has a batch of mad stone birds glaring up at him. Now he thinks that whoever did it is lurking around his property."

Finn stared at me for a moment. "I still don't understand."

"What does a farmer do when a fox is stalking their hens?" I peered up over the tall grass just in time to see the man with shining black hair ride south on his perfect black horse. "They go fox hunting."

The dirt road the Lir man raced down cut along the side of the valley, heading straight south. There were no trees surrounding the lane, or even a long, stone wall to offer a bit of cover.

"This was your plan?" Finn asked as we strode south along the dirt road out in the open for all to see. "You had the brilliant idea to go up to a castle and send a madman charging away on his horse?"

I bit my lips together.

"And now we just saunter along after the angry laxe and hope he doesn't notice?" Finn asked.

"Well, no." I untied the string at the end of my braid and shook my hair free. "Honestly, I was hoping we'd find someone with a loose tongue, eager to complain about the chivving child who'd frozen a flock of birds and murdered a man. But this works as well."

The Lir man rode so far ahead of us, he and his black horse were hardly more than a dark spot on the road.

There weren't many choices for where the man could be going. Along the road, there were only the long buildings and the mine. Still, I couldn't bring myself to stop walking. Not because I was afraid he'd sneak off the road, but out of fear of what he might do to the child. A child I'd sent him after.

I wove my hair into a tight braid as the man stopped his horse beside one of the long buildings.

Finn cringed. "I wish we had a bit of cover. Just a shrub."

The Lir man strode into the second building without glancing in our direction.

"Oh, you made him mad," Finn said. "Very, very mad."

"This way." I tugged Finn off the dirt and into the weeds and wildflowers that surrounded the road.

Vegetable gardens had been planted alongside the buildings, and a few women labored amongst the plants.

I kept my eyes front, locked on the second building as we cut between the garden and the first stone home. At least, it seemed like a home in a sad sort of way.

Built two stories tall and longer than four normal houses stuck side by side, signs of people living packed together spilled through the windows. Washing hung out to dry, the scent of overcooked food filled the air, and murmured words carried on the breeze.

I sensed the women staring at us but didn't look their way. I couldn't, not when the shouting began in the second building.

I couldn't understand the words at first, but I recognized the anger of the shout and the terror in the reply.

Do not let more innocent blood fall on my hands.

"Keep her away," the Lir man shouted. "Keep her inside. Keep her locked up."

"She is," a woman begged. "She never leaves my sight. I swear to you."

"There was a child prowling around my home," Lir growled.

"There are other children," the woman said. "It wasn't her."

"You shouldn't stay here," a voice whispered behind me.

I gasped and spun around, ready to fight for my life, only to find a little girl with black hair and brown eyes staring up at me.

"She is the only one who would be foolish enough to dare," Lir said.

"Come on." The child took my hand. "We can wait below until he's gone. It's best to stay hidden when the master is angry."

"Thank you," I whispered.

"If not her, then who? Which one has been prowling?" Lir shouted. "Someone here has got to know."

"I don't know," the woman said. "I have been in here with Cinnia. I sit with Cinnia. My whole world is watching her. I don't know what anyone else does."

The little girl led me around the side of the building.

I glanced behind to Finn.

He widened his eyes at me but followed all the same.

The girl stopped at the corner of the building. Chewing on her top lip, she glanced up at the windows before running for an open cellar door against the side of the house.

Lir said something, but I was too far away to make out the words.

"Go." The girl pointed at the steps leading down into the darkness below. "Go on."

"It wasn't Cinnia!"

I froze at the woman's shout.

"We have to help her." I looked to Finn.

"Cinnia?" the little girl said. "She doesn't need any help, but we have to hide. You can't let him find out you went to the pond."

The child stood, pointing into the dark as though she hadn't said anything strange.

"Go." Finn nodded me toward the steps.

"Thank you." I hurried down the stairs, blinking against the darkness in the cellar below.

Barrels and baskets lined the walls of the short-ceilinged room. The scent of wet dirt and fresh-dug vegetables made it hard to believe I'd just stepped out of a bright shining morning.

"All the way to the back." The girl darted in front of me and beckoned me to follow. "Once he knows it wasn't Cinnia, he'll go on a tear. It's better if we keep out of the way when he does that."

She stopped at the back wall and turned around to face us. "You are very big, so it might feel tight to you. Sorry."

Before I could ask her what might feel tight, she'd already leaned against a barrel and begun shoving it to the side.

"Do you need help?" Finn asked.

"I can do it." The child dug her toes into the dirt, pushing with all her might.

The barrel inched sideways, and a tiny slat of light appeared in the back wall.

"Who's out there?" a voice whispered.

"It's Evie." The little girl dropped to her knees. "Scoot over. We've got to make room for guests."

"What?" the voice squeaked.

I knelt down as Evie crawled through the hole in the wall behind the barrel.

"Just make room," Evie said. "The master's on a tear upstairs."

I inched toward the flickering light.

A little boy sat huddled at the back of the dirt cell.

The space was only ten feet deep and not even as wide, but I could tell they'd spent a lot of hours trapped inside. Someone had etched pictures into the dirt walls, and a stack of dirty blankets had been neatly folded in the corner.

"Who are they?" the little boy asked.

I crawled into the chamber. "My name is Ena, and this is my friend Finn."

"You've got to close the door behind you," Evie said.

"Right," Finn said.

I slid out of his way as he wrestled the barrel back into place. It wasn't until he'd blocked us in that the feeling of being trapped settled into my stomach.

"This is a lovely place you have here," Finn said.

"Why are they here?" the boy asked. He looked to be older

than Evie, but I wasn't sure if it was only the thinness of his cheeks and fear in his eyes that made me think so.

"I went to the water, to check on the man," Evie began.

"Is he still there?" A wrinkle formed between the boy's black eyebrows.

"He is." Evie nodded. "But they were there, too. And then they walked straight up the hill to the birds."

The boy glared at Finn and me. He balled his hands into tight fists as his shoulders crept toward his ears.

"Then they walked straight up to the estate and spoke to the master," Evie said. "Followed him here, too."

"Why?" the boy said. "Why would they do that?"

"Because we're looking for someone." I sat against the wall opposite the boy, arranged my skirt around me, and laid my hands in my lap.

Neither of the children spoke.

I waited another moment before pressing on. "Finn and I are looking for someone very special. And I think the person we're looking for knows an awful lot about how the man ended up in the pond and how the birds turned to stone."

Evie bit her lips together while the boy glared at her.

"You see," I said, "there are some children who are so special, older people are afraid of them. And when grownups get afraid, sometimes they hurt people. Or send special children away to places they don't want to go."

"No one should be afraid," Evie said.

"Evie." The boy hit her in the arm.

"She never meant to hurt anyone." Evie hit the boy back. "She was only defending herself."

"Quiet," the boy growled. "We don't know them."

"You don't," Finn said, "and you're right to be wary of strangers. But we are here to help."

"You can't help," the boy said.

"I think we can," I said. "I think you know who made the

strange things happen by the pond and on the hill. And, if you can be brave enough to trust us, we can help her. There's a place where she wouldn't have to be afraid of her magic. Where she wouldn't have to defend herself."

"Liar," the boy said.

"Breathe, Dorran," Evie said. "You've got to remember to breathe."

"Shut it, you." Dorran took a deep breath.

"Look," Finn said, "where I come from, there's a lot of magic, and it's wonderful. The people born with magic in their blood don't have to hide. They're trained and protected."

"You're from the Sorcerers Guild." Evie's chest sank.

"You shouldn't have brought them here." Dorran rounded on her.

"We're not from the Sorcerers Guild," I said. "We don't even like them. But whoever sank the man and froze the birds, they need help. They are going to be noticed or accidentally hurt someone they don't want to hurt. It's only a matter of time before the Sorcerers Guild comes for them."

"They've tried," Dorran said. "A lady in purple robes went to the estate. The master sent her away."

I looked to Finn. My own fear was reflected in the wrinkles on his brow.

"Can you tell us who it is?" I asked.

"No," Dorran said.

"We'll just talk to them," I said. "If they don't want anything to do with us, we'll go."

"We're not allowed to tell." Dorran glared at Evie as he spoke.

"He's right," Evie said. "We can't tell you. We made a solemn vow."

"Then you shouldn't break it," Finn said. "But maybe you could tell the one with magic that we're here. Let them know we want to help them, and that there's a place where they can be safe that's far away from the Sorcerers Guild and the master. That way, if they want to talk to us, they can, and you won't have broken your vow."

"Maybe," Evie said at the same time Dorran said, "No."

"Either way, it's up to you," Finn said. "Just know that all we want to do is help."

"There is no help." Dorran crossed his arms and pulled his knees up to his chest as though trying to form a cocoon where he might be safe.

"We should go," I said. "Let you two have your hiding place to yourself."

"You can't," Evie said. "He might still be up there."

"We'll be careful," I said.

"And you think you could help." Dorran laughed.

"Why shouldn't we go up there?" I asked.

"It's only the diggers, women, and us children who are supposed to be around the miners' homes," Dorran said. "You're not allowed. It's the rule."

"The master makes rules for everything," Evie said. "He owns everything in the valley. The mine, our houses, the whole town. If you don't follow his rules, he'll boot you out."

"Or worse," Dorran said.

"If you get booted out, there's no way to earn coin," Evie said. "That's when people starve or freeze in the woods. You can't let him catch you where you shouldn't be. You could die."

"Well"—I pushed myself onto my knees—"thank you for being so brave in protecting us. But Lir does not own me or my home. I have no fear of him." I crawled to the barrel and shoved it aside. "We're staying at the tavern in town. If the one with magic wants to speak to us, that's where we'll be."

I crawled out into the cellar, the awful feeling of abandoning those poor children gnawing at my gut.

Even though I'd told the children I had no reason to fear Lir, I still stood at the bottom of the cellar steps listening for a long while.

There was no hint of angry voices or whimper of distress coming from above.

What if Lir hurt the woman? It would be your fault, Ena. More blood on your hands.

I crept up the steps and peered around the front of the building.

The shining black horse still waited by the road.

"Hasn't the man got anything better to do?" Finn whispered. "Should we crawl back in with the children?"

"We can't let them think we're afraid of him," I said. "Why would they trust us to save the sorci if we're afraid of their master?"

"It's sick."

"I just don't understand it. He can't actually own the whole valley, can he? The Guilds wouldn't let one person own that much."

"I don't know." Finn took my hand, drawing me around to the

back of the building. "But I'd rather ponder the matter far away from here."

The women were still working in the garden as we cut back through. I didn't look away from them this time. I studied them instead. Their worn faces, etched with worry lines. The rounding of their shoulders that didn't look as though it could ever go away.

I looked to the mine in the distance. I couldn't see anything inside the great black hole in the ground.

"Liam should be here," I said once we'd stepped back onto the dirt road.

"He's got a monster stalking the camp, remember?"

"This isn't a normal sorci run." I dug my nails into my palms, willing my pulse to slow. "Suppose Evie actually sends the sorci to us. Do we just bolt for the mountains?"

"Yes."

"But what about the people in this valley? Are we just supposed to abandon them to Lir?"

"First off, we don't know that he's actually that bad." Finn raised one finger. "Second, short of killing him and hoping a better man takes over as master of these sad people, I don't know what you think we could do." He raised a second finger. "Third, the Guilds are our enemy, not the laxe. As much as I truly do not like this Lir man, he's not the one we're fighting against."

I grabbed Finn's hand before he could raise a third finger. "It seems wrong to ignore people who are being hurt just because their enemy is different from ours. Aren't we all tilk? Does it matter what face the monster wears?"

"Yes, because at the end of the day the Guilds are the root of every evil that destroys lives in Ilbrea. If we spend all our time hacking away at evil leaves, we'll never stop the Guilds for good."

I froze in the center of the road. "You think we can stop the Guilds for good?"

"I bet my life on it every day. Call me a hopeless optimist if you like, but it is freedom for all of us that I fight for, and I can only see one way to make that happen."

Finn looped his arm through mine and dragged me forward.

We cut off the road and through the fields below once we were level with the town. The terrain didn't hold the chilling feel of the tall grass or the crisp neatness of the estate. It looked like normal land leading to a normal town.

Even as we stepped onto the dirt lane that led between the farthest south of the houses, I was still searching for some proof that what the children had told us was true. That Lir genuinely owned everything.

The flowers in front of the houses no longer seemed soothing as we passed by. The blooms were a threat to the owners of the homes. If they did not tend their garden, they would be cast out.

And where would the people go?

I'd left my home and ended up with the Black Bloods. But if I'd been on my own, truly on my own, I don't know what I would have had to do to survive.

Finn chatted with people, getting directions as we weaved through the labyrinth of streets back to the tavern.

The same barkeep greeted us and offered us a table and a hot meal. Finn beamed at the prospect of food, and I tried to smile convincingly along.

The woman who'd glowered at me the night before brought out a tray of meat pies.

"Thank you," Finn said. "We took a nice healthy walk this morning, and I am ready for a good meal."

The woman's face brightened to an expression just above loathing.

"May I ask a question?" I said.

"Didn't you already have all your questions answered this morning, my love?" Finn pushed my plate toward me.

"Nearly." I dug my heel into his toe under the table. "Someone mentioned a tavern in town that's owned by a fellow called Lir. Is this the place?"

"The Lir family owns everything in the valley," the woman said. "We are all fortunate to be allowed to work his land."

She stalked back to the kitchen.

"You are lucky she didn't take the food with her," Finn whispered. "And did you really have to try and break my toe?"

"Yes."

I ate my meat pie without tasting it, trying to look like a pleasant wife instead of someone who wanted nothing more than to run from the valley.

"How long do we wait for the child?" I asked once Finn had finished his fourth helping of food.

"A few days, I'd say. We've got the coin for the room, and we'll still get back to camp before your brother or Liam go completely mad worrying about you."

An odd feeling grew in my gut, one I'd thought I had banished forever.

"I wish Emmet were here." Saying the words felt strange, like someone else had taken control of my mouth.

"Are you feeling ill?" Finn leaned toward me.

"Emmet would storm onto the estate and tell Lir he didn't have the right to control the people of the valley."

"Ahh." Finn leaned back. "I see. You wish a version of Emmet that doesn't exist were here. The real Emmet Ryeland would not go to the odd little castle and tell Lir he's a chivving cact. He'd go pummel Lir and then burn the castle."

"You're exaggerating."

"I'm not."

"What about the mine?" I looked up to the ceiling. There wasn't a cobweb or speck of dust in sight. "Would he sit around wondering what Lir mined that granted him such riches and power? That little girl said Lir sent a sorcerer away. What in this world could give Lir the power to turn a Guilded sorcerer away from their hunt for a sorci?"

"By the gods, I'm glad Emmet's not here." Finn doubled over laughing. "I can see it perfectly in my head. He'd stomp right up to the entrance of the mine looking like a demon fresh from the forge, glowering so badly most would scatter at the sight of him. He'd stride straight to the center of..."

"Keep going." I looked to Finn.

"No." Finn narrowed his eyes at me. "I don't want to give you any foolish ideas."

"It's not foolish at all," I whispered. "There's something wrong with this place."

"Yes." Finn nodded. "It's called a madman owns everyone. All the homes. All the shops. This is what happens when a rich slitch decides who lives and who dies."

"Lir sent a sorcerer away. That's not possible. That's not something the Guilds would ever allow someone to even attempt without the person foolish enough to do the demanding ending up dead."

Finn rubbed a hand over the stubble on his chin.

"There is something going on here, Finn. Something that scared the tracker badly enough to send her racing back to the mountains. Shouldn't we at least try to find out what she knew? Bring the best information we can back to Liam?"

"I love you, Ena Ryeland. I swear to the gods I do, but if we get ourselves killed sneaking around a chivving mine, I will haunt you in the next world."

"Good." I squeezed Finn's hand. "Dead or not, I don't know what I would do without you."

I have made many mistakes in my life. Some, I cannot bring myself to regret. Others, I would tear the stars from the sky for the chance to change.

Pain and I have long been acquainted. Grief is a feeling my heart knows well.

I understood the greed of the Guilds. Their love of power and abundance of hate.

I didn't understand the horror one common man's hunger for power can inflict.

I should have known.

I should not have been bold enough to think I could help.

I should have learned from the blood already on my hands.

The night wasn't cold enough to warrant wearing my coat, but, as the fabric of it was darker than the sleeves of my shift, I wore it anyway.

Finn and I strolled arm in arm to the edge of town, me doting on him and whispering sweetly in his ear, him nodding and beaming at every person we passed. My nerves didn't begin to shout until we'd reached the southernmost home in town.

There was only a narrow trail leading toward the mine, almost as though the town wasn't meant to acknowledge the hole in the earth near their doorstep.

Once we'd slipped into the shadows behind the last house, we moved more quickly. There were low bushes along the way, but nothing big enough to offer any real hope of hiding. So, we just kept walking, counting on the dark of the night to shield us from prying eyes.

The mine was farther away than it had looked from the top of the valley or even from the miners' homes where we'd met Evie and Dorran.

I looked toward the cluster of buildings. Candles burned in the windows.

I wanted to ask Finn if he thought that was where all the miners lived and if those three buildings would be able to house enough workers to keep a mine running. But the only noises around us were the wind, the soft sound of our footsteps, and the low hoot of an owl. Somehow, it seemed like speaking might break whatever treaty we'd made with the night. I swallowed my questions, foolishly certain I'd have time to ask them later.

I slowed my pace as we neared the mine.

Finn kept beside me, one hand already on the hilt of his knife.

Two lanterns hung by the mouth of the mine. Silhouettes of men moved in the dim light. One pacing. Two standing together, only shifting slightly as though trying to ease the burden on their sore feet.

I took Finn's arm, stopping him behind a low bush. I knelt down, shutting my eyes and trying to reason through how to talk my way past the men.

"Do you want me to knock them out?" Finn whispered. "I can try to do it without hurting them too badly."

I shook my head.

"Unless you can flirt enough to lure all three of them away at once, I can't think of a better plan."

The mine sliced into the hillside, but the slope wasn't at a steep enough angle that I'd have a hope of climbing down from above and slipping in unseen.

"You shouldn't be here," a voice whispered behind me.

I fell to the ground, reaching for the knife in my boot.

"Chivving stars and gods, girl." Finn grabbed my hand, blocking me from my knife.

I looked up to find Evie staring down at me.

"What are you doing here?" I pressed a palm to my racing heart.

"Following you," Evie said. "You said to tell the one who put the man in the pond to find you at the tavern, but you're not at the tavern."

"Evie"—I pushed myself to my knees—"did you put the man in the water?"

She shook her head. "But I told the one that did what you said, and you're not in the tavern."

"We're going to go back to the tavern," Finn said. "We've just got a little chore to finish first."

"In the mine?" Evie cocked her head to the side.

"We need to know what they pull out of the mine," I said. "We're not going to take anything or hurt anyone. We just need to have a look."

Evie bit her lips together. "If you get to look, then you'll go back to the tavern, and then you can take the one who made the man go in the water where she'll be safe?"

"Yes," I said. "I promise. But right now, you need to go where you'll be safe."

"I'm safe here." Evie stepped out from behind the bush. "Come on. She'll get nervous if we make her wait too long."

The child strode straight for the three men.

"Evie," I whispered after her. "Evie!"

She just kept walking.

"The child is chivving mad," Finn said.

"Come on." I stood and chased after Evie. Finn's footsteps thumped quietly behind me.

We'd only been running toward them for a few moments before all three guards saw us coming. They all stopped, turned to face us, and drew their swords.

"Evie, stop." I caught her arm.

A shock, like lightning had struck my skin, shot through my hand.

I gasped, swaying as spots danced in front of my eyes.

"Ena." Finn grabbed me around the waist.

I blinked, trying to get my gaze to focus on Evie.

"Stop," one of the guards ordered. He looked down at Evie. "You? What are you doing here?"

"They need to look inside. I'm sorry." Evie drew her hands back.

A whoosh and a crack sounded as she shoved her hands forward, and all three men fell to the ground.

"Evie?" I ran after her as she strode into the mine. "Evie, stop."

"You said you needed to see," Evie called back. "So hurry up."

I leapt over the men lying on the ground. Their chests were moving, but their eyes were blank as they stared up at the night sky.

"Evie!" I ran after her.

"Ena, wait." Finn thumped behind me. "Oh, by the gods and stars this is a terrible idea."

The lanterns cast an orange glow into the entrance of the mine. The light flickered off the dark gray stone that matched the rock the entire town had been built of.

"Do you have a lantern?" Evie looked at me.

"No." My fingers fumbled as I pulled my lae stone from my pocket.

The blue glow shimmered off the rock, casting strange shadows like the whole world had suddenly been plunged deep underwater.

"That's pretty." Evie wrinkled her forehead, staring at the lae stone. "Is it magic? Are you magic?"

"No." Finn pulled out his own lae stone. "But we have a friend who is, and he made these for us."

I gripped my lae stone tighter. It had never once occurred to me that Liam himself had created the light I carried with me.

"Hmm." Evie turned down the tunnel. "We should keep going. I've only been down here once, and I don't remember much of it."

I followed the child deeper into the darkness. "Why have you been down here, Evie? Lir doesn't make you mine, does he?"

"No." Evie's voice bounced down the tunnel. "She asked me to come down here with her. She was too scared to come alone, and she wanted to see it. Didn't work out so well in the end though."

"Why?" I asked just as Finn said, "Who's she?"

Evie stopped, staring into the dark for a moment before turning toward us. "She never means to hurt anyone, but when she gets scared, she can't always make the magic stop. The men scared her."

"I'm sorry," I said. It didn't feel like enough, but I couldn't think of what else to say.

"Don't be," Evie said. "Just help her."

"We will," Finn said.

"Come on." Evie took off down the tunnel, running through the darkness as though she had no concept of fear.

Finn and I chased after her.

The walls of the tunnel crept closer together the farther down we ran, leaving barely enough room for a cart to pass. The roughly hewn stone had the same dark coloring as the rock by the entrance. As the shadows of the lae stones shifted against the harshly cut angles, it was easy to believe we were swimming down toward some terrible beast.

You will not drown.

"Finn," I said as the tunnel curved and the slope dove deeper still, "does this sort of rock look familiar to you?"

"A bit." A faint trace of fear tainted Finn's voice.

"By the Guilds." Evie stopped short just in front of me.

I wobbled, trying to keep from knocking her over.

"I definitely don't remember this," Evie whispered.

I held my lae stone high, though its dim blue glow barely carried far enough to light the chamber we'd entered.

Tunnels led off in five different directions, not counting the path we'd just run down. The chamber was larger than the clearing the Black Bloods gathered in at night. The size of the space seemed obscene for the three carts that sat in the middle and the one cage of tools tucked behind us.

"Evie," Finn said as he stepped in front of us, heading toward the carts, "how many miners live in the houses with you."

"I'd say..." Evie stared up at the ceiling. "I'd say thirty-four, if you count the three guards out front I knocked out. If you don't count the night guards, thirty-one."

"Such a large space for thirty-one miners," Finn said.

"What do they mine down here?" I asked.

"Rocks," Evie said.

"What sort of rocks?" I bent down to look into Evie's eyes. "Big rocks, like they use for building houses?"

"No," Evie said. "Little rocks. If they find one, the miners are given frie. They all drink and celebrate outside. Then the biddies get angry because the men trod on their gardens."

"Do you know what the little rocks are used for?" I asked. "Are they diamonds?"

"No. They mine rocks, not jewels." Evie ran after Finn.

"Why would they want little rocks?" A heavy fear settled across my shoulders. I looked up the tunnel we had traveled, waiting for one of the guards, or Lir himself, to come charging out of the darkness.

"Do the Guilds buy them?" I asked.

"Chivving cact of a slitching paun's nuts," Finn said.

"Oh dear," Evie giggled.

"What?" I looked to Finn.

"We need to get out of here." He leapt out of one of the carts.

"Why? What did you find?" I ran toward Finn.

He tore past me on his way up the tunnel.

"Finn." I chased after him. "Finn, what did you find?" I grabbed his arm.

He held his hand out. A tiny shard lay in his palm. A simple sliver of black rock that shimmered in the light of my lae stone.

There was something in the tiny shard that seemed familiar and alive all at the same time.

I'd seen mountains of the dark stone without feeling fear—the pendant around my neck that brought me so much comfort had

been melded of the same rock—but the tiny, out of place frag-
ment drained the heat from my body.

I pressed my palm to the stone pendant hidden beneath my
bodice, needing to feel its warmth against my skin.

"This doesn't belong here," Finn said.

"What doesn't?" Evie ducked under my arm to look into
Finn's palm.

"Nothing." Finn tucked his hand into his pocket. "We need to
get to the tavern. We need to leave this valley."

"Yes," Evie said. "She'll be waiting for you, and she is not good
at waiting."

Evie tore up the tunnel.

I took a deep breath before racing after her.

"Evie," I said, trying to keep my words even while I sprinted
up the slope, "if you are the one who put the man in the pond,
you can tell us."

"I've said it wasn't me."

"I know that," I said, "but you've got magic. I saw it."

"I know I've got magic," Evie said, "but I'm not the one who
put the man in the pond or froze the birds. She's waiting for you."

The child ran faster, moving so quickly, I wondered if her
magic were somehow helping her to fly up the tunnel.

Finn's footsteps kept close behind me as we ran, but he said
nothing.

The brisk air of the summer night surrounded us as we
reached the opening of the tunnel. The men still lay on the
ground, their blank eyes turned toward the stars.

Evie ran up the dirt path toward the town without even bothering to check that Finn and I still followed.

I had a hundred questions I wanted to ask of her, of Finn. I
even had questions I wanted to shout to the gods, but with the
night pressing in around us, there was nothing to do but run.

A stitch pinched my side, and my breath grated my throat as
we reached the southern edge of the town.

"Evie," I panted, "we've got to slow down."

I reached forward to catch the child's arm, but she dodged away from me without even bothering to look behind her.

I slowed my steps, forcing myself to walk between the stone houses.

Evie slowed before she rounded the next corner.

"If your friend"—Finn spoke between gasps as he took my arm—"if she's waiting for us at the tavern, we can meet her there."

Evie turned toward us. "She isn't at the tavern. She can't come into town. She's most definitely not allowed in town."

"Right," Finn said. "Of course. But why not?"

"It isn't safe for her," Evie said. "People upset her. She's not allowed to be upset."

"Then where is she?" I asked. "If you tell us, we can get our bags and go meet her. You won't have to stay with us."

"No." Evie turned and kept walking down the street. "I have to stay with you."

Evie led us down the twisting paths of the city without hesitation.

I kept my arm draped through Finn's, though I don't know what innocent defense I could have come up with for following a child through the streets at night.

By the time we neared the center of the town, my breathing had slowed. The scent of flowers and stone filled my nose as we moved from one pool of lamplight to the next. We passed a woman with a heavy basket in her arms, a boy chewing on a hunk of bread, and an elderly woman muttering to the shadows as she shuffled through the night.

Nothing seemed strange or out of place. The town had the same odd uniformity as it had in the daylight. There was nothing to explain the tingling on the back of my neck.

"Are we leaving tonight?" I whispered to Finn as our path became familiar.

"Yes," Finn whispered back.

We followed Evie down a curving alley and onto a wider road.

She stopped dead in the middle of the street, cocking her head to the side like a dog hearing a noise beyond my comprehension.

"Oh quatter wats." Evie shooed us back into the alley.

"What?" I pressed myself against the stone side of a cobbler's shop.

"He's waiting for you in the tavern." Evie chewed on her top lip. "The master's there."

"How do you know?" Finn asked.

"I don't know." Evie wrinkled her forehead. "There's too much noise in the tavern, and I can feel the people being angry and tense. I can smell the master, so I know he's in there, and he's downright furious. I don't know why there would be so many people sitting in a tavern and not drinking if it isn't about you."

"Our packs are in there." I shut my eyes. "Our supplies and our coin. We need our packs."

"I can get them," Evie said.

"No." I grabbed Evie by the back of the dress before she could step out of the alley. "You are not going anywhere near that tavern."

"But you just said you need your bags." Evie twisted out of my grip.

"I'll get them," I said. "Finn, you wait with Evie. I'll pop up, grab our bags, and be right back."

"You'll get caught by the master," Evie said.

"It's not worth it," Finn said. "We'll manage without the bags."

"I'm not stealing from people who are barely surviving." I wiped my hands on my skirt. "It's only one story up. You'll barely notice I'm gone."

I stepped out onto the street before Finn could stop me.

51

Low voices carried from inside the tavern, though I didn't see a hint of anyone standing guard around the building.

The large rocks the town had been built of may have been a cheap convenience for the Lir family as they cleared debris out of their mine, but the wide-set stone offered perfect handholds for me to climb.

I loved the burning in my muscles as I scaled the wall to our window. The precision of it, the dependence on every part of my body, made me believe for one beautiful second that I was in control. That my own skill and strength could somehow change the course of things.

I gripped the sill as I pushed the window up. There wasn't even a lock to block my way. I was in the room before I had time to truly think through how I was going to get our bags out.

There was no light in the little room. I squinted through the shadows to the corner where Finn and I had left our packs. I couldn't see anything in the darkness.

As I reached into my pocket to pull out my lae stone, a board creaked in the far corner of the room.

I spun toward the sound.

A man stepped out of the shadows by the fireplace.

I gripped the lae stone in my pocket as I recognized Lir.

His black hair and clothes made him look more demon than man. His pale face twisted into a smile.

"Lir," I said. "What a pleasant surprise."

Lir stepped closer to me. "Is it a surprise? Do you think so little of my people? Did you think none of them would tell me you'd been poking around my valley?"

"I figured they would. When you control people's lives, the line between loyalty and fear becomes so thin there are few brave enough to break away."

"Who sent you?" Lir moved closer still.

I stepped toward him, letting my lips lift into smile. "Who do you think?"

Lir gave a low laugh. "I won't play games with you. This tavern is filled with loyal men. I have more waiting in the shadows to tear you to pieces. Tell me what I want to know, and your end will be considerably less painful."

The crystal edges of the lae stone bit into my palm as I clutched the rock.

Finn will be fine. Finn has gotten out of worse before.

"I was hired by the Sorcerers Guild," I said. "The Lady Sorcerer doesn't like being told she can't take the children she wants."

"I made her a fair offer," Lir said. "If she's unwilling to pay, that's her own trouble."

A rolling hatred bubbled in my gut.

"It's funny how you strut around this valley as though you own the land," I said. "You keep the miners tucked away and the rest of the people living in your stone town too frightened to speak of the man hidden in the pond."

Lir's eyes narrowed.

"You're nothing more than a rich fool in a fancy house." I leaned in so there was barely a foot of space between us. "You don't own anything. Never forget, we all live and die by the will of the Guilds."

"You know—"

I dug my heel into his toe and swung my lae stone for his temple. The impact of the stone against his skull shook my arm, but I held on to the light as Lir collapsed to the ground.

The thump of his fall stopped my heart from beating.

I froze, waiting for a dozen men to charge out of the shadows.

The dull sounds from below, murmurs and movement I hadn't even noticed before, stopped.

You will not fail them.

I held my lae stone toward the corner of the room where our packs had been. The blood on the stone shone purple. Bile rose in my throat.

Our packs were gone. Every hint that Finn and I had ever been in the room had vanished.

Footsteps crept up the creaking stairs.

I glanced around the room one more time.

Not a hint that we had ever existed.

I shoved the bloody stone into my pocket as the footsteps stopped at the door.

The floor creaked under my boots as I leapt over Lir and to the window.

The door burst open behind me.

"She's in here!" the barkeep roared.

I sat on the windowsill and twisted my body over the open air, hanging by my fingers for a split second before dropping to the ground far below.

"Stop!" a voice shouted from the shadows.

I did not stop. I raced toward the place I had left Finn and Evie.

Four people carrying makeshift weapons tore out of an alley. A woman led the pack, brandishing a garden spade.

I do not want to hurt these people. I cannot hurt these people.

I rounded the corner into the shadows where I'd left Finn, but he wasn't there.

Fear coursed through me, but I kept running, desperate to find a way to escape the growing mob that chased me.

I cut out of the alley and onto another winding street.

A faint, blue light glimmered to the north. I headed for the glow, hoping against hope that Finn would be there waiting for me.

A scream carried from the west.

I glanced behind to see flames rising from the roof of the tavern.

A man with a club and a woman carrying a kitchen knife faltered as the fire danced against the night sky.

I ran faster, pushing my legs as hard as they would go. I needed to head to the woods, find Finn in the safety of the trees. I reached the blue glow. The shade and shape were right for a lae stone, but I didn't dare stop to pick it up.

My feet sloshed through a puddle as I rounded the next bend in the road.

"Ena."

I recognized Finn's voice the moment before he grabbed my arm, hauling me out of the way as the puddle I'd just run through caught fire.

The woman with the garden spade screamed as flames leapt onto the hem of her skirt.

"This way." Evie waved us forward. A blue glow shot from behind my shoulder and into Evie's waiting hand. She tossed the lae stone to Finn. "I told you there were people waiting in the tavern."

"Lead on," Finn said.

He kept me in front of him as we raced through the streets.

"Where are we going?" I asked.

"To meet her," Evie said.

Another round of screams carried from behind us.

I risked looking back. The fire had spread to other rooves.

"Evie, did you start the fire?" I asked.

"Only the little one." Evie darted between two buildings as a group of men raced toward us. "It must have been her. I told you she isn't good at waiting."

I kept close behind Evie, resisting the urge to pick her up and carry her as the pounding of boots came closer.

Finn roared behind me.

I pulled my knife from my boot as I turned toward the sound.

The men chasing us had bottlenecked at the mouth of the alley.

Finn sliced through the first man's throat and shoved him back, knocking the others over.

"Stop playing around," Evie called back to us.

"Sorry," Finn said, "hard to resist stopping people from killing us."

We sprinted out onto another street, then through an alley so narrow I was grateful we'd lost our packs.

An open field waited for us beyond the stone buildings.

My moment of gratitude at being able to see in all directions soon vanished as the overwhelming feeling of being watched by a hundred hungry predators made every blade of grass seem like a deadly foe ready to kill me.

"I see them!" a voice shouted behind us.

"Oh dear," Evie said. "Oh dear."

"What is it?" My words rasped in my throat.

"There are too many people coming," Evie said. "She won't like it."

My legs burned as we raced up the hill, scrambling over stone fences, terrifying the animals we tore past.

The woods came into view, their silhouette like jagged teeth devouring the horizon.

"We're coming!" Evie shouted. She gasped in air before shouting again. "We're coming!"

I wanted to shush her, but there was something in her tone that made me quite certain the child was saving our lives.

The ground leveled out as we reached the top of the rise.

I glanced behind just long enough to see the string of torches following us and the massive blaze that had swallowed the center of the town.

"We're coming!" Evie shouted again as she raced into the woods.

I turned my eyes front, squinting into the shadows to try and see where she was running, but unwilling to pull the lae stone from my pocket.

Evie's steps slowed as she veered south.

"We're here," Evie said. "I'm here."

For the first time, there was a hint of hesitation in her voice.

"I've brought them," Evie said. "I did just as I said I would. Come out."

Evie stopped, turning around in a circle as she peered into the darkness.

The crashing of a dozen men carried from the edge of the woods.

"We have to keep going." I reached for Evie's arm.

She shook me away. "It's too late to turn coward. It's run now or stay here and wait for the master's rage."

A girl stepped out of the shadows. Her long black hair shimmered in the starlight. She led another black-haired girl out from behind a tree. Dorran stepped out beside them, worried lines wrinkling his brow.

"Good." Evie turned to look at me. "We're all here. Now, where do we go?"

52

I stared at the four children for a moment before remembering how to speak.

"To the river," I said. "We have to move as quickly and quietly as we can."

"Come on, Cinni," the tallest girl said to the one beside her. "We're going to run as fast as we can, all right?"

The girl nodded.

I cut around them, heading east.

I couldn't look back to check on them as we raced through the woods.

I could hear their panting and the steady, heavy thumps of Finn's boots, but there were too many branches and roots to dodge to allow me to watch the children.

We were miles from the river. Finn, Evie, and I had already run for miles. I wanted to stop, to ask the children if they needed to stop, but I didn't know how close behind us the townspeople were.

I pictured the whole forest catching on fire in a blaze of wrathful magic. I didn't know if any of us would be able to escape the flames.

My breath came in exhausted gasps, my feet throbbed, and my legs felt as though they'd been filled with stones. But I kept running.

"Stop," Finn panted behind me.

I swayed, catching a tree branch to keep upright as I turned to face him.

Dorran gripped a stitch in his side, gasping for breath as though he were about to drown.

The two girls held hands as they looked from Finn to me. Evie danced from one foot to the other as though unable to stop moving.

"Hop on my back," Finn spoke to Dorran. "I can carry you."

"We can slow down if you like," Evie said. "They headed too far south. They aren't very close right now."

"Are you sure?" the taller of the other girls asked.

"I can hear them." Evie nodded.

The taller girl looked to the smaller girl, who gave a tiny nod of her head.

"All right," the taller girl said. "We can go slower."

"Good," Finn said. "But we still need to keep moving."

"Right." I turned east again.

I wished I had my waterskin. I wished I had my pack, or the chivving stones Liam had given me so I could protect us from whatever horde Lir had sent after us.

I pressed my stone pendant to my skin, needing to feel that its constant warmth hadn't disappeared.

"We're just going to keep walking."

I turned at the whisper.

The taller girl leaned close to the smaller. "We love walking, don't we? We're going to walk and walk and then we'll find a nice place to rest."

"Sounds lovely," Evie said. "We can all climb in a pile and sleep together, right Dorran?"

"Yes." Dorran's voice wavered as he spoke. "We'll be in a nice, safe place where the four of us can sleep."

"We'll be ready for sleep," the taller girl said. "A nice long walk like this, and we'll be absolutely ready to curl up. That will be wonderful."

The smaller girl gave a tiny nod of her head.

"When we get where we're going," I said, "do all of you want to share a tent? Or do we need one for each of you? We have enough to go around."

"Together," the tallest girl said. "Wouldn't you like that, Cinni? If we all stayed together?"

I glanced back in time to see the smaller girl nod again.

"Do you have cotton to stuff in my ears where we're going?" Evie asked. "I don't want to spend the rest of my life listening to Dorran snoring."

"I do not snore," Dorran said.

"You do," the taller girl said.

They kept on that like as we trekked through the woods. There was a soothing patter to the way they spoke, like it was some sort of game they were all very good at playing.

With my knife in my hand, I searched through the shadows for any sign of attack.

An owl hooted from its nest, and we spooked a family of deer but didn't see any hint of another person before we reached the edge of the river.

"First, I want to sleep late," Evie said, "then I want to eat cake, then I want to lay in the sun all afternoon—"

"And end up with a pink face," Dorran said.

The soft rumble of the river carried through the trees.

"We're going to have to be very quiet," I whispered. "There's a bridge over the river, and I need to make sure we can all get across it."

"I'll go." Finn crept past me.

"Finn," I began.

"You should learn to take turns, Ena," Finn said. "You wandered off without me last time. Now it's my go."

He slunk out of the trees before I could think of a good argument for keeping him with me.

I beckoned the children forward to the very edge of the forest.

The starlight glinted off the water as the river raced south. It was a beautiful thing, and also an obstacle I feared we could not cross. I could swim, but not well enough to carry four, or even two, children with me.

"Look at the river," the taller girl spoke so softly, her voice might have been nothing more than a trick of the wind. "You've never gotten to see the river have you? It's so pretty and fast."

A branch cracked as footsteps sped toward us.

"It's like the water is dancing," the girl said.

Finn raced out of the shadows. "Follow me. Quickly."

We ran after him without question.

I fell behind, letting the four children get between Finn and me.

The two girls still moved hand in hand, while Evie ran in front and Dorran in back. The four of them were like a little unit, like the legs of one giant spider, dodging around tree branches and jumping over roots, while all staying the same distance from each other.

It wasn't until the bridge had come into view that I realized they weren't moving around each other. They were all centered on the smaller girl, as though silent Cinni were the axis their whole world rotated upon.

"There." Finn pointed into the shadows.

A freight boat bobbed next to the river dock.

A feeling of blissful relief flooded through me.

Finn slowed as we neared the boat.

I scooted around the cluster of children to reach his side.

"Did you check inside?" I whispered.

"Not yet," Finn said. "I wanted to get you first."

"We'll go in together then," I whispered.

I stopped at the edge of the dock and looked to Evie. "You all stay here, and Finn and I will be right back."

Cinni flinched.

I bent to look into her dark eyes. "We will be right back, and then we'll all get on the boat and float far away from here. All you've got to do is be brave for a few more minutes."

"Don't worry," Evie said. "I'll take care of us."

"Good girl." I followed Finn out onto the dock.

Even while tiptoeing, the aging wood thunked beneath my feet, but the sound was swallowed by the noise of the boat clunking into the pilings of the dock.

The boat was more than twice as wide as a wagon, and most of the middle was taken up by a cabin.

Finn climbed down onto the boat before pulling out his second knife.

I gripped the hilt of my own blade tighter as I lowered myself onto the deck.

The river racing around us and the knocking of the boat against the dock were the only noises I could hear.

Finn pointed to himself and then to the door of the cabin.

I nodded and pointed around the back side of the deck.

I didn't like turning my back on Finn to circle the cabin. It seemed wrong for us to separate, but we needed to search the boat. I crept quietly along, peering into the shadows between the crates of goods and open water barrels, pressing my back to the cabin wall as I looked around the corner.

I kept waiting for a noise from Finn, listening for any hint of a struggle inside. I paused at the far corner and took a breath before peeking around the back of the boat.

A man sat in a chair, a dark blanket draped over his body, letting him blend in with the stacks of goods around him. His head lolled to one side, and he'd propped his bandaged foot up on a crate.

I'm not sure if I froze for a minute or a heartbeat.

Then I pressed my knife to the man's throat and held my other hand over his mouth.

He jerked awake at my touch.

"Shh," I whispered in his ear.

He made a noise against my hand. I pressed the edge of my blade into his skin.

"If you make a sound, I will kill you. If you try to fight me, I will kill you." I tightened my grip on his mouth. "I don't want to hurt you, but I will. You are going to stand up very slowly. If you move too quickly, I will slit your throat. Now, stand up."

The man lowered his bandaged foot from the crate, wincing as he set it on the ground.

Slowly, he stood.

"We are going to walk around to the front of the cabin," I whispered. "You're going to go very quietly."

I dug my shoulder into his back, guiding him toward the far side I'd already checked. We took three steps before he shot his elbow back, hitting me in the ribs, knocking all the air from my lungs.

He spun toward me as I stumbled, drawing his fist back to punch me, but I still had my knife.

The glimmer of the starlight off the metal caught his eye a moment too late.

I drove my knife into his side.

His eyes grew wide. He opened his mouth to scream from the pain.

I wrenched my blade free and kicked him hard in the stomach, knocking him toward the railing.

He coughed at the blow, gagging on the blood that had already begun to fill his lung.

I dodged to the side as he stumbled toward me.

A sound carried from the far side of the cabin.

I swung with my free hand, punching him in the cheek.

He sagged toward the railing.

I drove my knife into the side of his neck. He made a horrible, inhuman sound as I sliced through his throat.

He swayed as I yanked my blade from his flesh.

I dropped my knife and shoved him over the side of the boat and into the river below.

The splash as he hit the water covered the sound of my gasp as I saw the blood on my hands.

The warm stickiness had covered the sleeve of my coat as well.

I stayed stuck for a moment, just staring at my hands.

"Ena." Finn peered around the corner. "Did you find anyone?"

"No." I clenched my hands, hiding the worst of the red. "There's no one here."

"I'll get us untied." Finn disappeared toward the front of the boat.

I tripped over my own knife as I stumbled to the water barrel and plunged both my arms in, using the rough fabric of my coat sleeves to scrub the blood from my hands.

The soft sounds of footsteps came from the dock.

I snatched up my knife and dunked it into the barrel, washing the evidence of death away. I pulled the lae stone from my pocket and scrubbed it clean as whispers drifted from the dock.

I pulled my hands from the barrel and tucked my weapons away. My sleeves dripped onto the blood-stained deck.

I wedged myself between the barrel and the wall of the cabin.

The thump of a rope hitting the deck came from the front of the boat.

I pushed on the top of the barrel as hard as I could. "Please. Just tip."

The barrel crashed down with a splash that soaked my boots and washed away any trace that I had just murdered a man.

53

The children slept during our night on the boat. Finn and I didn't.

I had no idea how to steer a boat, so it became my job to get the children settled inside the cabin, and watch the shadows on either side of the river, searching for anyone coming to kill us.

I stole a spare blanket from the cabin. There were two beds, but all four children had insisted on piling into one.

The tallest tended to the others well enough that it felt wrong for me to hover. Evie waved goodbye, but the others didn't even seem to notice as I crept out of the cabin with my pilfered blanket.

I spent the night pacing the deck, searching for signs of approaching death. By the time the sun started to rise, my clothes had changed from a sopping-wet cold mess, to a damp cold mess. But somehow, pacing the deck in chilly discomfort didn't seem like enough penance for ending a man's life.

I tried to tuck the horror at what I'd done into the darkness where I couldn't feel it, but the look in his eyes when I'd stabbed him wouldn't leave my mind. I tried to burn the guilt away with anger at the Guilds. It was their fault I had to help the children in the first place.

But it wasn't the Guilds who had pressed a knife to the man's throat.

But they're the ones you have to outlive. A voice that sounded horribly like Emmet's rattled through my mind. *The have made a battlefield of our lives.*

"How long will it take us to reach where we're going?"

I gasped and spun toward Evie. The other three children all stood behind her.

"Don't sneak up on people." I pulled my blanket tighter around my shoulders.

"Is it going to be a very long time?" Evie asked.

"I'm not sure," I said. "I've never traveled on this river before. We should ask Finn."

"Finn," Evie called.

"Hush," the tallest girl said.

"I was just told not to sneak." Evie shrugged.

"What's wrong?" Finn peered around the corner from the front of the boat.

"How long until we get where we're going?" Evie asked.

"Ah," Finn said. "We should be off the river by the end of the day. It's actually a nice little shortcut for us. Once the eastern mountain range is in sight, we'll hop up on land, and then it will only be a bit of a climb to your new safe haven."

"How much of a climb?" Dorran asked.

"It'll be a long way," I said. "But Finn and I will be with you, and it will all be worth it in the end."

"A climb will be nice," the tallest girl said. "I think you'll like a climb, Cinni."

Cinni didn't seem to have heard. She stared at the trees we floated past as though trying to memorize all their branches.

"Cinni"—I bent down to be eyelevel with the girl—"is that your name?"

"It's Cinnia, really," Evie said, "but we call her Cinni."

"Cinni, are you the one who put the man in the pond?" I asked.

Cinni's eyes flicked toward me. Her brow wrinkled, and her hands curled into fists.

"She's not mad about it." Evie took Cinni's face in her hands. "Ena and Finn are helping us. They aren't like the pond man."

"It was Cinni," the tall girl said. "She got out on her own. The man saw her using magic. He tried to snatch her."

I gripped my blanket to keep my hands from shaking. "What's your name?"

"Gwen," the tallest girl said. "I should have been watching Cinni. It's my fault the man ended up in the water."

"It's not," Evie said. "It's his for trying to snatch Cinni."

"I'd have done worse if he'd come after me." Dorran laid a defensive hand on Cinni's shoulder. "She was only protecting herself."

"So," I began, speaking slowly, trying to place all the words into an order that wouldn't upset the children, "Evie has magic and Cinni has magic, what about you two?"

Gwen and Dorran exchanged glances.

"Would you send them back if they were normal?" Evie asked. "Because there's no way they could go back to the miners' homes now."

"We wouldn't send them back," I said, "but it will make a difference as to what happens once we get to our home."

"It's all four of us," Dorran said. "We were all born cursed."

"We're Lir's pack of bastards," Evie said. "Well, some of them. We've got more brothers and sisters, but none of them have got magic."

I sank down to sit on a crate. "How many children does Lir have?"

"There are twelve of us," Evie said. "There were fourteen, but two had to be buried."

"They still count," Gwen said. "All of the children born in the miners' houses were Lir's."

"But we're the only magic ones," Evie said. "I told Gwen about you, and she said the four of us should go with you."

"I had to get Cinni out," Gwen said. "She can't travel alone, and I couldn't leave Evie and Dorran there without me."

"Well, you're with us now." I pressed my face into a smile. "And soon we'll be someplace where there are other people like you. People who can teach you and help you."

"Not the sorcerers." Dorran furrowed his brow.

"Where we're going is far away from the grasp of the Sorcerers Guild," I said. "So I need to ask you to be very brave while we're on our journey, but I promise you, it will be worth it."

Cinni nodded.

The children spent the morning on the deck of the boat. Dorran and Evie bickered. Gwen and Cinni sat together, Gwen talking while Cinni studied the trees.

I ransacked the cabin, shoving everything of use I could find into two sacks. I found enough hardtack to make a man sick, and a few packets of spices. I found a coin bag tucked beneath the top of the table with enough in it to feed a small family through a long winter. A crate hid glass flasks of frie. Finn pouted as I dumped the frie and filled the flasks with water from our one remaining barrel.

Finn never asked why I had knocked the other barrel over. I was grateful.

I'd searched the crates and cabin three times before the forest and hills gave way to a beautiful view of the eastern mountains.

I had never imagined I'd be so happy to see the range that had loomed over me my whole life.

"Is that it?" Evie pushed herself up onto the rail that surrounded the boat. "Do we only have to walk as far as the mountains?"

"It's a bit farther than that." I lifted Evie down. "But once we get to the woods, things will be safer."

I didn't allow my mind to wander to the monster that lurked within the trees. Liam had promised to kill the beast. I had to trust him. Without that, I would be lost.

"Everyone up here, please," Finn called from the front of the boat. He stood behind the wheel like he was the captain of a great ship in a daring story about the sea. "I'm going to ram this boat into the shore, and we're all going to hop off very quickly before the river realizes what a foolish idea that is."

"What?" Dorran squeaked.

"Just hop off the front of the boat and scamper away," Finn said. "It'll be easy."

"Come here." Gwen took Cinni's hand and led her to the low part of the rail that had been tied near the docks. "Do you understand what we're supposed to do?"

Cinni didn't move.

"Cinni." Gwen stared straight into her sister's eyes. "I need you to understand that we have to jump."

Cinni nodded.

"Let's keep it quiet for you." Gwen fished in her pocket and pulled out a strip of cloth. Two bundles of fabric had been sewn to the sides. "Hold still." She tied the fabric around Cinni's head, pressing the bundles of cloth over her ears.

I waited for Cinni to rip the fabric away, but instead, the child's forehead relaxed a tiny bit and her eyes stopped darting between the trees.

"Get ready to jump," Finn said.

Gwen held tight to Cinni's hand while Evie shoved Dorran forward.

I grabbed the two sacks I'd stuffed full and carried them to the rail.

"I hope this isn't an awful idea," Finn said.

A horrible scraping came from beneath the hull as rocks and

dirt met solid wood. The boat shuddered and lurched against the shore.

Evie was the first over the side, leaping down with a joyful shout.

Cinni and Gwen jumped next.

I heaved both bags over the rail before dropping to the ground five feet below. The damp earth swallowed my boots as I landed.

"Jump!" Finn shouted.

"It's too far," Dorran said.

I yanked my feet free from the dirt.

A scream carried from above me as Dorran flew from the boat and landed face first in the mud.

The boat scraped against the shore with a horrible grating noise as the river dragged it back into its current.

Finn vaulted from the boat, landing on his hands and knees beside me.

The hull of the boat rammed into a rock in the shallows with a great crack.

"Why did you throw me?" Dorran spat dirt from his mouth as he struggled to his feet. His entire front had been coated in a thick layer of mud.

"You weren't jumping." Finn shook the filth from his own hands.

The current pulled the boat away, twisting our vessel downstream.

"I could have died," Dorran growled.

"If you think that was death-defying, you might have a difficult time adjusting to your new life," Finn said.

"Finn." I slogged toward the girls, having to wrench my feet from the mud with each step. "We're all on land. Can we just be happy with that?"

"I'm muddy and wet because he tried to murder me," Dorran said.

"Quiet, Dorran," Gwen said. "You have to stay calm."

"Easy for you to say," Dorran shouted. "I'm going to freeze to death in mud-packed clothes."

Cinni screamed.

At first I wasn't sure where the sound was coming from. Then the pitch of it cut so deep into my ears I could barely think.

By the time I looked to Cinni, Gwen had already wrapped her arms around her sister. I could see Gwen speaking but couldn't hear the words past Cinni's scream.

"Stop it!" Evie's eyes grew wide with horror. "Cinni, you've got to stop. You'll hurt them."

I followed Evie's gaze.

The mud surrounding Finn and Dorran twisted and shifted as though the muck had suddenly come to life.

"Run!" Dorran tried to scramble through the mud, but the dirt around his feet had solidified.

Finn made it farther. He'd nearly reached me before the ground trapped him.

A heartbeat passed where I wasn't sure if I should run toward Finn to try and free him or away from whatever foul magic trapped my friend.

"Cinni, enough!" Gwen shouted.

The screaming stopped.

I looked toward the black-haired sisters.

Gwen held Cinni's face in her hands.

"I'm sorry they shouted, Cinni," Gwen said, "but you're not helping them. I know you want to. I know you're trying to protect us, but you have to let Dorran go. He can't breathe properly, Cinni."

I looked toward Dorran.

The mud on his clothes had solidified, clamping around his torso. He breathed in shallow gasps. The filth on his arms and face had hardened too, turning him into a statue of fear.

All the mud on Finn had hardened as well, but his face hadn't been coated in the muck.

"Cinni," Finn said, "please let us out. I know Dorran was upset about the mud, but we'll get him washed up. We'll light a nice fire and dry him off, too."

"Take a deep breath," Gwen said. "Finn and Ena are helping us. You've got to relax and let them."

Cinni shut her eyes.

"Good girl." Gwen kissed her sister on the forehead.

"Very good," Evie said, "but are you going to let all of us out, or should I?"

I looked down to my feet. The mud around them had turned to stone. I hadn't felt it happen, hadn't even been watching the ground I stood on. I had assumed my capture would come with pain, but it didn't. My feet were simply stuck.

"I'll do it." Gwen stepped away from Cinni.

The ground around the two of them had hardened as well, but a little column had grown beneath them, lifting them above the danger, protecting them from Cinni's spell.

"Uhh." Dorran groaned. "Ah oo, ee."

"What?" Evie said.

"Ee." Dorran tried to speak, though his mouth had been trapped open. "Ee."

"This should be interesting," Evie said.

Dorran's eyes rolled back in his head, like he would have closed them if his frozen face had allowed for it.

A warm breeze, like the first promise of spring, twisted and swirled around me. The wind carried the scent of honeysuckle.

The mud squelched as I began to sink even farther.

Pulling with all my strength, I dragged my left foot free.

Finn cracked through the top layer of dirt surrounding him and ran toward the swaying grass above the riverbank.

I wrenched my right foot up and staggered a few steps before grabbing the two sacks and following him.

I didn't look back at the children until the grass swished around my ankles.

Dorran fell to his knees on the cracked ground, panting and pink-faced.

Gwen held Cinni tight and whispered in her ear.

Evie grunted with each step as she made her way to my side. "Can we go to the forest now?"

"We should rest for a moment," I said. "We'll get Dorran cleaned up and then—"

"We have to go now." Evie widened her eyes at me. "Dorran likes being muddy. It's good for his skin." The little girl mouthed a word to me that looked horribly like *horses.*

"Come on then." My words sounded false to my own ears. "No time to waste. Once we're in the trees, we can all sit for a rest and get washed up."

"But—"

"You heard her," Evie cut across Dorran. "It's time for adventure, so let's get cracking."

Finn took one of the sacks from me. "What are we going to do?" he said in a low voice over the soothing tone of Gwen's coaxing and the grunts of Dorran climbing to the edge of the bank. "What are we going to tell Liam? What are we going to say to Orla?"

I hoisted my sack onto my shoulder. "We tell them at least we got to her before the Guilds."

A frozen terror wrapped around my spine at the mere thought of what the Sorcerers Guild would make of a child like Cinni.

"We tell all the Black Bloods they should be chivving well grateful to us," I whispered.

Bits of hardened earth still clung to the tops of my shoes. I shook my feet, trying to kick the fragments free, but the magic clung to the leather and laces of my boots.

"So just straight to the forest then?" Evie pointed across the sweeping field to the mountains beyond.

"For now," I said, waiting for her to tell me there was some danger only she could hear.

Evie wrinkled her forehead for a moment before nodding and heading off toward the forest.

I let Finn lead the children as we crossed through the weeds and brush. I kept well behind our little pack, searching for horses and men. I wanted to ask Evie why she thought there were horses. If she had only heard the sound of hooves beating the ground, it could just as easily have been deer. But Cinni was still shaking, and I was too terrified of the damage frightening her might cause.

The bright sunlight beat down upon my face. My hands cramped from gripping the neck of the sack I carried over my shoulder. Birds dove and swirled through the sky. Everything was as peaceful and normal as I could have asked for.

We rounded a low slope and cut out onto a wide, flat plain. Without the rise blocking my view, I could see a village perched on top of a hill to the north. Around the edges, farmers had planted their fields and penned in their livestock. It was a pretty scene. Like Harane might have looked from a far enough distance.

A tingle pulled at my feet. The urge to walk up into the village and slip back into an easy life lured me north. But the life that tempted me was a lie. Pretty or not, whether they knew it or not, the people who dwelled in those little homes lived and died at the will of the Guilds. No matter how tired I was, peace was not worth that sacrifice.

Finn paused at the western edge of the mountain road. He took a moment looking up and down the wide dirt path. He raised one hand, beckoning me forward.

I cut around the children and to his side. "What?" I whispered.

The grass rustled as Dorran crept closer to us.

Finn gave a tiny nod toward the pretty village.

I followed his gaze.

Up the mountain road, on the barren dirt between the houses, more than a dozen horses had been tied between buildings. People wearing black stood near their mounts.

I let out a slow breath and looked south down the road.

There was nothing in that direction. We could run south, but even if we'd still had the boat, determined men on horseback could catch us traveling by foot or by water.

"Into the forest then," I said. "On we go."

I hurried the children toward the woods as quickly as I could without risking upsetting Cinni. I glanced north as often as I dared, searching for any sign that someone had decided to follow us. No men or horses emerged from the village to chase us.

The scent of the forest surrounded me as we stepped into the trees, wearing away the edges of the worry clenching my stomach.

"This way." Finn cut southeast. "Once we get in a bit farther, we can stop and get everyone cleaned up and fed."

The children followed Finn without complaint.

Evie dropped behind the cluster the others had formed to walk by my side.

"Have you been in these woods before?" Evie asked.

"Sure," I said. "Not right here, but it's all the same forest, really."

"Oh." Evie bit her lips together. "Are there usually lots of animals in the mountains?"

A cold dread trickled through my veins.

"Why do you ask?" I kept my voice calm.

"I can hear the horses," Evie whispered, "but that's all. I've never been in a forest where there are no little animals before."

Finn led us on a winding path up the mountains. I kept waiting for the monster to come thundering through the woods ready to kill us all. If I had been able to think of another safe place for the children, I would have led them out of the trees, but I didn't know where else to go and couldn't risk the open with soldiers prowling so close by. Our only refuge was the camp.

I warned Finn of what Evie had said when we stopped by a brook to wash away the worst of the mud. He didn't know what else we could do either. So we kept climbing.

Every step seemed to grant a bit more freedom from the Guilds and give the monster a better chance of killing us with his claws.

But we kept going, climbing higher and higher as the sun sank.

I searched the trees, looking for a place that could offer enough high branches for each of us to perch in safety while we waited through the darkness. My body longed for sleep, but I knew I wouldn't be able to allow myself any rest, not with the chance of a beast seeking our flesh.

The sky had faded to gray when Evie grabbed my arm.

"Are you all right?" I asked. "We'll stop climbing for the night soon."

Evie stared at me, her breath coming more quickly.

"Evie." I took her hand in mine. "Evie, what's wrong?"

"I was wrong. It's not just horses," Evie whispered. "There are smaller creatures, too. That's what all the animals are hiding from."

My worry ebbed for one foolish moment. "Smaller is fine. This is a forest. There should be small animals here. And even small animals hunt other animals."

"But why are they hunting us?" Evie said. "Why are there dogs chasing us?"

"Finn, run." I seized Evie's hand and dragged her up the mountain, outpacing Finn.

"What's happening?" Finn ran beside me.

"Someone's caught our scent."

None of the children cried or questioned as I led them south, hoping against hope I might find something to protect us.

I didn't know who might be in the mountains, let alone coming closer to us with dogs. In the end, it didn't matter what monster chased us. All that mattered was that we couldn't be caught.

A low groaning came from behind me.

"Hush, Cinni," Gwen panted. "You're fine. We're all going to be fine."

The barking of dogs carried through the trees.

I strained my eyes, searching the shadows for any sign of a creek or pond, anything that might shield our scent.

"I can stop them," Evie said. "I can do it. I can stop them."

"No." I held tight to Evie's hand.

Crack.

The sound split through the woods, sending night birds scattering toward the sky.

"Breath, Cinni," Gwen said.

"Up ahead," a voice shouted from far behind us.

Crack.

Trees on either side of us fell to the ground.

"I can do it," Evie said.

I didn't answer as I dragged her around the curve of a slope. A wide patch of boulders waited on the other side.

The dogs howled.

Crack.

The tree above us toppled, twisting away from the boulders as it fell, sliding down the slope toward the dogs.

Evie wrenched her hand free from mine and turned toward the sounds of the approaching men.

"No, Evie." I jumped in front of her.

"It's a sorcerer," a voice shouted from far below. "It's got to be."

Finn grabbed Evie and me, shoving us into the shadows behind a boulder.

"How did they find us?" Finn said. "How could they possibly have found us?"

"Emmet said there's a traitor. Maybe even in our camp." I shut my eyes, forbidding my guilt from overwhelming me. "I thought we left too quickly for anyone to betray us."

"Ena," Finn said.

Dorran whimpered.

The smell of the children's fear cut through the cool scent of the shadowy forest.

"Round them up!" a second voice shouted.

I opened my eyes.

"We fight." Finn met my gaze. His eyes held no fear of death.

"I'll do it," Evie said. "I can stop them. I can kill them."

"No." I tucked her hair behind her ears. "I will not let you carry that burden."

Cinni whimpered as the barking of the dogs came closer.

A tiny fracture cut through the place in my heart where hope had dared to dwell.

I looked to Finn. "Tell him I'm sorry."

I dropped my sack and ran.

Back around the shelter of the boulder and onto the open side of the slope, letting my silhouette cut through the gray of the twilight.

I reached up, smacking a branch with all my might, cracking it off of the tree and breaking the skin on my palm.

The dogs howled.

I didn't try to keep my blood from dripping onto the ground. I pumped my arms as I ran, coating the forest floor with my scent.

The pounding of horse hooves thundered up the hill behind me.

I'm sorry. I'm so sorry.

A cliff blocked my path. I ran at the rock face, leaping up and grabbing hold with both hands. I climbed as fast as I could, digging my toes into the cracks, not caring about anything but surviving for one more minute.

One more minute for Finn and the children.

One more chance for them to find a path to escape.

One more moment before Evie knew what it meant to have blood on her hands.

"Stop!" a voice shouted from below when I was a foot from the top. "By order of the Guilds, I command you to stop!"

"Not a chivving chance." I dragged myself up and over the ledge as the cliff began to collapse around me.

I rolled away from the rocks as a bright orange light flashed toward me. The heat of the spell burned my skin, but I didn't stop, even as I screamed in pain.

I scrambled to my feet and kept running.

Shouted orders came from below, but I couldn't make out the words over the rasp of my own breathing.

The world swayed around me, and fatigue pulled at my limbs.

Just a little farther.

The damage of a long ago avalanche marred the slope in front of me. I raced south, trying to find a path that might lead me up and farther east.

The barking of the dogs came from the north as the animals gained on me.

Another cliff blocked my path. The stone wall jutted out around the edge of the rise, trapping me on the hill of loose debris.

"Up this way!" a voice shouted from below.

I ran to the rock face, searching for any imperfection that would allow me to climb. There was no handhold to be found.

Men in black uniforms appeared at the bottom of the slope, flanking a man in purple robes.

Dogs streaked out of the trees, barking madly as they raced toward their quarry.

I pulled my knife from my boot and pressed my back to the stone.

I hoped Lily would be proud that in the end I had done something worth being murdered for. I hoped Emmet would survive the fire of his rage whole enough to still be of use in this horrible world. I hoped Liam could forgive me, even if he could never have loved me.

The man in purple raised his hands. Green crackled between his fingertips.

Darkness and cold surrounded me.

I don't know how long I lay panting in the darkness. It might have been minutes or hours before I realized I was not dead.

I unclenched my hand, and my knife fell with a clatter. The ground beneath me was smooth as I rolled over and pushed myself to my hands and knees.

My palm stung where the tree had ripped open my skin. My fingers trembled as I pulled the lae stone from my pocket.

The blue light gleamed off the black rock surrounding me. A wide tunnel with a high, perfectly-carved arch in the peak of the ceiling stretched out in front of me.

I looked to the rock behind me and pressed my bloody palm to the stone. The mountain did not budge.

There are legends in this world that will terrify you. There are monsters that no man can slay. There are stories that hold truth and histories rotting with lies.

There are some answers that should never be brought into the light.

I did not have that wisdom as I ventured alone into the darkness.

Ena's journey continues in Ice and Sky. *Read on for a sneak preview.*

ANCIENT MAGIC LURKS IN THE SHADOWS.

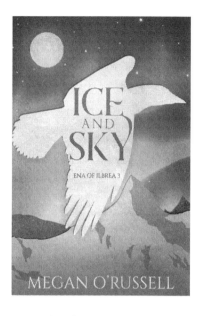

Continue reading for a sneak peek of *Ice and Sky*.

I am not innocent.

I have killed. I have harmed. I have tried to do good and ended up hurting the people I cherished most.

I cannot argue any punishment the stars torment me with. I deserve to burn.

I have waited for the sky to turn to ash as the gods declare my guilt.

I am still waiting.

There are legends of people living deep beneath the stones of the eastern mountains. I had heard the stories long before I knew the Black Bloods were real.

But somehow, even after the magic and monsters I'd seen, I didn't believe the tales to be true.

I was wrong.

The only sounds in the black stone tunnel were the soft plodding of my feet and the rhythm of my own breathing. I don't know how long I walked down the high-arched corridor before the walls began to sway and exhaustion finally won the battle against my own will to escape.

I lay down on the ground, gripping my lae stone in one hand and my knife in the other. Bundling my coat around me, I pressed my back against the wall as sleep swallowed me.

I don't know how long I slept. When I awoke, nothing had changed. There was no sun to judge time by. As far as I could tell, there was nothing in the world beyond the little pool of blue light cast by my lae stone.

My throat burned from thirst, and my stomach longed for food. But I didn't know if I'd been asleep for hours or for days.

Finn might have made it to the camp before I woke up. Or he might have been taken by the Guilds. There was no way for me to know.

I clutched my lae stone tight, trying to convince myself that the answer to that question was worth journeying through the darkness.

My legs trembled as I stood up. My feet ached as I kept walking down the tunnel.

There was no change in the walls, no slope or corner. There was nothing but darkness and moving forward one step at a time.

The pounding in my head began before my hands started to shake.

I had seen bare bones once in a passage created by the mountains. I wondered if the person who had been trapped had been like me—whisked away from Death's embrace so the mountain might torture them more. I wondered if anyone would find my bones, and what they might think of my fate if they did.

"I'm sorry." My words crackled in my throat. "Whatever I've done to offend you, I'm sorry."

I stopped and leaned back against the wall, resisting the temptation to lie down and sleep. Warmth radiated from the stone. I pressed my palm to the heat.

"Actually, I'm not," I whispered. "Punish me if you like. I am willing to die if that is the price you demand, but I am not sorry for saving those children." My breath caught in my chest. "For trying to save those children."

I thought of the four of them—Evie, Gwen, Dorran, and Cinni—captured by the Sorcerers Guild, trapped in the stone tower in Ilara. I shut my eyes, sending a plea up to the stars that Finn had led them to safety.

My eyes stung, but I didn't have any tears to shed.

I tried to distract myself from the pounding in my head and the pain in my body as I kept walking down the chivving tunnel. I pictured Finn arriving at the camp, all the children safely with him. It was a happy image, a valiant success. Finn and I had not only protected four innocent sorcis. We'd also managed to keep powerful magic out of the hands of the Guilds.

Then I got to the bit of the fantasy where Liam found out Finn had returned without me, and the stinging in my eyes came back.

I banished the fantasy from my mind and kept walking forward.

The blackness that lurked in my chest had always seemed an ally before. A place where I could hide hurts and memories that were too horrible for me to bear.

The blackness I journeyed through taunted me. I was the thing the world did not want to see. I was the pain the mountain could not stand. I had been tucked away and would stay hidden until I died.

I screamed at the high arch in the ceiling. My rage tore at my throat and echoed down the corridor. There wasn't even the sound of a scurrying rodent to answer me.

"Keep walking. Even the eastern mountains cannot be endless."

I knew my own words weren't true. But my lie was enough to keep me moving for a while longer.

My throat ached, and my tongue felt as though it might crack with every dry breath I drew. The pain in my legs changed from a dull throb to terrible cramps that left me limping.

I'm not sure how long it took for the pounding in my head to develop a noise my ears could hear. Not long after the sound began, the tunnel started swaying before me. I staggered as I tried to make the walls and floor stay in place.

I wanted to lie down and sleep, but I was afraid if I allowed myself to rest, I wouldn't have the strength to stand back up again.

"If you want me dead, just kill me. If you want to torment me, then bring fire or knives. Do not make me wander down here."

I waited for the mountain to answer.

"Did you save me so you could have the pleasure of watching me die slowly?" I tucked my knife into the sheath in the ankle of my boot and laid my palm on the smooth stone of the wall. "I am not a child of stone. I'm not a Black Blood. You shouldn't have let me in. Was it a mistake? Can you even make mistakes?"

The stone stayed silent.

I took my hand from the wall and lifted the pendant from the top of my bodice. The stone held a blissful and familiar warmth.

"Please. I just want to get back to camp. I want to help. I want to fight."

I pressed my forehead against the stone wall.

"I just want to get back to him."

I let my eyes drift shut as I waited for rocks to tumble down and grant a bloody end to my captivity.

The pounding in my head amplified.

I pushed away from the wall and kept walking. I wished there were a branch in the tunnel, anything that might give me a choice besides following the mountain's will or lying down and waiting to die.

The pounding in my head developed a new texture. A strange and constant rumbling.

I wondered if it might be a sign that my body was giving out. I'd never seen a person die from thirst before. Through all the misery we'd suffered in Harane, we'd always had water to spare.

As I walked, the sound grew louder. The texture of the noise became familiar.

I moved as quickly as I could, limping as I ran toward the rumble. The ground beneath my feet lost its smooth perfection as the peak of the tunnel dropped to a less impressive height.

"Oh, please."

The end of the tunnel came into view. The walls disappeared, opening up into a vast blackness my lae stone was not large enough to light.

I ignored my fear of what could be lurking in the blackness and followed the sound.

A waist-high wall blocked my path.

I scrambled over the stones, falling to my knees on the other side. I lost my grip on my lae stone. The light rolled away, stopping under a bench.

Cool moisture greeted my palms as I crawled toward my lae stone. The ground was not hard beneath me. As I lay on my stomach to reach for my light, something soft touched my cheek.

Moss.

The ground was covered in moss. A plant with pale green leaves twined around the legs of the stone bench.

I wanted to touch the leaves, but the low rumbling called to me. I crawled toward the sound, not trusting my legs to carry my weight.

Another wall blocked my path. My hand slipped as I tried to pull myself onto the ledge.

The rocks were slick with water.

Gritting my teeth, I made myself stand.

The blue glow of my lae stone shimmered across the water cascading down from a fountain.

I dipped my hand into the pool and drank.

The coolness raced past my lungs as I drank and drank until I thought I would be sick from the wonder of water.

I was so desperate to quench my thirst, I didn't even have the sense to question how a statue of a woman had ended up in a fountain in the belly of the eastern mountains.

Order your copy of Ice and Sky *to continue the story.*

ESCAPE INTO ADVENTURE

Thank you for reading *Mountain and Ash*. If you enjoyed the book, please consider leaving a review to help other readers find Ena's story.

As always, thanks for reading,

Megan O'Russell

Never miss a moment of the magic and romance.

Join the Megan O'Russell readers community to stay up to date on all the action by visiting https://www.meganorussell.com/book-signup.

ABOUT THE AUTHOR

Megan O'Russell is the author of several Young Adult series that invite readers to escape into worlds of adventure. From *Girl of Glass*, which blends dystopian darkness with the heart-pounding danger of vampires, to *Ena of Ilbrea*, which draws readers into an epic world of magic and assassins.

With the *Girl of Glass* series, *The Tethering* series, *The Chronicles of Maggie Trent*, *The Tale of Bryant Adams,* the *Ena of Ilbrea* series, and several more projects planned for 2020, there are always exciting new books on the horizon. To be the first to hear about new releases, free short stories, and giveaways, sign up for Megan's newsletter by visiting the following:

https://www.meganorussell.com/book-signup.

Originally from Upstate New York, Megan is a professional musical theatre performer whose work has taken her across North America. Her chronic wanderlust has led her from Alaska to Thailand and many places in between. Wanting to travel has fostered Megan's love of books that allow her to visit countless new worlds from her favorite reading nook. Megan is also a lyricist and playwright. Information on her theatrical works can be found at RussellCompositions.com.

She would be thrilled to chat with you on Facebook or

Twitter @MeganORussell, elated if you'd visit her website MeganORussell.com, and over the moon if you'd like the pictures of her adventures on Instagram @ORussellMegan.

Feather and Flame

Printed in Great Britain
by Amazon